Happy Reading

♡ Emmy

Meanmna
Book One of the Daearen Realms

Emmy Gatrell
Relevant Daearen

Meanmna: Book One of the Daearen Realms
ISBN: 978-0-9912851-1-2
Publisher: Relevant Daearen
Cover Art: Norman Wong
Edition 1.0

For my family:
Jon, Prescott, Hadrian, Kevren & Dijouri
Without your love and support, I couldn't have made my dreams come true.
Love you all!

ONE

"That's it! I can't study! Time for a non-fat quad vanilla latte!" I said it with flair, tossing my book across the room and jumping on my bed, almost hitting my head on the low, angled ceiling. I wasn't ten anymore and I needed to stop doing that, but who doesn't like jumping on beds, right?

"Quit being so dramatic, Sarette. It can't be that difficult." Mathew grabbed my math book, tossing it to land perfectly in the middle of the desk with a thump. "Yeah, I'm sure you're never going to finish without a cup of coffee, and you probably need to go get a new candle." I couldn't quite hear the rest of whatever he said, but he mumbled something about having a crazy chick for a best friend.

"I just need to get everything in order—and, *then* I can get focused," I said.

Mathew stood up, stretching out his six-two frame, purposefully smacking his hands on the low ceiling just to startle me. I jumped, as I always do when he does that. "You know they have medicine you can take for OCD, right?"

"Quit being a dick." I stood and put my hands on my hips. "I told you I needed coffee hours ago." I looked at him—beautiful and perfect, with his dark brown hair and aqua blue eyes. He had filled out this summer, too. He had gone away on vacation as a tall, skinny, dorky kid and somehow came back still dorky, but a rather reasonably-built man, or at least well on his way to becoming one. Too bad we've known each other since we were in diapers. You can't have feelings for someone you've known that long. It's kind of creepy, not unlike those people who counted the days until Miley Cyrus or Selena Gomez turned eighteen.

"Earth to Sarette." Mathew was holding my coat in his outstretched hands. "Where'd you go this time?"

"Nowhere. Just remembering when you peed in my bed." I grabbed my coat from him and ran down the stairs from my attic bedroom.

"I was three, and that was fourteen years ago!" I heard him shout as I went down another flight of stairs and rounded the corner to the kitchen.

7

"Hi, Mom."

My mother was leaning back on our farmhouse sink, holding her iPad. If I had to guess, she was playing Words with Friends. "Hey sweetie, I thought you needed to study." A giant boom sounded through the house, shaking the doors of the china cabinet. Mom looked up and yelled, "Mathew Michael Conner! You are too big to be jumping down the stairs! You're gonna break my house!"

With a sheepish grin, he rounded the corner into the canary yellow kitchen. "Sorry, Mom." He leaned over to kiss her on the cheek.

When I say *leaned over*, I mean it. At barely five feet tall, Mom looks like a little person next to him. I wish I looked like her. Shanna Miller was blessed with black hair, but hers was so black that it didn't look natural—it looked like something that came from a bottle of dye. Her dark blue eyes always seemed a little sad. I'm not as lucky; I have sandy brown hair, perpetually frizzy and overly thick, and hazel eyes that change color with my mood, or at least it seems that way. I'm not as short as my mom; I'm five-foot-six, but at least I got her curves.

"Need. Coffee. Now," I spoke my best approximation of a robot with my arms moving mechanically. I'm such a geek.

Mom didn't need to hear about the candle. She hated all that stuff and absolutely forbade me to play around with "things beyond my understanding", whatever the hell that means. I hated lying to her, but I tried to rationalize that I wasn't really lying, I was omitting. Integrity can be a bitch, though. How would I feel if someone intentionally left out critical information when I asked them a question? Yes, omission *is* lying, but I have a ton of crap to do. I can't get anything accomplished unless everything is just the way I need it. It just is what it is. Maybe Mathew is right about my having OCD.

With a quick turn to the kitchen island, I grabbed Mathew's keys off the counter and yelled "Shotgun!"

"You don't need to call shotgun when it's only the two of us. Besides, I think you should drive. I've got a date later that I have to get ready for."

Yup, that's right. It's Friday and MMC has things to do. His newfound good looks make Friday the day that we don't hang out anymore. "Are you to the S's yet? You seem to be working your way through the senior class girls pretty efficiently—so efficiently I might think you have a plan of sorts."

I stopped talking and took in Mom's and Mathew's responses, both of their mouths dropping open at my accusation. "What? Come on. There must be a plan involved. Start with the A's and work your way to the Z's. Or, begin with the brunettes over five-foot-five and then on to blonds over five-foot-five. I don't know how you are deciding who is next, but there is a plan. I just haven't figured it out yet." Truth be told, I know I am the only person in the world who could say that to Mathew, and I know I'm pushing it.

"Just because you can't get a date doesn't mean I need to be antisocial too." Now Mathew was pushing it.

"Thanks for keeping it classy." I shrugged away the hurt, set down his keys, and grabbed mine.

"You two crabby pants need caffeine and it's on me." Mom padded over to her imitation Coach purse to fund our caffeine mission. She searched through her wallet, made a slight shrug, grabbed a fifty, and handed it to Mathew. "You can keep the change for your date. And try not to be out too late," she said with a smile. "Sarette, your curfew is 11 p.m. and please only go to the coffee house," she said with a don't-even-think-about-going-anywhere-else look in my direction. "Now, both of you say I'm sorry to each other and get moving. I'm going to take a bath. I'll probably be asleep when you get back, so goodnight," she said while heading to her bedroom, probably looking forward to a couple hours by herself. "Oh, and Mathew, please tell your mom to call me tomorrow. Love ya, guys." As she shut the door, it felt like she was pushing us out of the house. But after seventeen years as a single working mom, she deserved whatever she wanted.

We looked at each other and simultaneously said, "You're sorry," then raced toward each other yelling, "Jinx, pinch, poke! You owe me a Coke." Pinching and poking ensued. I think between Mathew, Mom, Mama, and me, we owe ourselves around forty-eight kabillion or so Cokes, although my math might be off a bit. I looked at Mathew's stupid "I won" smirk, but I could not stay mad at him. I stuck my tongue out at him instead. We've known each other our entire lives and my life story is woven with our shared experiences— good, bad, and indifferent— we share a bond that I suspect even real siblings don't have together.

Our shared lives started on day one of our existence. Looking into the nursery from the outside, our moms met while in the hospital on December 21, 1998. Both were looking fondly at their newly-born babies lined up next to one another in little Plexiglas cribs—each of us wrapped in hospital-issued blue, white, and red-striped blankets. I guess our moms bonded because they were both alone in the hospital, neither of our fathers stuck around and neither had any other family. They were both twenty-something single parents alone in every way until they found each other. They instantly became best friends.

At the hospital, Mom invited Mama and Mathew to stay with us until they got on their feet. Mom had just inherited a large home from her parents in Adrian, Michigan and there was plenty of room for all of us. We were practically raised as siblings. Early on, we started calling Mathew's mother "Mama" and my mother "Mom" to distinguish between the two. As luck would have it, the house next door went up for sale right after we were potty trained. Mama and Mathew were able to have their own place while we all still had our family unit. It was a win-win.

"Let's go! It's freezing out here." I reached for the car door handle on the driver side.

"I don't *have* to go out tonight." Mathew folded his hand on top of the hood and looked guilty. "Do you want me to cancel my date? I didn't know it bothered you so much."

"Dude, it's all good. Just a mini pity party for me—I'm over it. I'm just destined to hit refresh on Facebook while bouncing between Words with Friends and Dice with Buddies. Enough of my fabulous Friday night plans—let's go." I slinked into the car.

"Are you sure?" Mathew got in and closed the passenger door behind him.

"Yes, I'm fine. You should go get ready for your date. I have to get to the store before they close, so I'm going to head there before I get coffee."

"I really am sorry . . . I was just trying to be funny with the whole antisocial thing."

"Ha, ha, ha. Mathew it's only a joke if the other person laughs . . . I said I was fine. Seriously, dude, I'm just pickier about who I will go out with. That's why I'm not going out. You, on the other hand, apparently are using a systematic, almost mechanical approach to who you date. Just to be clear, I turned down Shane today for winter formal and I'm—"

"You what? Why did you say no? I don't get it." He leaned back against the seat with a look of disbelief.

"I'm not interested in dating the 'most popular guy in school,'" I said as I used my fingers as quotation marks. "He just wants to see me naked. Like I said, not interested."

"You're weird. Are you really stopping to get candles first?" he sighed.

"Yup."

"Is it going to be quick?"

"I'm going to take a long as I need to make it right. Why?"

"Well, I could use coffee but I have some homework to do and I have to get ready. I think I'm going to bail. Is that cool?"

"Yup."

"I'm going home." Mathew reached for the passenger handle and sprung out of the car. "Love you!"

"Love you, too. Have fun! But, not too much fun. I have no desire to be an aunt yet!

"Bitch!" he exclaimed.

"Dick!"

With a giggle and a smile, the fight was over. Mathew ran across the lawn and went into his house as I started the car. *Darn it, I should have started it already.* The windows were solid ice. I went back into the house to stay warm while the windows defrosted. When I walked into the living room, I noticed the picture of my dad was gone off the mantle. *Mom is crying again, I thought and* turned around. I went back outside and got in my cold car. It whined loudly in protest as I backed out of the driveway.

TWO

I was still trying to stop thinking about my dad when I pulled onto Maumee Street with one of my favorite songs, "Ain't Life Grand" by Widespread Panic, playing on the radio. Music always reminds me of my dad. I say "reminds me", but that's wrong—you have to have actually met someone to be reminded of them. I don't even know him. I think I look like him, but if I squint and tilt my head, I can see mom's contributions, too. I have Dad's hair, at least from what I can tell in the only picture I have of him. There's only a quarter of his face and hair showing, but that's more than I've seen of him in person. He has a beer in his hand and is standing with a gaggle of folks outside some venue, waiting to see Widespread Panic. The picture is slightly blurry and out of focus because it was blown up from the original. That's my dad, though, blurry and out of focus.

I wanted to park on the street and started looking carefully for someone who might be leaving as I drove through. Adrian is a beautiful old town with broad sidewalks, small shops, and a never-ending supply of small town gossip. But, like many cities in Michigan and across the States, it lost jobs in manufacturing when big box stores moved into town. Adrian is a two college town, Adrian College and Siena Heights University, so it has held on better than a lot of small towns. I circled around the block again, still in search of a parking place.

"There's one," I shouted as I turned onto a side street and saw an empty space. "It's official. I'm going crazy. I'm talking to myself and that's *got to* be one step closer to crazy land." I paused, "And now I'm talking to myself about talking to myself! Maybe there's a magic candle to ward off the crazies."

Muttering to myself as I pulled into the spot, I heard a slight laugh behind and to the right of me. I threw my car into park and spun around, half expecting someone to be there. Seeing no one, tears sprang to my eyes. "And now I'm hearing things; maybe I *am* going crazy." At least I *thought* I heard something, but I definitely felt the melancholy that must precede losing one's grip on reality. I blinked the tears away, checked my reflection in the mirror, and got out. It was a beautiful winter day. I'm not the biggest fan of the cold, but you can't complain about a sunny and clear December day in Michigan.

I hustled past the Croswell Theatre and walked quickly to get out of the vicious winter wind. The bell chimed as I went into Visions. There were no other customers in there, which wasn't surprising; it had been that way every time I went to the shop. Stuff crowded the tiny space, and the windows were always shuttered. I'd often wondered how the place stayed in business, but I was glad it was there. I'd also wondered why the religious right in the area had allowed a mystical bookstore to open in Adrian; maybe it gave everyone something to complain about together, for unity. That is not to say there is not a pseudo-open discussion as to whether Visions is good for the community. There's the occasional op-ed piece in the paper, which is a thinly-veiled attack on the occult and insinuating the devil's commercial agenda, but no one has been brave enough to protest in person. Cowards. Whatever.

I waited a few seconds, taking in the smell of sage, incense, and a mixture of other organic smells while my eyes adjusted to the crazy ambient lighting. When I could see again, I noticed the Christmas lights hanging haphazardly from one piece of furniture or fixture to the next, giving a multi-colored glow that added to the ambiance. Wind chimes were clinking and ringing as the air from a small oscillating fan blew past them. Bookcases lined all the walls. I smiled when I saw the bookcase that contained the novels about vampires, fairies, witches, werewolves, and such. Celine, the shop's owner, had a handwritten sign hanging over it that read "FICTION?" as if she had a question about whether or not that stuff was real.

The case to the left displayed all the candles. I needed a new water candle. I have no idea why mine always burned up so much faster than the others. One would think that a "water" candle would burn slower. Nor do I understand why I shouldn't purchase a batch of them at one time, but Celine said you get better results from a new candle that has recently had the appropriate spell cast. Apparently spells have a short shelf life, so I come here a lot. A candle burning in each corner of my room has always helped my paranoia. I've often felt like I was being watched. The candles seemed to keep me safe in a bubble. That's why I preferred being at home most of the time.

There was no real order of displays in the cramped little retail space at Visions; Celine felt there was no need for such accouterments. "You'll know when you find what you need," she always said. I started moving carefully around a table of crystals. A giggle from near the counter startled me. I turned quickly, lost my footing and began to fall. I could always count on my clumsiness to make most days interesting. I grabbed the table to avoid a thunderous fall. Somehow I made contact with a crystal and cut my hand on the jagged points. Taking a deep breath, I looked around to see who might have witnessed my escapade. *No one.* "Great," I said aloud and threw up my hands in a victory pose. That's when I heard another giggle. I turned slowly and this time I saw a child poking her head up from behind the counter.

"You're funny," she said with a little awe in her voice. "Your colors are so pretty. I've never seen them look like that."

I wasn't sure what she meant about colors; I was wearing earth tones. Feeling more embarrassed than anything, I nodded and smiled at the girl. She came around the counter. Standing before me was a strawberry-haired pixie, about five years old and as cute as could be, with big green luminescent eyes and pink cheeks. She had a silver band across her forehead that looked like a crown. She was holding a clear crystal wand with an amethyst spirit crystal on the end. A spirit crystal has a large quartz in the center, like a spire, and small crystals growing out of it. It's shaped kind of like a pineapple, and this one was the most beautiful one I had ever seen. I'm not sure why a kid would have one since they are very rare and are indigenous to the Magaliesberg Mountain region of South Africa. *Thanks, Mom the geologist. I feel smart.*

"Hello. That is a beautiful wand for a beautiful girl!"

"Thanks!" She grinned, twirled around, and said, "So, do you know what kind of the fair people you are yet?"

"Huh?"

"Paige ..." Celine said as she walked through a beaded curtain from the back room. A sign hung above the opening that read "Employees Only", quite comical since Celine was the only employee. She stopped, her eyes widening when she saw the little girl. Turning to me, Celine said, "I see you met my . . . um . . . niece . . . Paige."

Breaking the totally strange silence, I walked to Paige with my hand out. "Hi, Paige. I'm Sarette." She looked at my hand like she had no idea what to do with it. That's when I noticed the blood. "Oh, shoot! I cut my hand on the crystal." I grabbed a tissue from the Kleenex box on the counter to clean it up. The bell on the door rang. Glancing up at the mirror behind the counter, I saw the door slowly swing open and then shut, but no one was there.

"Got anything to keep me from losing the rest of my mind?" I asked Celine. She was staring with a frown on her face at something behind me and to my right. After a moment, she smiled and gently patted me on the arm.

"Oh, sweetheart. That's an old door. You're not going crazy. So, why are you here besides the coo-coo candle?"

"Is there a coo-coo candle?" That half-laugh—more of a snicker— sounded behind me again. This time I pretended I didn't hear it. No need to alienate anyone else with my crazy weirdness. "My water candle burned up again."

Celine gave another quick look behind me.

"I'll get it!" Paige yelled as she ran around the crystal table and past me, glancing and giggling to the door as if there was something there. *That's it. I'm leaving here and checking into a mental hospital. What the hell is going on?* For as long as I can remember, I've had the feeling of being watched. The feelings had grown increasingly intense since last spring, and for the past week, I had been hearing and seeing things. Like laughing when no one is there and doors opening without assistance. Then there was the weird buzz I felt coming from the crystal that I had just cut my hand on. *Wait a minute. I did feel something, didn't I?*

I went back to the table to take a better look at the crystal. It was a translucent dark green stone with little white swirls that appeared to be moving inside of it. About the size of a baseball, it had a relatively smooth bottom and several jagged edges on top. I clasped the crystal in my hand and felt a little buzz or tingle again. "What kind of crystal is this? It looks like it's moving. I've never seen anything like it." I looked up to Celine, who had a strange look on her face.

"I didn't realize I had put that out. It's not time yet." Celine sighed and looked past me, shrugging her shoulders. "It's an amazonite crystal."

"Amazonite? I didn't realize they could be translucent." I looked down again and saw it was opaque, rather than the single shade of see-through green like before. Now there were different shades of green throughout and white swirls that looked like solid veins. *I am losing my mind. I'm going to have to go three towns over so nobody sees me check into the crazy house.*

"No, you're not," said a voice that I'm pretty sure I only heard in my head. I put the amazonite down on the table and looked up.

"You know? I think I'll wait until next time for that candle. I don't feel very well, and well, um, I . . . you know . . . I have to go." I started for the door.

"Why don't you take the crystal?" Paige said. She was smiling as she stood in front of me with her little arm holding it up. "It should help you see things beyond your understanding."

She did not just say that. I didn't want to start screaming and make a run for it, so I forced a smile and looked at Celine. "How much do I owe you?"

Celine smiled a strained smile. "On the house," she said. "It found you. It's time."

I'm not going to ask what time it is, I'm sure it's not time to get ill. I'm going to have to find a new magic store when I get out of the loony bin.

No! I heard in my head, a little more forcefully this time. I took the crystal and ignored the buzz I felt.

"Um, thanks. I guess I'll see you soon." I nervously grabbed the knob, opened the door, and headed to the street, looking in all directions.

"I can't wait to see you again!" shouted Paige. I smiled and waved to her, then I turned around and started walking. *I'd love to see you again too, little girl, but it will be at least seventy-two hours before I get out of the nuthouse.*

"No!" I heard the voice again—this time out loud and coming from behind me. I sprinted toward my car. I kept hitting the unlock button on the keyfob, just to make sure the door would not be locked when I got there. I jerked the door open and, panting, got in as fast as I could. After a moment, I looked in the rear view mirror. Someone was sitting in my backseat staring at me. I think I screamed before I fainted.

THREE

I have to be dreaming again, I thought as I wiggled my toes in the grass. I raised my gaze and looked around. *Yep, the same place, the same dream.* The same green rolling hills and trees covered in strangely colored flowers. The sun was high in the sky and I felt its heat on my face. Looking toward the mountain range in the distance, I felt the urge again. There was something I was supposed to get to on the other side of the mountains, but I could never get any closer than this. I try every time I have this dream, but something felt different this time. Something sounded different too. There was water gurgling, splashing and lapping to my left. The compulsion to try to get to the mountain left me. I needed to see the water—it was calling me, and like a moth to a flame I ran to it, into the forest, ducking under trees, jumping over brush. The twinkling blue water called to me through the limbs and leaves ahead. My heart was pumping and I could hear the water, even over the erratic beating of my heart. I ran as fast as I could in the long flowing dress I'm always wearing in these dreams. I broke through the trees and skidded to a stop. On the shore was a man dressed in jeans and a band tee shirt, Phish maybe, but I couldn't tell from where I was standing. *Who the hell is he? What the hell is* he *doing here? What am* I *doing here?*

"Hello, Sarette."

I glanced around, looking for a weapon. *Wait! This is a dream. Nobody can hurt me in a dream.* I took a deep breath. "Who are you?"

He smiled and crossed his arms in front of his chest. *Yep, he works out.* He chuckled and looked over at me like he could hear my thoughts. I blushed and looked down. *Wait a minute! This is my dream.* I looked up. "I asked you who you are." That sounded much more confident than I felt. *God, I'm even a wuss when I'm sleeping.*

"You really need to stop putting yourself down," he said. "Also, for the record, you are *not* going crazy. This is all normal . . . well, *mostly* normal." He smiled.

God, he has a great smile, I wonder how many years he had braces? I had to do two cycles over five years and my teeth aren't that good. Why do I keep looking at his lips?

17

He laughed again. His hair looked almost black and was run through with dark red. His eyes were dark green, his lips totally kissable. "If you would like me to stop hearing what you're thinking, you should probably wake up and talk to me. I'm the guy sitting in your back seat." He winked and disappeared; I started yelling to an empty space.

"My backseat? What? Oh wait! That's right; there's a telepathic ax murderer sociopath sitting in the backseat of my car, waiting to chop me into little pieces. I'd rather stay asleep for that! Thank you very much. Get it over with already; I'm already crazy. Just finish me off!"

"I'm not an ax murderer sociopath, and I have already told you that you're *not* crazy. Wake up, please. I'd really like to talk in person, on your plane." It sounded like he was right next to my ear. His voice was oddly soothing in a Barry White or grandpa sort of way.

"Ok." I closed my eyes, but nothing happened. I waited a couple more seconds and reopened them. "Um. Still here. Am I supposed to be doing something to get out of here? You mentioned a plane?" Looking around, my eyes suddenly felt very heavy. I closed them again.

My face felt cold and wet and was pressed cockeyed against the window. *Great! Yay me! I'm sure I'm looking super-hot with my face smashed against the window and drool running down my chin. I can't wait until these pictures land on Instagram.*

I lifted my head off the glass and heard the deep voice from the backseat say, "Well, I'm not going to put any pictures on Instagram or Facebook, or any videos on YouTube. I promise."

"Please don't kill me. Take whatever you want." I grabbed my purse and whipped it over the seat without looking.

"Didn't we just go over this? I do not have an ax. I am not a sociopath. You are not crazy. And, we really need to talk . . . Sarette? Please look at me."

I slowly opened my eyes but didn't turn around. "Dreams are not real," I whispered, and started repeating a mantra. "This is not real. This is not real. This is not real."

"Sometimes dreams are real, Sarette," he said softly. "I promise I am not going to hurt you. Please turn around."

Was he pleading? Why would an ax murderer beg to see me? I slowly turned around and gasped. There he was!

"It's you!" *The man of my dreams, I mean, the man* in *my dreams, in not of.* He chuckled and looked straight at me. "Are you still reading my mind? Because you need to stop. There's a lot going on up here." I pointed to my head while making the crazy sign. "I don't even know who you are and you know my thoughts! That takes a lot of nerve. I don't remember inviting you into my head." *I'm rambling! Stop talking! Why is he smiling at me?*

"Sorry, I won't read your mind anymore, now that you're ready to see me." He paused. "Well, you're going to see more strange things. But for now, we need to talk about—"

"Who are you? What is going on? This is it, isn't it? The moment I realize I am totally and completely insane. I'm a paranoid psychotic, aren't I? You're a figment of my imagination, here to help me understand my craziness."

"For God's sakes, Sarette! You are not crazy, but you are very likely to drive *me* crazy if you don't stop and listen." He took an overly dramatic deep breath. I almost said something, but he put his hand up to stop me. I hadn't noticed before, but he had a slight accent I couldn't place. *God, that's sexy.* He took another deep breath and started again. "My name is Elwin. It's a pleasure to meet you, finally. I've—"

"What do you mean finally? You've been watching me? Are you some kind of stalker?"

"I've been sent here by your family. I'm here to help you get ready for the journey to meet them." He put his arm across the back of the seat and nonchalantly looked at me with a half-smile, acting as if he had uttered the most reasonable statement in the world.

"Wait. What? My family?" I exploded. "I don't know what kind of crazy crap this is, but my *family* is my mom, who is at home crying. Mathew is on a date with a girl whose name starts with an S, I think. And Mathew's mom, Peggy, is . . . I haven't any idea where she is or what she's doing, but she would not have sent some hunky guy to prepare me. She's never had a dating problem and she would have kept you for herself." *Did I really did just say that?* I turned back around, started the car, and said, "It's time for you to get out."

"Listen, we really need to talk. I can help you understand what's been going on. I can help you understand who you really are. When you are ready to talk, I'll find you." He put his hand on the door handle and got out of the car. *Wow! He's tall and he's smirking again. He had better not be reading my mind—it's my crazy mind.* He leaned down and looked at me through the window. "I know this is a shock, so please think about it. I'll be seeing you around, Sarette Miller." He shut the door and started walking away.

I watched him in my rearview mirror until his outline started to go blurry and he disappeared. I shook my head in disbelief. This is too much—much too much. I am going crazy.

No, you are not. Goodnight, Sarette. I heard in my head.

I headed back home with no coffee, no candle, and my last shred of sanity gone.

FOUR

The dashboard clock said 8:05 when I pulled into the driveway. I put the car in park and gazed up at my house, wondering what, if anything, I should tell my mom. The kitchen lights were on. Mom was probably checking Facebook or re-tweeting some inspirational meme with an ocean photo and an unattributed motivational quote. She has to work early tomorrow so she should be calling it a night any minute. I can't talk to her about what Elwin, the mystery man, just said. The topic of my dad would make for a day trip on an emotional rollercoaster. I learned a long time ago that if I wanted Mom to keep acting like Mom, I should not bring him up, ever. She gets so sad and tries to push through, but it takes so much out of her. It's also hard for me to watch that.

What if what Elwin said is actually true? Wouldn't Mom like to know that she could see him, my dad, again? My dad! Okay, I needed to talk to her. Now! But, what the hell would I say? *Hey, Mom! I totally disregarded what you said and went to the freaky bookstore in town. There, I came to believe that I am completely insane—like "bring-your-insurance-card-and-commit-me" insane. Of course, I'm only crazy if what this really hot guy—I mean, smoking hot guy—said isn't true. My family, who has been watching me, would like to see me. Not my family as in you, but rather my dad's family. Surprise! You know dad—the guy you met when you were finishing your dissertation? The guy you fell so completely in love with that you have never gotten over him? Wait, Mom. Please! Mom, don't cry. You don't need another bath. Come back!*

"Ahhhh," I said as I dropped my head on the steering wheel, accidentally hitting the loud and obnoxious car horn. I sat up and covered my mouth with my hands—like that helped. Mom was looking at me through the blinds. *Smile. Okay, you can do this—you have to do this now.* I took a deep steadying breath, got out of the car, and started walking toward the house. *Maybe if I walk slowly enough, she'll go to bed before I get there.* I rolled my eyes at my own ridiculousness.

When I reached the front door, I saw that someone had taped a piece of paper to it. It had been folded in half, but I could tell it was handmade, the kind of paper you see at a craft show. My name was written on it in beautiful swirly calligraphy. The Scotch tape that held it in place ruined the aesthetics, but I guess wax would have been a pain in the ass to clean off later.

I opened the note without removing it from the door; I'd hate myself if I ripped it. There were only two words on the inside: Good luck! I carefully took it off the door and quickly looked around. I could see someone walking away from me about four houses down. He turned to look at me. It was Elwin and he was waving. As his outline started to blur, I heard in my mind, *I can listen if you want me to. I might be able to help with the conversation.*

No, thank you, I answered back. I gasped when I realized I was communicating with him telepathically.

See? You're learning already.

I heard him in my mind, and then he was gone. I was smiling when I walked into the house.

Mom was sitting at our huge kitchen table. She must have just oiled it because the parquet pattern was shining like gold, thanks to the light coming from the chandelier above. Mom had made that Mason jar light fixture. She is such a do-it-yourself-er—she prefers me to call her an "up-cycler."

"Hey, sweetie. You weren't gone very long. Are you caffeinated appropriately?" Mom asked. She was wearing a bathrobe, her hair wrapped up in a towel. Her eyes were a still a little red. She looked back down to her iPad. She was playing Words with Friends; she must have already updated her Facebook status.

I stood there, just watching her for a moment as she studied her board; then she looked up again and asked, "What's up? You walked in with a huge cat-that-ate-the-canary smile on your face. Now you're staring at me and frowning like you are a million miles away." She clicked her iPad off. "It's a boy, isn't it? Must be someone I wouldn't approve of." She tapped her chin, deep in thought. "A biker. That's it, isn't it? I truly do not approve of the new no-helmet laws, so wear one, okay?"

I couldn't say anything. I must have made her nervous. Switching course, she started again. "Listen. I know sometimes it seems like I favor Mathew. But as soon as you have a date, I'll give you fifty bucks, too . . . That sounded terrible. Let me try again—"

"Mom!" I cut her off. "It's about Dad; I think it's about Dad. Elwin said *family,* not Dad specifically." Mom looked like I had just slapped her. "I'm sorry."

She raised her hand. "I've told you everything I can about your dad. You know that. I have always been honest with you about your father's time with me." She looked so sad and mad at the same time. But then I saw a twinkle in her eye. "Elwin? I knew there was a boy involved. I just knew it!"

I sat down across the table from her and took a deep breath. "You know I'm quirky. I like my things certain ways. I have strange habits. I always think someone is watching me." Her eyes grew large, but she didn't say anything, so I began speaking fast before I lost my nerve. "I guess around the end of the school year last year, things got weirder. I can't really explain it. That 'being watched' feeling was a bit more constant—an ever-present anxiety. I hear things—voices. Not random commands or anything Son-of-Sam like, but more like discussions. Sometimes answers to what I'm thinking just blurt out of thin air. I see things that aren't really there. I became so worried that I looked up my symptoms on Web MD and it said, 'You are crazy. Check yourself into the loony bin immediately.' I'm exaggerating and paraphrasing, of course. Things started getting really bad about a week ago. No more feelings of being watched. Instead, I *knew*— I absolutely *knew* there was something or someone by my side almost all the time—but I could not see anything or anyone. Tonight I went to Visions. Yes, I know you don't like me to go there, but I had to go. That's another thing or feeling that I can't quite explain. I'm absolutely driven to that place. Today when I was there, I cut my hand on a crystal. Oh, let me show you." I looked around for my purse. "Shoot! I must have left it in the car." I started to get up.

"Sit. You can get it when you finish." She waved her hands, motioning for me to continue.

"So, I met Celine's niece, Paige." *What was that look? Mom's heard that name before.* "I was feeling really crazy because I kept hearing things and tried to make a hasty exit. Paige stopped me on the way out and she gave me the crystal that I had cut my hand on. Then I left, thinking of driving myself to the loony bin." *Should I tell her I freaked and fainted because there was a stranger in my car? No. I'm going to keep that detail to myself. Should I mention he showed up in my dream? How about my apparent newfound telepathic abilities? Not now.* I cleared my throat and continued. "Outside the store, I met someone named Elwin." *Should I mention how sexy he was?* I was blushing and decided not to say anything about that. "He said my family wants me to see them and he was here to prepare me for the journey." I stopped talking and looked at her, waiting for her to respond.

Mom pursed her lips and tilted her head a little to the left. "And then?"

"Well, then I freaked out."

"Did he say anything else?" She was calm—a little too calm.

"He said that when I'm ready he can help me understand what's been going on and who I really am." I looked down and started picking at a frayed edge of my sweater.

"It's not time yet," mom mumbled under her breath.

"What?" I looked up.

"Nothing." Mom paused for a moment and held her poker face. "Well, when you decide, he will know and find you." She slid her chair back and stood up. "Why don't you go get your purse? You can show me the crystal."

In a bit of a daze, I stood up. "Okay." I tried to smile, gave up, and went outside to get my purse. Mathew's truck was still gone. *It must be one hot date with little Miss S.* I walked around to the back passenger side, opened the door and leaned into the backseat. It smelled like rain in my car and I wondered if that was what Elwin smelled like. I hurried back inside with my purse in one hand and my crystal in the other.

When I returned to the kitchen, I found it empty. Mom was not there, but there was a note on the table:

Sarette, I need to think. Let's talk about this tomorrow after I get back from work. I love you. Try not to make any decisions tonight.

I picked up the note and sitting under it was a crystal that looked just like mine.

FIVE

I threw my purse on my desk and placed both crystals on my nightstand, staring at them until I could finally break my gaze. Then, wiping away the beads of sweat gathering on my upper lip, I took off my heavy sweater, headed to my dresser, and changed into a tank top and boxer shorts. It might be winter in Michigan, but houses in Michigan are wrapped like mummies in winter to keep in as much heat as possible. Hot air rises, making my attic bedroom feel like the seventh level of hell.

I lay down on my bed and stretched out, mentally and physically exhausted. I needed to sleep a dreamless sleep. I've only had two dreams that I can remember. The one where, up until today, I would walk to the mountain range in the distance. The second dream started within the last couple of years and is more of a nightmare. I'm standing at the back of a town square—a town in the Old West. The square is filled with people who are fuzzy and out of focus. There is a stage on the other end of the square, and a man is standing on it, giving a speech. He's a blurry silhouette, speaking words that I can't hear, but they give me a creepy, ominous vibe that I continue to feel even after the dream ends. I always wake up terrified, but I have no idea what terrifies me.

I rolled to my side and looked at the crystals again before turning off the lamp. Staring up at the glow-in-the-dark stars that had been super-glued to my ceiling since my childhood. I knew there was no way I could think about today's happenings and not edge my way a little closer toward insanity. Could it be true? *Don't think about it . . . Time to sleep. Count sheep. 1, 2, 3, 4. No, not sheep. Think of all the two-letter words you can: aa, ab, ad, ae, ah, am, an, as, at . . .*

I fluffed my pillows, looking for cooler parts of the bed, but something was not quite right. Ah ha. My candles were not burning. I didn't have a water one anyway, so what was the point? Besides, it would not be safe to leave them burning if I did fall asleep. I decided to name every Widespread Panic song I could think of: "One Arm Steve" . . . "Ain't life grand" . . . *Elwin's eyes are so pretty! His black hair with red overtones is so hot.* "Christmas Katie" . . . "Doretha"... *He has nice arms. I wonder if he plays guitar. Who doesn't dig a guitar player? Stop thinking about him!* I punched my pillow. More Panic songs: "Surprise Valley" . . . "Diner" . . . "Disco". *What if I could meet my dad? Why did Mom look so strange when I mentioned Paige?* "Blue Indian" . . . "All Time Low" . . . "Climb to Safety".

"Grrr! This is pointless!" I sat up, clicked the light back on, and looked at the crystals again. *Where did Mom get hers?* I got up and walked over to the doors that lead to the roof of the porch below. The flat space is large enough to hold the orange vinyl couch that we found in the trash. We enjoy hanging out there in nice weather, but without having any railing, the area can be dangerous in winter when the roof gets icy. Overcome with a sense of urgency around today's events, and specifically the journey Elwin mentioned, I looked out the window and started talking to myself.

"Of course, I'm going to say yes. What other choice do I have?"

In a blink, Elwin was standing outside in the yard, looking pleased as he leaned against a tree. He gazed up at me with that half-smile of his. *What is that smile is all about? It's always there, and so inviting. Is it just a tic?* My heart started racing at the sight of him, and I felt like Juliet opening the door to Romeo as I walked out onto my makeshift balcony.

Near the edge of the roof and from this short distance, I could see that Elwin was frowning. He disappeared from the yard momentarily and then popped back up in front of me on the balcony. He placed his hands on my arms and started to rub them up and down.

"You're going to freeze out here. Do you want to put on warmer clothes?" He nodded toward the house without breaking his eye contact with me. "I can wait for you."

Being this close to him, I felt surprisingly hot, even though it was minus eighteen degrees with the wind chill factor and I was not wearing a coat, shoes, or hat. I realized I could die of exposure. "You're right," I said with a quick smile and turned to head inside. "Why don't you come inside for just a minute? *What has gotten into me? I just invited a strange guy into my bedroom in the middle of the night.* I crossed the room and sat on my bed. "In or out? Shut the door. It's freezing."

Elwin walked into my room, shut the balcony door and leaned back on it. He crossed his arms and smiled. I grabbed my hot pink Hello Kitty pillow and put it across my lap. Playing with the fringe along the side of the pillow, I sat in uncomfortable silence, not knowing what to say.

"You really didn't need to decide tonight. But, I'm glad you did." Elwin paused. "We can start training tomorrow."

"Training for what?" I inquired.

"Your journey."

"What journey?"

"To see your family."

I took an exaggerated inhale to find my center. "What family?"

"You ask a lot of questions."

"Listen, I'm still not so sure that I haven't gone crazy. So, if you wouldn't mind, could you start providing me with the info I need to figure what . . ." I waved my hands around the room, ". . .this is all about? I would super-duper appreciate it!" I ended with my arms out and watched as his eyes got bigger. *What is he staring at?* I looked down and noticed how transparent my tank top was. I didn't have on a bra. I pulled the pillow up over my chest and buried my face in it. I could have died of embarrassment.

I felt Elwin sit down on the bed next to me. "Sarette, if I could give you all the answers right now, I would. But I can't because most of it is not my story to tell. Besides, that's not why I'm here. My job is to get you ready. Where we're going is not an easy place to get to, and it will be dangerous. But your grandmother and father wouldn't have sent me unless they trusted me completely." He reached over and absentmindedly tucked a loose hair behind my ear.

"My grandmother and my father?" I could barely whisper. "Where have they been the last seventeen years?" I felt tears coming.

"Due to some complicated situations, it was safer for you to remain a secret. But your father has always kept an eye on you, kept you safe, and has been waiting to meet you. I will prepare you and get you there safely; that was my promise to your family, and it is my solemn oath to you." Elwin stood up and faced me. He clenched his fist and put it over his heart, bowing his head.

I couldn't help but giggle at the pomp and circumstance. "What are you? A knight or something? And what's with the disappearing act? Am I going to learn how to become invisible? Are we going to a different dimension?" He smiled as I kept rambling. "Give me something to go on. I have a wild imagination and by the time I see you again, I'll probably have convinced myself that I'm a fairy princess or something." Still clenching the pillow tightly to my chest, I waved and circled one hand as if to say, 'anytime now'.

Elwin stood up straight, crossed his arms over his chest, and looked at me intently. He was even taller than Mathew. Suddenly nervous, I started to avert my gaze downward. Somehow, I settled on his lips and lost my train of thought. I swallowed hard and looked into his eyes. He was smiling, having caught me in such a state of longing. He took a step closer, bent down, and brought his face a couple inches away from mine. For a brief second, I thought he was going to kiss me. But he kept moving until I could feel his breath next to my ear. That sent an involuntary shudder through my body. Slowly, he moved his breath from my ear, down to my shoulder, and back up to my ear. I tried not to show how much it affected me, but surely he must have noticed.

"Well . . ." His voice was soft, breathy, and torturously seductive as he whispered in my ear, "As a matter of fact, yes, I am a knight, or something.

The disappearing act is complicated, but I'll teach you how to do it. I promise." It sure seemed that he was talking about something more than physically disappearing. "Yes, sometimes I'm invisible and other times I'm in a different realm." As I tried to compose myself, he lifted my chin so I could look at him. With a regretful look, he said, "Get some sleep, finish your math homework, and call me when you're done." I nodded and the magical moment was over. With only a couple of strides, he reached the other side of the room.

"I need your number if you want me to call you."

He turned toward me with his hand on the doorknob. "Just say my name toward the east," he said as he pointed out the window, "And I'll be here." He shut the door as he disappeared.

I lay down on my bed and was wildly kicking the air with my pillow over my face when I heard Elwin say telepathically, *Goodnight, Princess.* He punctuated his comment with a lilted laugh. All I could do was smile.

SIX

Saturday, December 13

I have always been able to wake up when necessary—it didn't matter if it was an afternoon nap when I had only forty-seven minutes, or an early morning project I had to finish before school. I wondered if that was one of my super powers. Perhaps Elwin could clue me in about that, too. I opened my eyes and stared at the stars on my ceiling. I had slept well for the first time in a really long while. No dreams!

I turned my head to stretch and caught the time on the clock. "Holy crap! It's 10 a.m. I never sleep this late!" I said to myself. "Never mind the super power thing. Maybe this whole scenario has me a little off. At least I'm not calling myself crazy anymore."

I swung my legs over the side of my bed, set my feet on the floor and caught my image in the dresser mirror. I didn't look any different, but I definitely felt different. I padded over to my desk and got my phone out of my purse. I scrolled through my texts and found five text messages and a missed call from Mathew.

11:59 p.m.: Do you want help tomorrow with math?

7:00 a.m.: Going jogging. Want to come?

8:00 a.m.: Back from jogging. R u up yet?

9:00 a.m.: Seriously, you never sleep this late. Call me.

Missed call at 9:15 from Mathew.

9:58 a.m.: I'm coming over and breaking in!

I hit the call button and wrestled with putting on a sweatshirt single-handedly as I walked toward the balcony. I could hear a phone ringing, which meant Mathew was on the lawn below.

"Geez, Mathew. Stalk much?" I opened the door and shouted to him as I walked to the edge of my roof. "Can't a girl sleep in without you getting all crazy?"

"I have known you my entire life and you have never slept past 8 a.m.— ever. Excuse me for worrying." He looked relieved as he gazed up at me and shut his phone dramatically. "You want coffee? Steph bought me some gourmet stuff I can bring over."

"I knew you were on the S's," I shouted as I heard Mathew opening the kitchen door. "I'll be right down after a quick shower."

I sauntered back into my room and noticed the crystals sitting on my nightstand. Mom had some serious explaining to do. I grabbed clean clothes and headed downstairs to the bathroom.

As I got out of the shower a few minutes later, I could smell coffee. When I turned the corner into my kitchen, Mathew was checking email on his phone.

"Hey, thanks for worrying about me," I said as I grabbed my favorite square blue coffee mug. It was heavy and huge, with an etched Celtic-looking knot design. It fit my hand perfectly, which meant I could fit four fingers inside the handle. I'm not a big pinky-raising person. "How was your date?" Leaning back on the counter I looked at him. "Which Steph was it?"

"The date was awesome. You don't know her. She lives in Toledo; met her in the field house at Siena Heights University. She's thinking about going there next fall. She loves the small campus and that the school is run by Dominican nuns. Did you know that the Dominican sisters are millionaires? Creating social change from the inside out, in companies like Dow, has really paid off. Maybe I should see if I could audit a business class there next semester." *Wow, He looks happy. He should be happy, I guess.* "She wants to meet you, too. Maybe we can go see a movie next weekend. What do you think?"

"Third wheel, sounds like a lot of fun." Disappointment must have shown on my face. I took the towel off my damp hair and tossed it toward the laundry room door.

"Maybe Steph has someone she can bring. Or, is there someone you could ask?"

"Why do I need a date? It's not like we can chat in the movies anyhow."

"You might not feel like a third wheel at all. At least, not until we go out for coffee afterward. You could bail then." He was begging with those puppy dog eyes of his; I could tell he really liked her.

"Let me think about it, okay?" I took another sip of my coffee, looking at him from over the rim of my mug. Elwin's face popped into my mind. It wasn't really Elwin's face, but rather a smirk and his green jeweled eyes. I've never seen a color quite like that one. All of his features came into focus in my mind. His strong arms made me wonder how it would feel to have him hold me. I could feel the heat creeping up my face. *Stop it, Sarette!* I quickly took another drink of coffee, hoping Mathew hadn't noticed.

"You must have had a good night. You're blushing. Did you end up meeting a guy when you went to get coffee?" He rambled on without waiting for me to respond. "Was he a college guy? Siena Heights or Adrian? Football or track? Frat guy?" I didn't say anything. "Come on! You have to give me something!"

What could I say? *Yeah, I met a guy last night! He's a knight, sent by my long lost family to retrieve me for some inner dimensional journey fraught with danger. I'm not sure if we'll be back by next Saturday or if we will have time for trivialities such as dating, but I can check to see if he wants to go to a movie with us!*

I took another sip of my coffee. "Well, yes. I did meet someone—outside of Visions. But I'm not really sure about him yet. He wants me to call him after I'm done with my homework."

"What's his name?" He smiled teasingly.

"Elwin. But like I said, I'm not sure about him yet. But, if our first date goes well, I'll ask if he wants to go with us."

"Good!" Mathew stood up, stretching.

I decided to employ a tactic that I know usually works with Mathew: change the subject to something that either annoys or flatters him. "Are you sure you're not on human growth hormones? 'Cause you are looking pretty ripped, dude."

"So, where is Elwin from?" Mathew smiled. "You don't think that I can't tell when you're changing the subject on me, do you?" He paused. "All right, no more questions for now . . . but soon." He walked over, put his hand on my head and mussed my hair. "Now, if you don't need any help with math, I'm going to head home. I have a date this afternoon."

"I'm all good. Thanks for the coffee, or rather thank Steph for the coffee."

He bent down and kissed my cheek before he headed out the back door. I refilled my coffee cup and headed upstairs to finish my homework.

SEVEN

Solve $3[3 - (5x - 6)] + 7x = 0$
A) 27/8
B) 7/4
C) -16/27
D) 70/31
E) None of the above

    I spent the next ten minutes working out the problem and checking my math. I circled A on the Xeroxed busy work and closed my math book. I looked over to my never-used alarm clock. It was 11:55 a.m. Mom was not going to be home until after 3 p.m., so I had some downtime. I thought about calling Elwin to find out if there would be food where we were going. Surely, the meals are served on jeweled sterling trays in other dimensions! That is unless my family members were vampires. *Crap, what if I'm a vampire? I hate blood.* I had never heard of a knighted vampire, though, so I figured Elwin probably wasn't going to bite my neck.

    I noticed a shimmer across the room. The rocks on my nightstand seemed to be glowing. I quickly walked over to them and picked up one in each hand. Neither stone remained opaque. Like I'd first witnessed at the store, they were clear dark green with white swirls inside. As I sat down on my bed, the two crystals accidentally touched one another. I was instantly being pulled out of my body. I closed my eyes, hoping to relieve the nauseated rollercoaster feeling in my stomach. An odd, electric feeling washed over me, then suddenly it all stopped. I opened my eyes to vivid greens and blues. I gasped when I realized where I was.

    Holy moly! I was in my dream, but it wasn't a dream. I was standing at the edge of the forest, looking at the lake. The weather was so beautiful! Sunny and about seventy-seven degrees, just the way I like it. I was completely overdressed in my wool sweater and jeans. The water was so blue it was sparkling like gemstones in the sun. My eye caught something in the water about twenty yards out. Someone was swimming out there. It was Elwin. I could only see his shoulders and head above the water.

I strolled down to the edge of the lake. I noticed that I was still holding the crystals together in my hands.

"Hey," I said as casually as possible. Startled, he turned around and started walking toward the shore. I could not stop looking as the water slowly lowered on his muscular body. Attentive and focused, I scanned his shoulders and biceps, toned and strong. His chest was defined and hairless. *Manscape or natural?* I wondered as I looked up to meet his smiling eyes. Tyra Banks on *America's Next Top Model* would say he was "smizing". I wondered if I could still watch that show when I got to wherever it is I was going.

"You're going to have to turn around so I can get out," he said.

"Huh?" I responded, not quite understanding. *Holy crap! He's naked.* I blushed. "Sorry." I quickly turned around and closed my eyes.

I heard him laughing as he walked out of the water and moved to my left. After a few moments, he cleared his throat and said, "You can open your eyes now."

My face heated even more when I saw the rest of his six-pack being hidden under some over-washed Phish t-shirt. "Phish? They're okay. Not fully my vibe," I spoke in an attempt to help cool my excitement. "I've seen a bunch of live music, thanks to my mom. I've seen more than thirty Widespread Panic shows with her. I find that few things are more exhilarating than dancing to a really good version of 'Ribs N' Whiskey'."

"No, I guess you wouldn't find Phish to be your vibe," Elwin answered as soon as he could get a word in edgewise. "I like Phish all right, but I actually I wear these because I think these are . . ." He pulled out his shirt and looked down, ". . . hysterically ironic." He was smiling. "Want to see why?"

"Sure."

He turned toward the water and raised his arms out in front of him. He was holding a stick in his right hand and said something in a language that I did not recognize. He lowered his hands, put the stick in his pocket, and cast me a quick look before he walked out on the water. Not *in* the water, but on *top* of the water. My jaw dropped open. He was only about ten feet out when he stopped and turned around. He laughed a little when he noticed my shocked expression.

"Can you guess how I did that, or *what* I am? By the way, your awed face is pretty darn cute." He laughed, and then mimicked me with wide eyes and his mouth formed into an "o" shape. He was still laughing when I shook my head no in reply to his question. He started gently waving his arms at his sides, and little waves started moving away from him on either side of where he was standing. It created what looked like a catwalk from him to the shore. They obviously have their own version of *Top Model* here.

"You see, I'm not actually controlling the water. I can ask it to do certain things and if it wants to, it will do what I ask. So the Phish shirt is me having fun, rather than being a fan."

"You talk as if water is a living, breathing thing," I said.

"Not breathing, but certainly living. All of nature is connected and balanced. It's our job here to make sure that balance remains. Do you want to try and walk out here?"

Without giving it a moment's thought, I walked out on the water and came right up to him. His mouth dropped open, which I thought was funny. I quickly made the "o" shape with my mouth the way he had.

"I've never seen anything like that," he said as he tucked a stray curl behind my ear.

"Anything like what? I hope I didn't do anything wrong."

"I didn't have to come and get you. You didn't even have to ask. Everyone has to ask. Wow." He was staring at me, smiling that beautiful smile I had already become so fond of.

"You still haven't told me what you are."

He leaned down a little, not quite face to face, but much closer than before. He clenched his fist and placed it over his heart as he said, "My name is Elwin Colin of the Water Fey. I am a knight of the High Spirit Court. And you . . ." He paused and looked sad. Then, he bent down so his mouth was right next to my ear and said, "And, *you* are my princess. A fairy princess."

"I'm a fairy princess?" I could feel his arms tighten around me as I fainted.

I sat up straight and opened my eyes. I wasn't sure how much time had passed, but the sun was still shining brightly overhead. I closed my eyes again and took a deep breath, trying to recover. I blinked slowly and saw that I was still in my dream, but now I was on the shore, trying to remember what Elwin had said. I couldn't have heard him correctly. A princess? That's absurd. I am just an ordinary and boring chick who likes coffee a bit too much. There had to be some mistake.

"I don't make mistakes," I heard a voice coming from my right. Elwin was sitting next to me. He sat up and started rubbing his hands together to dust the sand off. Smirking a little, he said, "It's not that I don't like a damsel in distress as much as the next guy, but the fainting thing is going to be an unnecessary hindrance. Try to not do that anymore."

"Funny. I don't understand how I can be a fairy, let alone a princess. Seriously, I'm a human high school student struggling to make sure I get into the right colleges, whatever those are."

"Well, first, it's actually *fey* princess. I used the more common human term, hoping that might ease the news, which it didn't." He was smirking and his eyes were laughing. "We can agree to disagree about there not being anything extraordinary about you. In fact, I think you are one of a kind, Sarette Miller."

"What does that mean?" I said, creating a breeze by flapping my sweater in and out. "Is it always this hot here?"

"Well, you are a little overdressed for where we are. We have two options. One, we go back to the god-awful cold in Michigan and figure out some way to keep warm. Or, you can go and put on your swimsuit and meet me back here." It seemed like he was flirting with me. I was not sure how, but his eyes looked hungry.

"I vote to go back to Michigan where I can make coffee to keep warm while we wait for my mother. If I'm going to faint every time we talk about this, I'd rather only faint once. I don't want to hear the story over and over again. Do you understand what I'm saying?"

"I'm picking up what you're putting down," stated Elwin in a cute but mocking tone. After watching me for the last year, he must have known that was one of my favorite phrases. He reached to my side and picked up my crystals. They must have stuck together like magnets because he was only holding one of them.

"Take these," he said as he handed them to me. "Close your eyes and pull the stones apart. I'll be right behind you." He reached down his shirt and pulled out a silver chain. The two stones on the pendant looked just like my stones, only much smaller.

"Okay." I closed my eyes and pulled my crystals apart. I got that same roller coaster feeling for a second, but when it stopped, I was back in my room, sitting cross-legged on my bed. I looked up just in time to see Elwin appear on my balcony. I jumped up, dropping the crystals on the bed and ran to open the door for him.

"That was so freaking cool!" I said excitedly. "What else can I do with these? A necklace like yours would be much more convenient than carrying these big crystals with me. So if I'm a princess, then … is my dad the king?" I was still angry about having no interaction with my family all these years, but curiosity compelled me to keep digging. "So where has my family been all this time? Why have my mom and I been all alone? Actually, it has been the four of us. You understand that I have to tell Mathew about this, right? There is no way on God's green earth that I could ever keep this from him and our moms." I abruptly stopped my nervous rambling.

"You understand that they might not believe you, right?" he said.

"Yes, but that doesn't change the fact that I *have* to tell them. Not right now though. Mathew just started dating someone and he doesn't need to be distracted. He really likes her. Oh, do you want to go to the movies with me and them next week? Mathew is ready for his girlfriend to meet his family and I'm up first." I didn't mean to ask Elwin out. It just slipped out.

"That would be nice." He was looking intently at me.

Jumping up from the bed, I grabbed my phone off my desk and texted Mathew to let him know I had a date for Saturday. And to tell him that I was breaking into his house to get some more of that yummy coffee. A few seconds later he texted back: who is your date? I work till 5. C u then. Just hit brew ;)

I put the phone down and looked at Elwin.

"All set for Saturday. And, next Sunday is Mathew's and my birthday and we always do something special together. I'll tell him about this craziness then. Come on, let's go hit brew."

EIGHT

"All right. Talk," I said as I placed a cup of black coffee in front of Elwin.

"I thought you wanted to wait until your mom got home."

"I changed my mind. I'd like to get a primer course first so I don't completely freak out in front of her." I sat down across the table from him and took a sip of my sweetened coffee with skim milk.

"What do you want to know?"

"Who is my father?"

"King Roland of the Spirit Fey."

"What or who does he watch over?"

"Well . . . everything. I guess you could call him my superior." He shrugged and set down his coffee cup. "In our world, Daearen, there exists a certain hierarchy. Each of the five elements is represented by a realm. Each has its own royal family in charge. Each has its own castle. And the balance in that realm—water, fire, earth or air—carries into this one."

"What about the Spirit Fey?"

"They watch over everyone and everything in Daearen. The Spirit Fey have an ultimate rule of the land. They have the most magic, the most power and are the only fey with the power to use magic *against* other fey. Your family rules our world."

"I'm just going to let that sink in for a little bit. Um, my grandmother? What's her story?"

"Your grandmother and grandfather Keltoi ruled side by side for many years. It was a most glorious reign, a time of productivity, tolerance, peace and harmony. Your family leads the fey with confidence and humility. Your father, King Roland, spent his life preparing to be king. He also, he told me, had an incredible wanderlust, and one day he left our world and came to yours. He didn't know it, but soon after he left us, our King—your grandfather—started getting sick. He died a very short time later. His death made it Roland's time to serve.

"Your father immediately returned to take over the crown. Your grandmother, the queen, vowed to stay by his side until Roland's sister, Princess Penelope and her chosen were mated and then they would step in and rule. However, Princess Penelope disappeared after her mate died, and never took her place as the queen. So, your grandmother stayed on the throne. You see, we must be ruled by both a queen and king or the balance is upset. Your father still has not chosen a queen, which is very unusual. That brings us to you. No one knew anything about you, except for your father and grandmother. They've had friends secretly watching out for you."

"What do you mean, he had friends watching out for me?"

Elwin took another drink and nodded his head toward the kitchen window above the sink. I automatically followed his gaze and looked. There was a blue dragonfly and a rainbow-colored butterfly outside the window. "I don't get it. I mean, dragonflies are pretty and I like butterflies, but they're bugs. Can I talk to bugs? Is that it? Or can I somehow make it so their wings don't freeze off? It's like zero degrees outside?"

"They are not bugs," protested Elwin, "nor are they a dragonfly or a butterfly. Go, take a closer look."

I spilled coffee as I got up and walked closer to the window. I glanced back at Elwin and shrugged. "Still look like bugs to me."

"Let me help." Elwin walked up behind me, put his hands on my shoulders, and bent down so his mouth was right next to my ear. A shiver of excitement ran through my entire body. "Take a deep breath and look again." He started mumbling something in an indiscernible language. The bugs flew down to the ledge. They shimmered for a moment, then, right before my very eyes, they morphed into two tiny people about six inches tall.

"Tiny people with wings!" I cried. "That's awesome!"

The dragonfly's wings had different shades of blue in a stained glass pattern. She looked at me and did the same hand over the heart bow thing Elwin did. I squinted and leaned in for a better look. She had a sparkling blue nightclub dress. Her eyes and hair were blue, set off by her alabaster skin. The butterfly also did the heart-fist-bow thing. She had bright green eyes and the most beautiful ebony skin I had ever seen. She was wearing a glittery white nightclub dress so short it showed off her long legs. Her wings were different colors, woven in an intricate Celtic knot pattern. The tiny women curtsied, then turned back into bugs and flew away.

"Wow . . ." I could not look away from the window. "That's one of the most amazing things I've ever seen."

Elwin was standing behind me with his hands on my shoulders. I felt safe as I leaned on him and rested the back of my head on his muscular chest. He sharply sucked in a little breath and hesitantly reached around me, clasping his hands together in front of my bellybutton. I wondered if I made him as nervous as he made me. The embrace felt so wonderful that I took a small breath and closed my eyes, enjoying how our bodies fit together. His breath was a little heavier than normal. I wondered what would happen if I turned around to face him. Would he kiss me, or politely pull away?

"So you must be Elwin!" a voice blurted out. I jerked out of Elwin's arms, turning around so fast that I almost tripped. Elwin caught me as I met my mother's eyes from across the room. She put her purse down on the table by the door and moved toward the kitchen where we were standing.

"Mom, this is Elwin. Elwin, Mom." I tried not to look too guilty. After all, I hadn't done anything wrong.

"Elwin," Mom said as she nodded her head in his direction. "I hear we have some issues to discuss." She waited until he nodded back before walking over to the coffee pot. "Coffee smells good," she said as she poured herself a cup.

"Why don't you go and get the crystals, Sarette. I have a feeling they're much more interesting now that there are two of them." She spoke calmly, walked over to the table and sat down. "Elwin, please sit down." She motioned toward the place in front of his abandoned half-cup of coffee. He cautiously accommodated her request. I stood there in awe. I had never seen her so businesslike. "Sarette?" Mom snapped. "The crystals?"

Without further hesitation, I took the stairs three at a time. As I reached the top, I heard my mom say, "So, is there news of my husband, the king?" A twinge of melancholy tugged at my heart. She knew more about my dad than she had revealed to me. I mentally unchecked the box next to "always be honest with me" on the trust meter and quickly grabbed the crystals off my bed. They were opaque and looking normal again. To be safe, though, I made sure they were apart—I didn't want to accidentally travel to another realm or plane of existence.

Hurrying back down the stairs, I rounded the corner of the kitchen just in time to hear Elwin say, "I'm sorry if this is a shock, the queen kept the change of plans from Roland too. Daearen has grown more unstable and Queen Paige is ill. She fears she will not be strong enough to pass on the crown if we wait until next summer like you and Roland agreed to."

Elwin looked at me as I sat down, and I felt my face flush with betrayal, anger and curiosity. I looked at my mom, and my eyes started to fill with tears. "You've been lying to me my entire life."

"No," she clarified, "I've been omitting parts. We wanted you to have as much normalcy as possible, for as long as possible. What your father and I had was a once-in-a-lifetime thing—destiny. But we couldn't continue to be together. It wasn't my fault, or your father's; it was the fact that I am totally human and only those with fey blood may enter the fey realm. That's why direct contact with humans is strictly forbidden by the fey. Your father was going to give up the fey kingdom so he could live here with you and me. He and I were completely in love and he didn't care about being king. We were living our life, our way, and on our terms—at least for a while anyway. Then, one day, everything changed." Mom's eyes glazed with unshed tears. "Roland said he needed to leave. His father had died and a throne must have balance to be effective." She paused and took a sip of coffee.

Elwin chimed in. "If a realm in Daearen doesn't have balance in all things, bad things happen here."

"What kind of things?"

"Tornadoes, flash floods, tsunamis, those kinds of things."

Mom set down her cup and regained control of the conversation. "When the Spirit Fey throne was left unbalanced it didn't create an event here, it created a void or darkness in Daearen, and there has been fighting within all the realms ever since that day. Sarette, when I told Roland that he was going to be a father, he wanted to come back, but I wouldn't let him."

"Wait! You talk to him? How come I've never talked to him?" I was practically screaming. "You guys didn't think I should know about this? I want to see my dad, now!" Tears were flowing down my face. I looked from Elwin to my mom. Elwin, his eyes cast downward, was kneading his hands together, and my mom sat there calmly. "I can't do this!" I pushed out my chair and ran up the stairs. I reached my room and flung myself across my bed, burying my head in the pillows.

Elwin came up the stairs and stood in the doorway. "Sarette," he began, but I raised my hand.

"Please don't!" I lifted my head just enough so he could hear me but not see my face. "I need to process. I know it's your job to get me to understand all this, but…" I took a deep breath. "…just give me time to think. Please."

He waited for a moment. "I need the crystals for now, so call me when you're ready to talk." I could hear movement behind me. He was probably doing the heart-fist-bow thing. "Goodbye, Princess." He was gone. I put my head back down and cried myself to sleep.

I felt someone sit on my bed. I shot straight up and opened my eyes.

"Mathew Michael Conner! You know better than to sneak up on me! People get hurt when they surprise someone in bed. You should know that."

"What people?" He chuckled. "Who, besides me, would be brave enough to walk in on you?" His face grew serious when I raised my head. "Have you been crying? Is it that guy you met? Did this college dude already turn into a dick? Where can I find him? I got your back." He made an over-exaggerated angry face, trying to make me smile. It didn't work. "Seriously, I hate seeing you upset. What's wrong?"

"No, nothing like that. The guy, Elwin, is amazing. I wish it were a guy thing; it would be easier to fix. I had a fight with my mom. Elwin was here and witnessed it. He was sweet and wants me to call him when I'm feeling up to it."

"You had a fight with Mom? You never fight with her. Was it about Elwin? Elwin is a strange name." He pulled my hair like he used to when we were six years old.

"Owww! What was that for?"

"So, about the fight . . ." Mathew waited. I didn't know how much to tell him, or if this was even the best time to spill the beans. "You probably need to process all this before we talk, huh?"

I nodded. He got up and headed for the door. "I've got a date with Steph tonight, but I will cancel if you need me. You know that, right?" I nodded my head again. "I'm here for whatever you need."

As I listened to his footsteps fading down the stairs, I felt a stab of pain in the middle of my chest. If I went to the fey realm, I would have to leave Mathew behind. Mom, too. I was completely pissed off at her, but I didn't want to leave her. And what about Mama? It's always been the four of us. They are the only family I knew, and I'd have to leave them and go to some unfamiliar place and be with people I'd never even met. I rolled over onto the bed, squeezed my Hello Kitty pillow, and stared at the spot where the crystals had been sitting.

I didn't bother to wipe the tears cascading down my face as I fell back to sleep.

NINE

I awoke at 8:02 p.m. and realized I had screwed myself into not sleeping that night. I could process all the new family history I'd just gotten, or I could call Elwin. I sat up and looked to the east. What time was it in la-la land anyway? Do they observe Eastern Standard Time? I went downstairs to the bathroom where a look in the mirror confirmed that I was a disheveled mess. I washed my face, freshened up, and discarded my wrinkled clothing. I ran back upstairs wrapped in a towel and donned a clean pair of jeans and a strapless baby doll top. I could always put a jacket on if I got cold. I quickly brushed through my hair, twisted it up, and clipped it in place. I slid into my strapped black flats and felt ready. I went to the balcony door, faced east, and called for Elwin. It was only a second before he materialized in front of me. I opened the door and motioned for him to come inside.

"You look nice all dressed up. Got a big date?" He walked past me, grabbed my desk chair, turned it around, and straddled it in one fell swoop. I shut the door and leaned back on it, crossing my arms to mimic his typical stance. I can't smize though; he definitely has me beat on that skill.

"No date—I've been crying and sleeping all day. I'm up for doing something, though. I'm not sure what; I just need to get out of my head for a little while. Also, it took me all of five minutes to get ready. I am in no way, shape, or form dressed up. You won't be able to miss me when I'm dressed up."

"I have no doubt." Elwin paused before he reached into his right jacket pocket and took out one of the amazonite crystals. It was the one my mom had kept all these years. He placed it on the desk and retrieved the other one from his pocket. He stood up and reached into his front pocket of his button-down shirt. I caught myself staring at his chest and averted my eyes. "I made something for you. I think you'll find it convenient. Turn around," he said as he made a twirling motion with his hand, "and close your eyes."

I responded without protest and closed my eyes tight. I felt like a little kid waiting for a surprise at her birthday party. I could feel Elwin's luscious energy swirling around me. I was startled and a chill ran up my spine when a cold object touched my skin near my heart. His fingers lightly touched the back of my neck and I felt him clasp a necklace. He left his warm hands on my shoulders and spoke into my ear, "You can open your eyes now."

"Wow, this is so beautiful." I looked at my reflection in the mirror, drinking in every detail. It was a thick silver rope chain made up of Celtic knots, one leading and turning into the next. The pendant resting on my breastbone had two pieces of my amazonite crystal. One side was a darker green with the white stripes and swirls, and the other side was a lighter, creamier green taken from the other side of the crystal. Both pieces were cut and shaped to resemble a yin-yang sign, however, it stretched into the shape of an oval rather than a circle. A simple two-strand, one in gold and one in silver, Celtic knot pattern framed the oval. I turned around and looked up at him appreciatively. "Thank you, it's so beautiful."

He swallowed hard. His hands, still resting on my upper arms, felt really warm. Looking up at him, I stood perfectly still, hoping he might kiss me. I was afraid to breathe for fear that it might cause this moment to end. Then, a sudden wave of nervousness and anxiety overcame me, and I had to look away.

"You made this?"

"Uh huh."

"You're such an artist." I lifted the pendant from my chest, smoothing my thumb over the surface, much like one might rub a worry stone. "Why are both pieces from my crystal?"

"That's how it works, two pieces of the same crystal. Mine is also made from yours. I haven't figured out why touching your crystal to your mother's worked."

"So how does *this* one work?"

"I put in a hidden latch so you can wear them at the same time and not have to keep one in your pocket. When you unlatch it, you can move the two pieces together and it will physically take you to the same place we were yesterday. If you sleep with the bigger piece nearby, your physical body will stay, but your spirit will enter the same location in the dream realm."

He moved his right hand from my arm and trailed his fingers across my ribcage, sending a warm quiver down my spine. I wondered if there was such a thing as a poisonous fey; I felt paralyzed by a sensuous exchange of energy as his hand covered my hand that was still holding the pendant. He then reached under my chin and raised my head to meet him eye to eye. This created the most intensely erotic sensation that I had ever experienced. I felt powerless to resist, and every cell in my body was begging him to caress me. His eyes looked hungry as our gazes locked. Then, I saw something momentarily flicker in his eyes. He gave a disappointed smile and took a small step back, removing his hands from my arm and chin. I suddenly felt cold.

"First test," he said, clearing his throat, "is to see if you can find the latch."

I looked down quickly and blinked, hoping he would not see the tears that had begun to swell at his rejection. I thumbed the pendant, searching for a discernible difference on the surface, but felt no edges indicating where a latch might be hidden. I started visually scanning it. One small loop in the silver strand of the Celtic knot was turned a different way from the others, so I flicked it gently with my thumbnail. Nothing happened, so I pressed in lightly. The center of the symbol split apart and the two crystals hinged so the backs were touching. I looked up with a victorious grin.

"Maybe I'm losing my touch," he said. "That took you all of ten seconds to figure out."

"It's so pretty. How did you make it?"

"I can't take all the credit. Your mother cut and shaped the crystals for me and I built the pendant at home."

"So how does it work? The stones touched, but I didn't go to the dream place."

"In this position, the halves are not quite touching." He pointed between the two pieces and I took a closer look. "To travel, you have to squeeze the two sides together. But, not now!" he cautioned.

He sat back down, straddling the chair as before, and hunched toward me with his arms clasped on the back.

"Do you know what their story is—my mom and dad?"

"That's not my story to tell."

"If I ask Mom about her story, how do I know she will tell me the truth? The *whole* truth! I am supremely pissed off with her, super confused and trying to keep my wits about me. She has been lying to me my entire life. Oh, wait. No, she's just *omitting* things. Part of the prep work for anything I do is research. I need facts. I'll get nothing out of talking to my mom." I sat down cross-legged on my bed and put my Hello Kitty pillow on my lap. "Start talking, Knight Boy."

Startled by my insistence for details, Elwin stammered. "Your mother has a crystal so she can spend her dreams with your dad."

"Why did she keep me from him?"

"It's really not like that. Your mom couldn't have introduced you to him. The crystal is for *her* connection. You mother and father are connected, joined as husband and wife, mates. No matter how much he loves you, he's just not connected to you in the same type of relationship. Their crystal is *their* unique link, their connection."

"So, are you and I connected?" I blurted. "I mean, when you showed up we didn't have any connection." *And apparently we still don't have one.* "So how does that work?"

"We do have a connection," he swallowed hard. "Your father has trained me for as long as I can remember to protect you, and I have been here since last May doing just that."

"You've been spying on me since last May? I feel so violated."

"I was not a peeping tom, Sarette. I wasn't peering in your windows or stalking you. I've been close by in case there was a problem. There haven't been any problems outside and you've always been excellent about protecting yourself in here." He spoke with his arm sweeping the room. "Your room has been a very safe place, thanks to the candles. Did your mom give them to you?"

"No, I bought them in town."

Elwin seemed surprised. "How did you know how to cast a protection spell on your house? I couldn't get within five feet of it."

"I've never cast a spell. The most I ever do is light my candles. It's not like I'm up here, chanting and dancing naked in circles with my arms stretched toward the ceiling. It's just me with a candle and a Bic lighter that I purchased for $1.99 at my local convenience mart."

"The Queen sent word a week ago that the timing has been pushed up. I've been trying to reach you here ever since. The water candle kept me out, so I'm not too concerned that you haven't got another one burning."

"So, what? A week ago you became a peeping tom?"

"Stop with the pervert stuff. No, I didn't peep. I could never make it close enough. Your protective circle was too strong. I needed a little help, so your grandmother came. I think you met her. She's Paige, the one who brought the crystal to Visions for you to find."

"What? The little-redheaded cutie? She was only five years old!"

"She didn't think you were ready to see her in her natural form, so she changed into something less imposing. Something 'cute', like you said." Elwin shrugged. "You really didn't do any ritual with the candles?" I shook my head no. "That's remarkable."

"Why aren't humans and fey allowed to be together?"

He raised his eyebrows a little bit. "It hasn't always been that way. Long ago, it was very common for a fey to fall in love with a human. The fey only truly fall in love once, but humans cannot come to Daearen. Many fey left to stay with the ones they love here in this realm. Our ancestors soon realized that with so many fey in the earth realm, our magic had weakened in our own. When Daearen became unbalanced, things like massive earthquakes, cities being leveled with fire and brimstone, the sinking of Atlantis, and Tornado Alley happened here. It took many years of laws, strict rules, marriages, and alliances to bring Daearen back into perfect balance."

"And then my father left and the imbalance came back. Why would my father leave if so much were at stake?" I absentmindedly reached for my pendant, found the latch, and clicked it open and flat.

Elwin noticed. "Totally losing my touch with the hidden clasp thing. It's too easy. Maybe I've spent too much time here. My magic could be weak."

"Are you like a rechargeable battery?" I giggled. "Or, do you go back to fey land and say 'up, up, Power Rangers!' and morph into super fairies?" A picture popped in my head of Elwin holding a wand and springing up with wings and sparkles. It started as a giggle that turned into a laugh. I kept laughing, harder and deeper to the point that I couldn't breathe. So hard that I started crying and couldn't see. I could still hear, though, and Elwin was laughing as hard as I was. He leaned back and fell right out of the chair, which made both of us laugh even harder. We were laughing so loud that neither of us heard Mom coming up the stairs. I don't even know how long she was there before she spoke.

"I'm not thrilled about you having a boy in your room, but I am happy to see you laughing." She leaned on the door jam with a hopeful look on her face. "Are you ready to talk?" She glanced at Elwin and said in an authoritative manner, "Alone."

Elwin looked at me and I nodded. He stood up and walked to the balcony door. When he opened it, a cold breeze whipped into the room. He turned around and said, "I'm not exactly sure when we will be leaving. But when it is time, we will have to go, no matter where we are in our training. Please call me tomorrow. There's much I have to teach you." He closed the door behind him, and on his second step his outline blurred and he was gone. The room instantly began to warm and I felt different. *Just a crazy crush, right? Get over it, Sarette. Our connection is different. He was clear: you are his job.*

I looked at my mom. "Ice cream?"

She smiled and we headed downstairs.

TEN

Mom put a bowl with two scoops of butter pecan ice cream in front of me and went back to get herself some.

With her back turned to me, she said, "I am sorry for not telling you the whole truth. I hope that one day you can forgive me." She tossed the empty ice cream container in the recycling bin and came to sit down. "Everything I have told you about your father is true. I spent the summer before my senior year of college in Tennessee working on my dissertation. It was a Saturday about two weeks into my field work when I went spelunking."

"Wait, wait, wait! This part is new. I didn't know you were a spelunker."

"I guess I forgot to mention that part. Anyway, I liked to take my time. The rope from me to the guy in front of me was sixty feet long. I was pretty much by myself when I noticed a faint glow in a crevasse off to the side of the main cave. That's where I found the crystal. It was so beautiful and I had never seen anything like it. I knew it was an amazonite, but it didn't belong there. The heft was inconsistent with the size, the planes of cleavage indiscernible. I figured I had something special, so I didn't tell my group. I just tucked it into my bag for later inspection." She wistfully looked past me as if she was someplace far away.

"When the group was done, they left and I stayed to do some cataloging of the samples I had taken. I also wanted to take a closer look at the strange stone. Outside in the light, the stone seemed to shimmer and alternate from a transparent crystal to an opaque stone, a quality I have yet to see documented in any textbook. After slogging through the recording of information and cataloging the samples, something drew my attention from the task at hand. I thought it was someone from the group coming back to get me, but it was your father. He walked out of the cave and approached me." Mom looked at me compassionately. "The rest of the story I have told you is true; we did immediately fall in love. We talked together for a couple of hours and that was that; we were rarely apart after that moment. It was near the end of summer and my work. Your father was planning to move to Michigan with me and we had plans for a future together. We did everything that summer, a summer I will never forget.

"One night we were laughing and planning the rest of our lives together when he doubled over in pain. He said it felt like his heart was ripped in two. He was gasping for breath, disoriented, but he was screaming and begging me not to call 911. He stumbled to the door, opened it, and collapsed. I couldn't move because of what I saw next. A brilliant red dragonfly flew in and landed on his chest. He was yelling at the dragonfly, talking to it as though it could understand his pleas. 'What's wrong? What happened?' he groaned. It was almost more than I could take. The sound of this man, the man I loved, crying and begging a bug for news. I was beginning to wonder whether he was insane when suddenly the dragonfly changed into a Fire Fey right in front of me." Mom looked at me. "Do I need to explain a Fire Fey?"

"No, please continue," I said.

"I was completely lost, confused by what most people would call a delusion. I had witnessed a firefly turn into a person-like thing. I could see this creature and Roland talking to one another, but I couldn't hear what they were saying. It was like I was in a vacuum that couldn't transmit sound. My mind was reeling and I was so off-kilter that I didn't notice the fey had left. Regular sound returned. I heard the door slam—that snapped me back to reality. Your father's face had a look of resignation and pride that I can't explain. I instinctively knew he was leaving, and I was losing my true love. He explained everything about his world, his role, and his need to go home. I think Elwin should explain those particulars since he knows far more than I do. Okay?" I nodded and Mom continued. "Roland should have gone back right then, but he stayed a little longer. That night at sunset, we pledged ourselves to one another and performed a binding ceremony. We had one night together as man and wife in this realm. The next morning I watched him walk into the cave and disappear from this world." Mom got up, grabbed the bowls, and put them in the sink.

"Elwin said that you see Dad in your dreams."

"Yes, with the amazonite crystal I can see your father in a dream state, but that's the only way I can see him. When we found out about you, he wanted to come back, but he couldn't leave. The people in both our worlds needed the leadership and balance he could provide. He needed to stay on the throne or life as we know it would dramatically change. I couldn't let that happen. We knew you would need to join him one day, but we wanted you to have this life, too.

"I know it's a lot, but you and I will still be able to see each other. I'm not abandoning you; I'd never do that. I have already asked Elwin to secure a lavakite crystal so you and I can still see each other in a dream state."

"I don't want to see you only when I'm dreaming. This is so unfair!" My stomach dropped into a pit as I thought about a new life without having my mom downstairs or just a text message away. My destiny had already been decided and I had no choice in the matter.

"There is one more detail that you should know. Once you arrive at your castle, Meanmna, you will have to choose your mate before you can ascend the throne—"

"Wait! What? I am expected to choose a mate? Like right away, get married?"

"Once you do and you're settled and have spent some time with your father, he can come back here." Mom looked sad but calm and apparently wanted to hear that I was okay with all of this.

Mom had seventeen years to prepare for this moment—I'd only had one day. It was so unfair. I was fighting back tears and started to feel a tightening of my chest. I closed my eyes tight, wrapped my arms around my waist, and tried to regulate my breathing. I kept my eyes closed when Mom started talking again.

"Sarette, I am sorry this is such a shock. I have dreaded this day since I found out I was pregnant. Maybe we should have told you sooner, but we wanted you to have as much of a normal life as possible. I'm sorry that this is unfair, but it is what it is. I think that's the real reason I didn't tell you sooner, we can't fight fate. I will no longer omit anything, Sarette. I'm excited to have my husband back. I would give anything if the three of us had just a little time together, but that can never happen. He will be able to come back to me once you and your mate become king and queen. Would I choose for you to get married at eighteen? No. But, I have no doubt you will find your mate once you reach Meanmna. I wish I could watch you fall in love."

I opened my eyes and looked at my mother for what felt like the first time, heartbroken and happy all at the same time. I reached over and grabbed her hand.

Mom squeezed my hand and said, "I wish we had some choices in all of this, but we don't. This is so much bigger than the three of us. I do not expect you to be completely okay with this situation. If there is anything I can answer for you, I will; do you have any questions right now? Or do you need to process?"

"I need to process."

"Well, you can process, but we have a lot to do. Perhaps you shouldn't see Elwin tomorrow for training. We need some gear for your journey. We could go in the morning. We can have breakfast in town then go to Cabela's. We should be able to get almost everything there, and then we can grab lunch in Dundee. Also, you should see if you can push up the birthday date for tomorrow afternoon."

"Do you really think that's necessary?" I said, hearing the pleading tone in my voice. "Our birthday is next Sunday, that's only one week away. There's no way I'll be trained by then. Don't you think I can wait to leave until after that?"

"No. Sorry, honey, but I don't. I can't train you for anything, but I can shop, so that's what we'll do tomorrow." Mom seemed unmoved by the enormous amount of emotional pain that was welling up inside me. "Text Mathew right away. You shouldn't wait to say goodbye. You will have to leave when it's time and not a second sooner or later."

"What about Mama? What am I going to say to her?" I felt the tears starting to trickle down my face.

"I'll take care of Mama. It's my turn for family dinner tomorrow; we will break the news to her then."

Our Sunday dinners were usually just the four of us unless Mama brought a date, which was always a little awkward. I hoped this would not be one of those occasions. I could not imagine having to say goodbye to my family while a stranger was sitting at the table with us.

"Dinner is at six, like normal," Mom reminded me. "Why don't you see if Elwin would like to come? Perhaps a demonstration or two will help with the non-believers among us. I think I'm going to leave you to process."

Mom smiled. I could see tears in her eyes as she kissed me on the head and gave me a big bear hug that I never wanted to end. She walked into her bedroom, shut the door behind her and started sobbing. Choking back my own tears, I loaded the dishwasher and headed upstairs.

ELEVEN

I texted Mathew as soon as I got to my room:

> Sarette: *Need to push up birthday to tomorrow, does that totally screw up your plans?*
> Mathew: *Not really. What's wrong?*
> Sarette: *Tell you tomorrow. Mom's taking me to Cabelas & lunch. I'll text when I get home*
> Mathew: *Going camping?*
> Sarette: *Not so much*
> Mathew: *Noncommittal answers worry me*
> Sarette: *No worries—we'll talk tomorrow*
> Mathew: *Text me. Love ya*
> Sarette: *Love ya 2*

I debated asking Mathew to come right over and talk about all this, but I wasn't ready. I couldn't believe I had to find a mate and get married, like now. It was a good thing I had someone in mind. Elwin had said I was his "job", but his eyes told a different story. I really needed to see him.

I put my phone down and walked over to the crystals on my desk, waving my hand over both of them. I felt a buzz over the second one, so I placed it gently on my nightstand. Elwin said if I fell asleep with the larger piece of the amazonite I'd go to the dream plane. He hadn't told me anything else, though, like what I would show up wearing. The first time I saw Elwin in my dream I was wearing a dress—and I hadn't chosen my attire. But the second time I was wearing my own clothes. I decided to put on my cutest pajamas just in case this worked and I ended up on the beach. I dug to the bottom of my dresser drawer and found the black, silky, never-worn pajamas Mom had bought me on sale. The one-piece jumper had spaghetti straps, buttons down the front and a red ribbon tie at the waist. It had never been my style, but now I pulled off the tags and slipped into it, enjoying the feel of the material against my skin. *But how do I look in it?* When I stood before the mirror, I was pleasantly surprised. It showed off my small waist and flared gently about my hips like a little skirt, even though it was actually shorts that hit about mid-thigh. The V-cut top didn't show much but still looked sexy. I knew I was trying too hard, but how was I supposed to get ready to be a princess? I just couldn't see myself running around a castle in boxers and a braless tank.

I left my necklace on—it really showed off my pale skin and I had already decided I would never take it off. I brushed my hair and talked myself out of putting on makeup before I climbed into bed. I was likely doing all this for nothing. After all, Elwin was clearly not interested in me personally. I'm his job! How many different times and ways had he said that? "Grrr!" I grabbed the Hello Kitty pillow and put it over my face, muffling the sound of my frustration. "Screw it!" I rolled to my side and looked at the crystal. As I reached to turn out the lamp, my hand gently skimmed the surface of the crystal and I felt the buzz again. Ignoring it, I closed my eyes and tried to calm my racing mind.

Tomorrow would be a big shopping day; Mom was taking me to Cabela's Outfitters store. I hoped I was not going camping in fey land. That would suck. And poor Mathew. What would I tell him? My life as I knew it was coming to an abrupt halt. Would it still be necessary to write that article for the paper? Would there be a GED program in la-la land? Would I even need to go to school? Would my friends at school even miss me? How would Mom explain my disappearance?

Trying my usual get-to-sleep routine, I began mentally listing songs that Widespread Panic had played: "Space Wrangler". . . "Superstition" . . . "Red Hot Mama" . . . "Love Tractor". . . *I wonder what I should wear to dinner tomorrow. Maybe I can find something at Cabela's. Elwin might like camo; you never know* . . . "Thought Sausage". . . "Imitation Leather Shoes" . . . "Georgia" . . .

I started hearing JB singing "Georgia" in my head. New Year's 2005 was the best show I'd ever seen. Hearing the boys play a cover from Ray Charles, that was a moment for sure. *Crap! I'm never going to see another show again either.*

This fairy princess thing certainly came with a lot of strings. I didn't really have a choice, though. Stay here and the world ends. Be a princess and there is no imbalance, as long as I never leave the kingdom. The thought of leaving the only family I had known hurt bad enough, but to be referred to as a "job" by someone who makes my heart race was even worse. *My life sucks. Fairy princess, my ass.* I rolled away from my crystal and start counting backward from one hundred. I had made it to sixty-seven before I realized I was dreaming again.

I looked around the dreamscape. It was nighttime and the stars' reflections were sparkling across the lake. The stars looked different there than they did on Earth; I didn't see any familiar constellations and many of them seemed to pulse as much as twinkle. When I looked down, I realized that I was still wearing the black one-piece. It was hard to imagine why I initially thought this looked sexy; I felt utterly ridiculous in it. I noticed a small fire about one hundred yards down the beach with a silhouette of someone sitting by it. *It has to be Elwin. He and I are the only two fey who can come here. I really need to get out of here before he sees me.* Before I had a chance to move, he turned his head and looked at me. *Crap! Why did I wear this tacky thing? Why didn't I back away three seconds ago? Wake up! Wake Up! Too late; here he comes.* I gave up hope of ending a potentially uncomfortable moment.

Elwin stopped about five feet away. His eyes slowly scanned the entire length of my body, moving down, then back up to meet my gaze. *This is too intense; I can't do this!* I looked away and down to hide my embarrassment.

Elwin cleared his throat and asked, "Would you like to sit by the fire?"

"That would be nice. Thank you."

He turned around and headed back to the dancing flames, and I walked behind him, silently cursing myself and swinging my arms wildly. I stopped just in time before he turned around and motioned to a big, thick blanket next to the fire. It was difficult to sit in the stupid outfit without showing my entire thigh. Elwin was such a gentleman, though; as if he'd read my mind, he reached into a bag and handed me a smaller blanket that I could drape over my legs. *I'm an idiot. He must think I'm an immature child with a crush. Let's face it, I am.*

"I'm not going to be able to train tomorrow. Mom is taking me to Cabela's for 'gear'. What kind of gear, exactly? Is it for camping? I hate camping."

"You'll be fine. You've never been camping. Therefore, you have no idea whether you like it or not. Your mom knows what you'll need," he said as he rearranged the coals with a stick.

"I also moved my birthday celebration to tomorrow afternoon. Mom said there will be no time for goodbyes when the time comes."

"That's true; we leave when we leave."

"Mom would also like it if you could come tomorrow. She's going to tell Mama—that's Mathew's mom—about all this, and she would like you there for backup and evidence that we're not crazy. It's at—"

"Six. I know. I've been watching you for a year, remember?" Elwin said in a clipped tone.

I'm making him uncomfortable in this stupid get-up. I should make up an excuse about why I'm wearing it... "I thought I would show up here in the long dress that I usually wear in my recurring dream since I'm entering the fey realm *through* my dream plane." I watched as his smile quickly came and went. I must have impressed him with my very limited knowledge of la-la land, but he had not looked at me since I sat down. In fact, he had avoided every opportunity to look at me. *I have to get out of here. I have made the biggest fool out of myself wishing for something I can't have. I need to figure out an exit strategy and execute it. Dammit!*

I stood up and tossed aside the blanket. Elwin was watching me out of the corner of his eye, but didn't move his head at all. "So, how do I get out of here? I have a big day tomorrow and need to get up early."

Grabbing the blanket, Elwin stood and draped it over my shoulders. His hands held the edges in place in front of me. *He's purposely covering me up! I have got to get out of here.* I took a step back, intentionally breaking his hold on the blanket; then clutching it myself, I turned and quickly started walking to the tree line. I could hear him following a couple of steps behind me. *Crap! I really don't know where I'm going or what I'm doing. I'd like to go home now! Just keep walking and don't look back, stupid little girl playing dress up. This is ridiculous! I have to ask him where to go or I'll just wander aimlessly.*

I stopped and turned quickly. He must have been looking down because he crashed right into me, knocking me off balance. Elwin reacted instantly, wrapping me in his arms and not letting me fall. We ended up in a dancers' dip position—me leaning backward and him leaning over me. I could not stop looking at his eyes. His hair was blocking some of his face. I removed my hand from his shirt and realized I had been clenching it so hard that my knuckles were turning white. I reached up and brushed my hand across his forehead, sweeping the hair over and behind his ear. He moved his head slightly and nudged my hand to the back of his neck.

"I do not think you're a stupid little girl playing dress up." His voice was thick and gravelly.

Oh, my God! He can hear everything I'm thinking! I gasped in shock as Elwin hungrily pressed his lips down on mine, searching, exploring, our tongues entangled in a dance. I reached behind his head and twisted my hands in his hair. *I need you closer.* I lifted up on my tippy toes, trying to get to him, but I was still bent backward and felt off balance. I heard a growl from somewhere in his chest, then he stood up straight, pulling me up with him. The entire length of my body was touching his, but I wanted him closer still. One of his hands left my back and moved slowly down my hip, thigh, and to the back of my knee. This movement caused part of his body to lose contact with mine. I moaned in protest and moved my hands from his hair to his back, trying to pull him back to me. Then, in one swift movement he lifted me and slid me along his body until my legs were wrapped around his waist. I gasped at the sensation. He started kissing my neck and then trailed his kisses upward to my ear, gently biting and sucking it. Then he paused to let out a contented breath into my ear, causing an uncontrollable shiver down my spine. I moaned, the sound new and unrecognizable, even to me.

His hands still under my thighs, Elwin turned us around and headed back toward the fire. He was gently kneaded my legs with his strong fingers, and I tried to adjust my position to force his hands where I needed them. He just pulled me in even tighter and let his rock hard stomach give my core the pressure it needed. By the time we got to the fire, I was panting with desire. He managed to lay us on the ground without removing my legs from around his waist and settled himself between my thighs. I unhooked one leg, sliding it next to his and rubbed it up and down his thigh. I left the other leg around his back. He paused from kissing my neck and looked at me. He moved slightly, bringing us face to face. One of his hands moved up my body, gently grazing my breast as he found the indentation above my collar bone and rubbed it lightly with his thumb.

Elwin brought his eyes to mine. "I've wanted to do this for a very long time." The lust in his voice caused me to shudder in anticipation. He lowered his mouth and gently kissed the indentation, opened his mouth wider and licked over the ridge of my collarbone, only to kiss the indentation again. I moaned again, softly this time, as he trailed kisses across my collarbone, stopping to nibble the base of my neck. He found the matching indentation on the other side kissed it, licked my collarbone, and kissed my indentation again. It was both delicious and excruciating. *God I don't want this to end!* I was desperate for him as I drew his shoulders to me in search of his mouth. I used my leg around his back to pull him even closer. I could feel him shaking. I was shaking. *If you ask, I would say yes.*

As soon as that thought popped into my head, Elwin pushed himself off me, quickly moved to the other side of the blanket, and left me lying on the ground. I lifted my head and looked at him, breathless and confused. *What the hell just happened?*

"I'm sorry," he said, his head in his hand. "I shouldn't have done that. This can't happen."

I sat up and crossed my arms over my chest, rubbing them to ease the sudden chill I felt. "I don't understand. What did I do wrong?" I turned my head away so he wouldn't see the tears in my eyes. *What's up with all this crying? I've cried more in the last thirty-six hours than I have in the last thirty-six months.*

"Please don't cry. I really hate to see you cry."

"Get out of my head!"

"Sarette," he said softly.

"Seriously! Get out," I snapped. The passion that had racked my body had been replaced with anger and hurt.

"I'm sorry."

"You already said that!" My voice was louder than I intended and I was flailing my arms in the air like a robot gone mad. He looked shocked. He had watched me for a year and knew that I never scream.

"Please, this is my fault. I shouldn't have . . . You don't understand. This . . . us . . . you and I can never happen," he muttered.

"Why? Why can't it? Mom told me what's expected of me. So you're right, I don't understand why this can't happen. So help me, please! My entire life has been ripped apart at the very seams. I've been told that I'm a fairy—"

"Fey," he interrupted.

"Whatever! I'm a fey princess, I have my own knight, and I am going on some dangerous journey that I need to 'prepare for'." I used my fingers as quotation marks. "I have no idea why I have to prepare; only that I have to. At a moment's notice, I am going to leave everything, *everything and everyone,* I love. I just found out I have to choose a mate and my own knight is giving me mixed signals! Please explain it to me. . . I just don't understand."

"Do you remember why I said I'm here, rather than someone else?"

"You said my grandmother and father trusted you."

"There's another reason, too. It was also safe to send me."

"What does that mean?"

He drew an infinity symbol with one of his hands as he said, "It is what it is, and I am who I am." He put his hand back down, smiled, and shrugged. "I'm not exactly spirit king material."

"But you are a knight, best of the best or whatever . . . or is that the Navy Seals? Army Rangers? I don't know. . . I'm rambling. Please continue."

"I am a knight. That doesn't mean I'm from a strong magical family, and *that's* who you are going to be expected to mate with. I'm not good enough for you, Sarette. If I die, nothing's lost. My second will take—"

"What do you mean, nothing's lost? I don't want to lose you!" Without even thinking, I scooted over to him. He hesitated for a second and then put his arm around me. I folded into his side, my head resting in the crook between his chest and shoulder.

"Sarette, it is my duty to get you to the castle safely, and I swear I will." I nodded my head against his chest. "But, if something should happen to me, my second is prepared to find you and they will get you to Meanmna safely."

"What's a second?"

"It's the same type of bond you and Mathew have. We have a word for that kind of bond: vaki. It means *true companion.* Think of a vaki as your second mate—your right-hand person, your conscript. I would lay down my life for my second and they would lay their life down for me. The only bond stronger than a vaki is that of a mazon. The word for your bonded mate is mazon. When two are bonded together in vaki or mazon, it's for life."

"Well, that's kind of cool. What happens if I fall asleep here? Isn't this a dream? How does that work?"

"If you fall asleep here, you'll just wake up in your bed tomorrow."

"Okay, 'cause you're really comfy." I snuggled a little closer so my cheek rested on his chest. He squeezed his arm a little tighter and started slowly drawing continuous loops up and down my arm. I let out a contented sigh. *This is nice.*

Yes, it is. I thought, then my eyes flew open. Now I was reading his thoughts!

"Do you want me to tell you a story to help you fall asleep?"

"As long as you start it with 'Once upon a time.' All good fairy tales begin that way. Ouch! You pinched me! Come on! That was funny!"

"Ha ha . . . Once upon a time . . ."

"Thank you."

He gently moved a curl across my forehead and tucked it behind my ear.

As I drifted to sleep, I heard him telepathically say, *Once upon a time, in a land in another dimension known as la-la land . . .*

TWELVE

Sunday, December 14

I opened my eyes the next morning and noticed that there was a fresh three inches of snow outside my rooftop door. No matter where I ended up on this journey, I would not miss winter in Michigan.

I needed coffee so I headed downstairs. Mom was in her spot, leaning against the sink with her iPad in one hand and her coffee cup in the other.

"Morning." She looked up and suddenly spewed the sip of coffee she had just taken.

"Mom, are you okay?" I hurried to her and started patting her back to help "un-choke" her.

"What are you *wearing?*" she managed to speak between coughs.

I looked down and realized I still had on the jumper from last night. "You bought this for me last summer, remember?" *Pretend nothing happened; don't blush. Think about something else, Hello Kitty, Old Joe, the 11 o'clock News.* It didn't work and I felt the heat rising in a wave across my face. I turned away to get myself a cup of coffee.

"Did you go and see Elwin last night?" She said as I was pouring. My hands were shaking as I nodded.

"Sarette, do we need to have another talk?"

"Mom, we had 'the talk' when I was thirteen. I've got the bases covered."

"Things work differently in Daearen. I don't want you to get hurt. I can tell you have feelings for Elwin, but, honey, that can never—"

"—never happen, I know. He made that perfectly clear last night." I looked at her. "I made a complete fool of myself, Mommy." My eyes filled with tears. *How do I have any tears left?*

Mom walked over and wrapped me in a hug. "Maybe we should see if your father can send someone else to escort you. If it's going to be too hard on you to be around Elwin, maybe that's what we should do."

"No, I would never do that. Elwin basically said he's expendable, so who knows what the consequences would be if I asked for a new guard? I just need to grow up and get to where I'm going. It'll all be fine after that."

Mom squeezed me again, then patted me on the butt, like a football player. "Let's get out here and do some shopping. Go get dressed, I'm starving." She smiled and went into her room. I finished preparing my coffee with way too much sugar and skim milk.

Then, just as I was about to go up the stairs, Mom stepped out of her room. She had tears in her eyes. "I don't think you're going to be able to stop yourself from falling in love with Elwin. I think it would be easier on you to say goodbye to him if you spent less time with him. You should leave in the morning," Mom rambled, nervously seeking answers. "Elwin is your father's most trusted knight and he can get you there safely with or without training you." I nodded slightly and started feeling that pain in my chest again. I knew she was right. "Elwin's a lot like your father, you know? I couldn't have stopped myself from loving him, even if I had known who he really was. You know how I always said it was going to be Mother Nature that destroyed the world, and not terrorists?" I nodded. "What I should have been saying is that I really pissed off the fey and now they are punishing the world for it. Crazy weather springs up here when there's fighting there. I'm sorry. This is so unfair. I'm sorry that you have the obligation to rectify my mistakes. I wish there were something I could do to change this situation. I'd give anything to go back to that day. I would make your dad leave right away and none of this would be happening now. But he didn't leave, and he cannot choose another queen because we performed the bonding ceremony. Your grandmother has ruled with him to keep the balance, but now she has fallen ill. If you do not claim the throne before she dies, the feminine aspect will not be represented. The court was missing male energy for only seventeen hours and that caused seventeen *years* of imbalance. Women are responsible for so much. If female energy is not represented, I'm not sure the earth will survive. This is my fault entirely. I love you so much, I'm so sorry!" With that, she broke into deep, wracking sobs.

Now it was my turn to comfort her. I gave her a hug and said, "Mom, I love you and I know you're sorry. You don't need to keep apologizing." I tried to lighten the mood. "I do have to ask you something very important, though. Why did we go to all those environmental protests if climate change is not caused by humans? Shouldn't we have been protesting the misrepresentation of fairy tales in human culture? Or knitting… I always wanted to learn how to knit. We could have skydived, Mom! Why didn't we ever do that? Or caving, clogging, quilting circle . . ."

Mom started laughing, "No honey, we are clearly impacting our environment. But the fey are too busy fighting to fix our mistakes. It's not just the environment that's impacted. Scientific advances, religion, civil rights, the increase of greed and selfishness—just about everything that makes humans unique—can be affected by the fey imbalance. Maybe we can find peace here if you bring it there. I'm going to miss you so much." Mom started to cry again and I joined her. *Tomorrow I'm going to say goodbye to my mom.* I begun to cry harder.

We held each other until Mom gently broke the tension. "Let's get ready."

She went into her room and shut the door behind her. When I rounded the stairs into my room, I saw a large box sitting on my floor. *Well, that's new. Whatever it is better not make me cry; apparently most things make me cry lately. Please don't make me cry again, Box.* I saw a note written in red Sharpie on the top.

Princess Sarette-
I think you should be mostly prepared now for the journey. I had the weapons made to fit your unique human qualities. Spend some quality time with your mother today. King Roland included something for her.
Until then,
~ Elwin

I tore the box open and found a bundle wrapped in brown paper. I took it out and unfolded it. Inside were two pairs of utility pants—the kind that carpenters wear, with additional pockets, latches, and rings to hang things on. Typical workman's gear would be beige or tan, but these were made of some sort of camo-like fabric with streaks of neon colors. I moved those to the side and found two black tank tops—nothing special. One long-sleeve cotton camo-print shirt. One set of camo-print long underwear. One light jacket, camo of course. *Awesome! Fashion forward! That's me!* I reached into the box for the next wrapped bundle of surprises. This one felt larger but squishier than the last one. I carefully unwrapped the paper and couldn't hold back my delight.

"Oh, wow!" I said to myself. I couldn't even tell what it was yet, but the shiny white material that looked blue one way and red the other was beautiful. I stood up and unfolded it to see the whole thing. It was a long hooded cape with large iridescent buttons down the front. I unbuttoned it and swung it around my shoulders. "Oooh!" I squealed at my reflection as I pulled up the overly large hood. It had fluffy white trim around it that couldn't be fur because there were tiny strands of different colors peppered throughout. The cape itself felt silky and soft on my skin and reached past my knees with the same trim on the bottom. I spun a little and noticed two small cut outs. Inserting my hands in the slits, I lifted my arms and flapped like a bird. *Don't do that again, dork!* I looked back into the bundle and saw a pair of fuzzy gloves sitting on top of a pair of snow pants that matched the cape. Written on the bottom of the paper in Sharpie was: "I've got your boots."

I looked into the box and very carefully picked up a sword by the hilt, removing it from its leather sheath. The hilt and the sheath were black with knot-work ingrained down the length of each side. I think it was shorter that the average sword, but I was not exactly a sword expert. The silver blade

59

tapered to an unbelievably fine point. I looked around and grabbed a piece of paper strewn on the floor. Holding the sword parallel to the floor with its blade facing the ceiling, I dropped the paper along the edge. *Holy crap!* The paper sliced right in two. I very carefully put the sword back in its sheath and without moving my body, placed the sword as far away from me as I could.

There was a small box sitting on top of another, and I picked it up. On the box below was a note in a different handwriting that read: "For my mazon, Shanna." It was from my dad. I gently passed my hand over the beautiful swirly script before I sat down with the smaller box that was shaped like a shoe box. I flipped open the lid and found a small dagger inside. Small crystals of various sizes, colors, and shapes decorated the handle. The blade was thin, about an eighth of an inch wide, and of some kind of metal that I had never seen before— purple with blue Celtic knots down the length. In the box was a small leather sheath that matched the sheath of the sword. I put the dagger in the sheath and set it beside the sword. Next, there was a piece of wood, but I had no idea what it was for. It looked like a stick to me. I set it down next to the dagger. At the bottom of the box was a small pouch made of the same leather as the sheaths. I opened the drawstring top and looked inside. There were about twenty crystals of different colors and shapes. I retied the string and put the pouch to the side.

"*Mom*! Come—"

"Don't scream, Sarette, I'm already here," she said as she rounded the steps. I was sitting on the floor still wearing the cape, which was puddled around me in a big circle. Her eyes swept the room and stopped on the sword and dagger. Her eyebrows rose a little. "Maybe you do need some training before you leave."

"I still need a couple of the rollup space bags and dry shampoo. I think I have everything else. Dad sent you something; it's in the box."

Mom quickly walked over and picked up her package. She passed her hand over the writing just as I had, and said, "Get dressed, I'm *beyond* starving now." She walked past me with the box in her hands and headed down the stairs without saying anything else.

Hey, Elwin! I screamed telepathically.

Princess, you do not need to yell, he answered back in a reasonable tone.

Sorry, um . . . Thank you for everything.

It was my honor, Princess.

Mom thinks we should leave tomorrow.

I think that's a good idea. Don't worry; I will keep you safe, Princess.

Can you please call me Sarette, Elwin? Please?

For now I can.

Thank you. I guess I'll see you at six for dinner.

Until six.

I felt the connection end abruptly. *Nothing like short and to the point answers to make a girl feel all warm and fuzzy.* I stood up, took off the cape, and finished getting ready for breakfast.

THIRTEEN

We decided on Alpha Coney Island because it was close to our house and they had an excellent breakfast that was cheap and quick. I ordered a giant three-egg, triple-cheese southern omelet smothered in country gravy. We sat in silence for most of the meal, and I wondered if this would be the last time I'd ever get to eat it. I decided to cut through the tension with a question.

"Mom, how exactly do you see Dad every night?" I nervously pushed what was left of the omelet around my plate.

"When I sleep, your father and I see each other through our amazonite crystal. We have our place, just like you have with Elwin. When I get a lavakite crystal for you, we will also have our unique place."

"How does that work?"

"Well, each crystal is linked to the location where it was found. A crystal can be bound between two fey—or in my case, a fey and a human—and bound by a drop of blood from each person."

"Can a connection ever be made with more than two fey? Like, can you, Dad and I see each other sometime?"

"No, it's binary; only two souls can be linked. It's that whole balance thing again, honey. Everything has duality and balance."

The waitress came by and took away our plates.

"Are you ready to go to shopping? Should we go to Meijer's first?"

"Let's go." I stood up with purpose and started bundling up to brave the cold weather. "I'm going to miss this, Mom."

"Me too, sweetie. But you are not leaving until we get a lavakite crystal because we need to be together to link it. So, maybe we do have a couple of days." She smiled and headed out the door.

Later that day, as we carried our purchases into the house, Mom said, "I think you should use my Oakley Kitchen Sink backpack. I'll be right back." She went into her bedroom and came back with a behemoth backpack, one of her prized possessions that I was glad I'd talked her into buying. I could definitely fit more in that thing than any other bag I had. It came with numerous zippered compartments, hooks to hang stuff from, and enough room to accommodate everything I would need for five days on the road. I was packing for eternity, though, not just five days. "Maybe you should pack now," she said gently, "just in case."

"Okay." I kissed her on the cheek and headed upstairs with the ginormous backpack.

In the first space bag, I packed my Hello Kitty pillow and Larry. Larry doesn't take up much space; he's a stuffed dog I've had since I was a baby. He looks like a beagle, but for some reason I tied bright orange yarn around his ears years ago. Now he sort of looks like a pigtailed X-Man with one eye. I rolled the bag down, emptying as much air as possible, and hooked up the vacuum to reduce the size even more. I wondered absentmindedly if they have vacuums in Fey-Ville.

Next, I grabbed one of the pairs of pants, one tank top, and the long underwear top. I folded them, stacked them on the desk, and added a pair of socks, some underwear, and a couple of bras. I put all the other clothing, along with several pairs of underwear, sports bras, and hiking socks, in one bag and vacuumed it down.

In the fourth and final space bag, I put extras of all my favorite beauty products, just in case I was allergic to whatever they had there. I put all four space bags into the backpack. I grabbed my overnight toiletries bag and put smaller bottles of everything in it. Except for the dry shampoo, I put in two bottles of that. I hate greasy-feeling hair. I tried to think of every possible situation and have something prepared for it: first aid supplies, sewing kit, flares, and flashlight. I made a note to ask Elwin about electricity. I hoped my iPad would work there. I reached into my purse and grabbed my phone to text Mathew.

Sarette: Does your big bday plan include food? . . . Starving

Mathew: That is the big plan. LUNCH SURPRISE!

Sarette: You certainly know how to make me feel special and your attention to detail is astounding! Ready?

Mathew: On my way

I grabbed the sword and box with the dagger, sat down on the bed, and waited for Mathew.

"Happy early B-Day," he said as he rounded the stairs. "Whoa," he noticed the sword sitting in my lap. "Are you getting into live action role playing now? What's with the sword?" He started walking toward me and everything hit me at once. *I'm leaving Mathew!* I burst into uncontrollable sobs. He quickly sat on the bed, folding me into his arms. "What's wrong?"

"I have to leave . . . My father needs me." I barely got the words out between sobs. I put my head between my legs to prevent hyperventilating. I felt Mathew rub my back like he always did when I was really upset. After a few moments, my breathing returned to normal and I sat up slowly. "I'm going to tell you a story, and there is a excellent chance you are going to want to commit me to a nuthouse afterward . . . I do have proof coming later, so just know it's all true, no matter how crazy it sounds. Do you understand the words coming out of my mouth?" He nodded and I began. "Once upon a time—"

"If you want me to take you seriously, you need to be serious," he interrupted.

"I am being serious. All good fairy tales start that way."

"Huh?"

"Save your questions until the end . . . Remember, all true."

I spent the next twenty minutes telling him the story. I was animated, confused, and occasionally pissed as I recalled the events of the last couple of days. When I was finished, he asked, "So, can you show me a magic trick?"

"No, not yet. That's why Elwin is coming to dinner, to show you and Mama the truth."

"I'm not sure we should tell Mama. I really don't know how she'll take this story."

"So, you believe me?"

"Of course I do. You're my vaki; you couldn't lie to me."

"I love you."

"Love you, too. Let's just play it by ear with Mama. I'm not sure if now's the time to tell her. She's not going to get here until 6:15 because a student needs help with downward dog or something else dog-related."

Mama Peggy owned a yoga studio in Saline.

"Elwin and I will follow your lead when she gets here."

"Ready for lunch?"

"Yeah, let's go to our last birthday date ever." *This sucks.*

Mathew and I spent the rest of the afternoon hanging out on memory lane. We took a two-hour lunch at the Chinese buffet, reliving our last seventeen years together over greasy, lukewarm noodles. We laughed and cried—at least, I was crying—Mathew would never. We drove by a bunch of our favorite places together. I made fun of him for having to finish his homework while I will never have it again. At least I *think* I never have to do homework again. I would know soon enough.

After hours of cruising, talking, and trying to find a way to not have it end, he went back to his house around four o'clock. Once back in my room, I grabbed my photo album from my desk drawer and shoved it into the backpack along with everything else. I put the backpack against the desk near my other stuff and went downstairs to take my last bubble bath in my home. *Why didn't I wait to pack my favorite orange spice bubble bath? I'm going to have to use Mom's warm vanilla sugar stuff. Great! Sad and hungry! Maybe I should go see if there are any Christmas cookies first . . .*

FOURTEEN

The clock read 5:55 when I heard the front door open.

"Hi, Mom." Mathew had arrived.

I yelled down the stairs, "I'll be right down."

I didn't care that it was negative sixteen degrees outside; I decided to wear my favorite summer dress: a blue spaghetti-strap sundress that hugged my curves. I put on some sweater tights (because I'm not a complete idiot) and my favorite black strapped flats. *I'm totally taking these shoes with me.* I took one last glance in my mirror and headed downstairs.

When I got to the kitchen, I gave both my mom and Mathew a kiss on the cheek. The three of us took a collective sigh and looked at one another. We didn't need to say anything; the three of us came together for a group hug and held each other for a few bittersweet moments until the doorbell rang.

"Let me get it," Mathew said and went to the door. I could hear the two guys talking for a second before they came into the kitchen. Mathew looked proud and Elwin looked amused. Mathew had probably just given him the hurt-her-and-I'll-kill-you speech. Since I would soon be in la-la land, I wasn't sure how enforceable the threat really was, but it was the thought that counted.

Elwin gave me a big smile when our eyes met. *I guess he's over what happened last night.* I smiled back, pretending to be totally fine. He walked to the table and opened up a wooden box. "I've brought something for you." Inside were two lavakite crystals lying on top of a red satin fabric; they were white with gold specks covering them.

"Why are these different than the one you and I have, or the one my mom and dad have?" I said.

"The lavakite crystals are used to bond vaki. It's a different bond than the amazonite crystals," answered Elwin. He looked at me and said, "Go get your spirit blade and we can bond these before Peggy gets here."

"First, tell me what a spirit blade is, and then I'll go get it."

"The purple dagger," Elwin replied.

I ran past him and took the stairs two at a time. Less than a minute later, I was back in the kitchen.

"Take the spirit blade in your right hand and prick a finger on your left hand, and then drop a little blood on that one." He pointed to one of the crystals. I did as he instructed and gasped when the blood was absorbed into the metal like a sponge.

Elwin smiled at me and said, "Now take your mother's left hand in yours and prick the same finger." He looked at my mom and said, "Drop the blood, My Queen, onto the same crystal."

Mom complied. The blood was absorbed into the crystal and then a spark of light, like a camera flash, burst from the crystal. Mom smiled and picked up the stone. She took it to her bedroom and returned a moment later.

"Mathew, are you ready?" Elwin said as he moved the other lavakite crystal to the center of the table. Mathew answered with a nod. Then Elwin looked at me and said, "Same as before, just use a different finger on the left hand." I nodded, then Mathew and I repeated the process. This crystal sparked just like the other one did. Mathew picked up the crystal and put it on the table by the front door.

"Sarette and Mathew," said Mom, "Please set the table. Elwin, if you wouldn't mind, help me finish dinner before Peggy gets here and reassure me that my daughter will be okay. That would make my nerves better, and I would greatly appreciate it."

The four of us had just completed Mom's instructions when Peggy walked in the front door.

"Sorry I'm late," she said. When she saw Mathew's crystal, she immediately zeroed in on Elwin. With a distrustful look, she crossed the room, deposited her hand in his and gave a firm shake. "You must be Elwin."

Elwin looked bewildered for a moment, but the look was gone when he spoke. "And you must be Peggy. It's very nice to meet you."

"Dinner's ready, let's sit." Mom shooed her hands at us like she was directing flies out the door. She had made one of my favorite comfort meals: ham, cheesy potatoes, and corn pudding. *I'm going to miss her cooking,* I thought as the five of us sat down. Mom was at the head of the table, Mama and Mathew were on one side, and Elwin and I were on the other.

We all started eating and fell into a comfortable conversation about nothing in particular until Mama Peggy said, "It is what it is and you are who you are." She waved her hand in the infinity symbol, as she had done many times before, but then I realized it was the same gesture that Elwin had used with me.

Elwin's eyes got big. He stood up so quickly that his chair fell over and hit the floor behind him. He did the heart-fist-bow thing and said, "Princess Penelope."

His head was still down, so he didn't see it coming. Peggy stood up so fast that her chair fell over and smacked the floor behind her. She sprang onto the table, jerked the carving knife out of the ham, and launched herself over Elwin's head in a somersault. On her descent, she grabbed his chin and put the knife to his throat.

"Holy crap! Are you a ninja?" I yelled.

"Language, Sarette!" Mom said.

In a menacing low voice, Peggy growled into Elwin's ear. "You cannot have them. Do you understand? You are *not* taking them!"

"Peggy put down the knife before the knight kills you," Mom said in a surprisingly calm voice. "Then maybe you can explain some things to me, like: A: Who the hell *you* are, B: Why Elwin thinks you are a dead princess, C: Why you think he's taking 'them', and D: where you got your ninja skills. But first, put down that goddamn knife." Mom stared at Peggy and waited.

"Language, Mom." I couldn't resist returning her scolding.

She shot me a warning look, then watched as Peggy walked back to her chair, sat it up, and plopped down on it.

"Elwin is Sarette's personal knight, her bodyguard," Mom said.

Elwin set his chair right and sat down next to me. I reached for his hand under the table. He laced our fingers together and placed our hands on his thigh.

All eyes were still on Peggy when I broke the silence. "So *are* you a ninja?"

Peggy looked at me and said, "No, I'm not a ninja, but there is more you need to know about me." Turning to Elwin, she demanded, "How did you know who I was?"

"I've seen a picture of you and Liam almost every day of my life. You have changed your looks, but your eyes are the same. When you said 'It is what it is' and moved your hand like that, I knew for sure who you were. My mom said she got that gesture from you." He smiled across the table at her. "I remember you, too. When my dad died, you came into my room every night for a week and didn't leave until I was asleep. Thank you for that."

"Care to elaborate, Mama?" Mathew, who had been staring at her from the side, found the courage to speak.

"My name is Princess Penelope of the Spirit Fey," she said in a very regal fashion. "King Roland is my brother." Looking at me, she said, "I am your aunt, Sarette."

"Aunt? But you're supposed to be dead!" I gasped, then turned to Matthew. "That means we're cousins. Cool! . . . Wait a minute. Mathew, you're a fairy too!"

"Fey," Mom, Mama, and Elwin said at the same time.

"Whatever!" I exclaimed. "And you each owe me a Coke."

"Perhaps I should start at the beginning," Peggy said, "Stop me if I use any words you don't understand." We all nodded in agreement. "When I was

67

growing up in Meanmna, there were quite a few of us training to be knights, including me and Roland and Elwin's parents, Sophia and Jeffrey, and Mathew's dad, Liam. We were all the very best of friends. That's why none of us were mad when Roland left. We actually supported his decision. He wasn't supposed to fall in love and not come back, but none of us were angry about that either. When my dad, King Simon, got sick, Liam and I were bonded." She looked at Elwin and said, "Your parents were there—you were too—but my dad died before Liam and I could step in.

"There were many formalities that Mathew's father and I needed to go through before we could step in to lead. We were so close to being ready, but then the attack on Beinn-Theine happened and Roland, Jeffrey, and Liam rode out. Only Roland came back. I lost my mazon and vaki— Elwin's dad—on the same day. I was angry, furious and heartbroken. I was almost ready to end it all when I found out I was pregnant. I couldn't stay in Daearen; something drove me to leave and I didn't even tell Roland. I thought it would be easier if everyone thought I was dead. I came here and found you, Shanna." She looked at my mom. "I chose this life with you as my sister-in-law. I used almost all of my magic to change my appearance and shield us from the fey. I do not have enough to go back."

Too stunned to say anything, the five of us just sat there staring into space or at our plates of food that had grown cold. Elwin squeezed my hand. "I didn't know," he said with a shrug.

"I believe you," I said and looked around the table. "So now what?"

"You can't take him," Peggy snapped to Elwin.

"Of course I can't take him; it's dangerous enough with one inexperienced royal, let alone two." Elwin picked up his napkin and muttered into it, "Someone else will have to come to get him."

Mathew stood up and yelled, "*He* happens to be standing right here!" Everyone looked at him. "Don't I get a say—"

"I don't get a say; why should you?" I interrupted.

"If Sarette is going, there is no reason for Mathew to go," Peggy interjected.

"Well, if that's true, then if Mathew goes, Sarette doesn't have to," Mom argued.

"Mathew is *not* going!"

"Well, then neither is Sarette!" With Mom's comment, the room erupted in yelling.

Finally, Elwin stood. Tapping on his water glass with a spoon, he said very loudly. "We are all losing by fighting!" Everyone looked at him. "We need every ounce of magic we can get to save us all. Do you not understand what has been happening for the last seventeen years, Princess Penelope? I am a knight in King Roland's court. I can not—I will not—keep this from him. Do you understand? I must be loyal and communicate to Roland that you are alive. Someone will come for Mathew soon, but it is not my place to take him." He looked around the table to make sure that everyone understood what he had stated. One by one, we all nodded. He walked to the window and opened it. The fey was there in bug form.

"Oh, show him first please," I said. Elwin looked at me disapprovingly and then nodded. I leaned over the table to Mathew and whispered, "Wait until you see *this*."

Elwin raised his hands to start the demonstration, but he was interrupted by the doorbell. "Expecting anybody?" he asked. We all shook our heads no. He reached behind him and removed a dagger that looked exactly like mine, and started toward the door. We were all frozen in our seats. It was surreal. My fairy warrior was going to greet a visitor, a visitor whom we had not invited. I had a feeling that Elwin was about to scare the crap out of some Jehovah's Witnesses. Elwin reached the door, opened it a little, and said, "Can I help you?"

"No, but I'm here to help you, big brother." A girl whose hair, eyes, and coloring were identical to Elwin's barged into the house. Elwin stood there with his mouth open.

"*Steph*? What are you doing here?" Mathew asked incredulously as he stood up.

"Big brother?" I said as I stood up.

"Since when do you go by your middle name, Elanora Stephanie Colin?" Elwin said, closing the door.

"Since I was on a covert operation from the queen herself, that's when." She smiled affectionately at him. "But I'll always be Nora to you."

"Somebody want to tell me what is happening here?" Mathew said as he walked toward the female version of Elwin. "Your name is not Steph?" She shook her head no. "You are Elwin's little sister?" She shook her head yes. "You are on a mission to do what? Get me to the castle?" She shook her head yes. "Was that all I was to you?"

She smiled, shook her head no, stood on her toes and gave him a little kiss on the lips. Mathew relaxed and took her into his arms, resting his chin on her head. I felt a little pang of jealousy in my heart. *Why can* they *be together when I can't be with Elwin?*

Peggy and Elwin spoke at the same time. "My mother sent you?" "Why wasn't I informed of this?"

Nora looked back and forth between Peggy and Elwin while staying firmly in Mathew's arms. "The queen saw a picture of you about six months ago, Princess Penelope. It was your eyes that gave you away. She recognized you and sent me to confirm her suspicions. I have watched out for Mathew ever since. Two weeks ago, the Queen sent word for me to meet Mathew and

69

be ready for this moment." She looked at Mathew and said, "I do like you. I think I might be falling for you, but it is my duty to get you to Meanmna, and I will do whatever it takes to get you there safely. Do you understand?" Clearly swept in up in the moment, Mathew started to bend down to kiss her when Elwin cleared his throat. They looked at him.

"Why wasn't I informed?" he asked again.

Nora shrugged her shoulders and said, "I don't know . . . more fun this way?"

"*Nora.*"

"*Elwin,* you have your own task. You have the priority package; I'm still your second if you die or something. Mathew and I won't leave until you two reach Meanmna. Okay?"

"Why would my mother do this to me?" Peggy asked no one in particular. She held her head in her hands.

Mom answered, "Because this is bigger than all of us, and we can't fathom what is really going on at this point." She got up and headed to the kitchen. "Who wants cake? I need cake."

FIFTEEN

I lay in my bed and looked at the stars on my ceiling for the last time. I ran through the plan we had come up with while eating cake. Elwin would pick me up at 8 a.m. and take me to meet Celine at Visions. Celine was a practicing witch and had put together supplies for us. After that, we would head to the cave where my mom and dad had met; it was the portal closest to Meanmna castle. There, Elwin and I would cross over into la-la land. My very existence was secret in Daearen; there had been rumors that had grown to legend, but the truth was still unknown. It shouldn't be too dangerous, as long as we kept a low profile.

Elwin and Nora had also explained the rift amongst the fey over the darkness that had come to Daearen. Some of the fey felt that my family, the Keltois, has failed in their duty and should step down and allow another family to take over the throne. Others felt that the only way the magic held by the spirit king and queen could be passed to another family would be to take the throne by bloody force. The fey who still support my family believes that because we are the only family to have ever held the spirit throne, we are the only ones who can. They think a solution will present itself and that I will be that solution. When I was presented to the court as an heir and chose a mate, the theory was that we should be able to appease almost everyone— except, of course, the fey who wanted to kill us.

Each fey is dependent on the balance in the Daearen realm. Once a fey has become unbalanced because of greed, power, changes—even love— darkness can take over their soul. There are no visible signs that a fey has turned. If the Keltoi family turned over the throne, we wouldn't know until it was too late and darkness came into power. If the Keltoi family lost the throne by force, it almost guaranteed that darkness would be in power.

I could be killed on the way. If not, I would have to choose my mate immediately. *Married at eighteen. Can't wait.* This mate would have to be strong enough to make up for my weak human half—one who is "good enough" for me, which Elwin *wasn't*, according to everyone, including him. I would get to be queen, but I could never leave or I would upset the balance, or the throne would be taken by force and I'd still die. *A winner all around!* At

71

least I'd have Mathew, and he'd have Nora. No fair. It is not Mathew's destiny to rule and, unlike me, he's a whole fey with plenty of magic, so there was no problem with their relationship.

Mathew and Nora planned to start training tomorrow. There was a good chance we could keep Mathew a secret until he reached the court. No fey had known Peggy was pregnant when she disappeared, and they certainly didn't know that she was still alive. It was, therefore, likely that his trip would be uneventful.

Elwin wanted to meet in the dream plane tonight so he could teach me a couple of basics before we started our journey tomorrow. I decided there was nothing I want to do less on my last night in my home.

Elwin?

Yes, Princess.

Please don't call me that. I only have one more night to be just Sarette.

You could never be 'just Sarette'.

I'm packing the amazonite away. I don't want to train tonight.

I don't think that's wise.

I don't really care what you think; nobody cares what I think. As of 8 a.m. tomorrow, my life is no longer my own. I just want to sleep tonight. It's the last night when it is not my duty to save the world. Okay?

Yes, Prin—I mean, Sarette. I'll see you tomorrow. Goodnight.

I quickly turned off the part of my brain that communicated with Elwin. *Distance, I've got to keep my distance from him; it can't end well for me. I'm sure it will be easy secretly traveling, just the two of us, across dangerous terrains with an unknown enemy lurking behind every corner. This sucks.* I got out of bed, walked downstairs, and knocked on my mother's door.

"Come in."

"Can I sleep with you tonight?" I asked as I stuck my head in her room.

"Sure, honey." She had been working. She moved the papers to the other side of the bed. I crawled in and she put her arm around me. She started brushing my forehead, just like she did when I was little. *My mommy. God, I'm going to miss her.* We lay there like that until we both fell asleep.

SIXTEEN

Monday, December 15

I woke up at six, jumped into the shower, then put on the clothes I had sitting on the desk. I had to admit, I looked kind of cute in the neon camo outfit. The utility pants, tank, and long john shirt made my boobs look big, my waist small, and my legs long and lean. I shoved my purse into my backpack and headed downstairs.

When I came into the kitchen, Mom said in sugary-laced sarcasm, "Awww, look at my baby girl all grown up to be a warrior princess."

"Nice one. The warrior needs coffee." I grinned as I reached for my cup and filled it with freshly brewed coffee. I had taken a quick sip before I headed back upstairs to put on socks and hiking boots. I grabbed my sword, my iPad, and the box with the dagger, stick, and bag of crystals in it. I looked around and headed down the stairs for my last time.

"Do you want me to make some breakfast for you?" Mom asked when I got back.

"No, I'm too nervous to eat. Do you know how I'm supposed to carry this stuff?" I motioned to the gear I was carrying.

"I haven't the faintest idea. An *iPad*?"

"I haven't been officially told it won't work there. Besides, I should have enough power to finish the book I'm reading." I put everything on the table and grabbed my coffee before I sat down. Mom joined me. We sat in silence, smiled and looked misty. I was not to going cry—yet.

At 7:30 the front door opened and Peggy walked in. "You didn't think I'd let you leave without saying goodbye, did you?" She got a cup of coffee and joined us at the table for another round of silence and smiles.

At 7:45, Mathew walked in and I jumped into his arms. He picked me up and held me. I couldn't help it, the tears came. Big fat tears dripped down my cheeks as he swayed me, lightly whispering words of encouragement and love. His words triggered some core resolve in me. *Yes, it will be okay. Yes, I am going to miss everyone. Yes, I can do this.* When he finally put me down, I saw Peggy and Mom hugging each other. They were crying. Mathew's face was also streaked with tears. I had to look away from the three of them and take a deep breath to steady myself. *You can do this, Sarette. It will be okay.*

Mathew answered a knock at the door at 7:55. Nora walked in ahead of Elwin and immediately wiped Mathew's tears away. "My brother won't let anything happen to her, I promise. He is the very best," Nora said.

Elwin followed his sister with a look that was equal parts pity and sadness. I felt like I was going to my own funeral.

Instead of a formal good morning, I said, "I need help with the sword and stuff. I have no idea how I'm supposed to carry it."

"I have something to help with that." Elwin reached into his jacket pocket, pulled out a wound-up piece of leather about three inches wide and let it unroll. It was a belt made of the same leather as my other items. He wrapped it around me, buckling it so it hung just over the widest part of my hips.

He opened the box on the table, grabbed the pouch with the crystals, and came back to me.

"What are the crystals for?"

"Lots of different things, but mostly they are healing crystals." He smiled as he reached around me like he was giving me a hug. He didn't break eye contact as he attached the pouch to a hidden D-ring on the back of the belt. I felt paralyzed as he brushed his fingers against my waist when he brought his hands to the front of my body. This seemed like a pretty intimate moment to be having in front of all these people, but I didn't really care. *Elwin won't be mine much longer, I'll take what I can get.* Elwin took out the stick from my gear.

"What's that for?"I asked.

"For now, it's a stick. It will be your wand once we bind it to you. Once bound, you cannot let anyone else handle it. Okay?" I nodded and he slid it into a hidden pocket on the side of my left thigh. The last boxed item was my dagger in its sheath. Elwin looked at me and said, "This is your spirit blade. The only times someone else should touch the blade are during a binding, or when you kill them." I nodded and tried to swallow the lump that had suddenly formed in my throat.

Elwin moved to stand on my right side. "Put your arm down. I need to line up the hilt with your hand." I lowered my arm. He adjusted my belt so it lay diagonally with the highest part on my left hip and the lowest part on my right thigh. He took the dagger and very gently slid the sheath through a loop where the belt rested on my thigh. Then he placed my hand on the hilt and made another adjustment. I stopped breathing when Elwin got down on one knee in front of me. "Pull the spirit blade." He watched me try to remove the dagger. It stuck a little so he moved the belt a bit more. "Try again." This time I removed it easily from the sheath, raised it up, and looked at the blade. "Good." He slowly moved his hands around my thigh and tied the bottom of the sheath to my leg. "Put it back and try again." Again, I pulled it out smoothly.

Elwin looked up at me, then stood, taking my hands in his own. We stared at each other until Mathew cleared his throat in an exaggerated fashion to break the hypnosis I was under. We both dropped our hands and guiltily slinked away from one another. I scanned the room to gauge everyone's reaction to the intimate display. Mathew looked amused, Mom looked sad, Mama looked regretful, Nora looked scared, Elwin, embarrassed.

"I guess I'm ready to…" I couldn't say it. I looked down and tried to take some deep breaths so I wouldn't start crying. I felt a set of arms around me. It was Mom. Mama walked over next. She kissed my cheek and joined the hug. Mathew wrapped his arms around all three of us.

Elwin and Nora were across the room whispering to one another. As soon as they saw me looking at them, they stood straight and watched us stoically. I unwrapped everyone's arms from me and said, "I'm ready."

Elwin nodded, grabbed my bag and sword, and walked out the door. Nora led Mathew out. Peggy looked at me again and squeezed my hand before following them out. My mom and I were left alone. She reached out and embraced me again. "You can do this, honey. I'm so proud of you."

"I'm not doing anything. There's a whole lot happening *to* me, but it's not like I'm *doing* anything. It's destiny, so I'm off. It's time to give up my free will and save the world," I stated in my best superhero voice.

"I think you're going to like it there, but I'm going to miss you." Mom put her arm around my shoulder and led me out. Everyone was lined up in front of a gray Honda Civic. I felt like I was approaching a firing squad. I gave Mom one last hug, took a deep breath, and walked to the car.

Mathew stopped me and picked me up to hug on his level. He whispered in my ear, "I'm going to see you very soon. Love you, Cuz."

"Love you, too."

He set me down and I turned to find Nora with her arms ready for a hug. I didn't really know her, but I needed all the support I could get right then, so I walked into her arms. "Elwin would never let anything happen to you. You know that, right?"

I nodded, then turned to the car door Elwin had opened for me.

When I got in, he shut the door and walked to Mathew. The two shook hands, then Elwin moved on to Mom. I could see she was saying something to him. He nodded and gave her a hug. Peggy grabbed him into a bear hug. She was crying. Nora and Elwin just looked at each other. They are vaki, so maybe they're communicating telepathically. After a minute, they hugged and he mussed her hair. I couldn't look at him when he got in the car. I kept looking at my family.

"Are you ready?" he asked.

I shook my head no and said, "Yes," at the same time. Elwin put the car in drive and we started to pull away from the curb. I turned all the way around in my seat, waving and faking a smile at my family. When we turned onto Maumee Street, I turned around and wept into my hands.

SEVENTEEN

I was still crying when we pulled into a parking spot near Visions.

"Do you want to come in?" Elwin asked. "This should be really quick." I was practically hyperventilating, so I shook my head no. "I'll be right back. Lock the doors."

Elwin got out and ran across the street. I forced myself to breath normally by leaning down and putting my head between my knees. After a few minutes, I heard Elwin scream telepathically, *Sarette! Get ready to unlock the doors!*

Startled to attention, I sat up and responded, *what's wrong?* I looked across the street at the store.

I'm coming! Elwin burst out of the shop doors in a sprint. He had a backpack over his left shoulder and his sword in his right hand. In my peripheral vision, I saw a dark object materialize out of a shadow. It screamed as it launched itself onto Elwin's back. It looked like the ROUS, or a rodent of unusual size, from *The Princess Bride*, but it had long human-looking arms and hands. Its back claws were trying to rip the backpack off Elwin. It reached its arms around Elwin, attempting to scratch his face and take his sword at the same time. I didn't think; I just reacted. I unlocked the car and ran toward Elwin, thinking only of his safety.

"Get back in the car Sar—" The rat thing covered Elwin's mouth and pulled his head backward in a lightning quick motion.

I felt something jump on my back. "No!" I screamed. I was trying to knock it off when my hand brushed against the spirit blade tied to my thigh. Out of instinct, I unsheathed it and sliced one of the creature's arms circling me. The cut started smoking. The creature let out a wail that sounded like two pieces of Styrofoam rubbing together. I used the opportunity to shake myself loose and turn just enough to stab it in the gut. I pulled the dagger out and ran toward Elwin, who was still wrestling with the first rat. I reached him at the moment he managed to throw that creature over his head. It landed directly front of me. I stabbed it in the middle of the chest.

"Car!" Elwin screamed.

Elwin and I sprinted to the car. I was shutting the door when Elwin threw it in reverse and crashed into a parking sign. I turned to look at the creatures as

Elwin slammed the car into drive and we took off. They burst into a flash of black smoke and vanished as we fishtailed our way down Maumee Street. We were still screeching tires when we turned on US 223.

I took a quick inventory of Elwin's wounds. He had three claw marks from his mouth to underneath his chin. There was a deep cut on his right bicep that was leaking blood and making a dark stain all over the bottom of his jacket sleeves.

"What were those things? What happened at the shop? Is Celine okay?" I knew the answers couldn't be good.

"When I walked into Visions, I could smell the roushum." Elwin looked at me and said, "That's what those things were. I was too late to help Celine, but I did find the bag she had ready for us."

"I don't understand? Why were those things here? What does all this mean?"

"This means that you are not a secret anymore, and that's not a good thing. We need to get to Daearen now. I can protect you better there, but this means our passage is going to be anything but safe." Elwin hesitated, then blurted out, "You shouldn't have gotten out of the car. You could have been hurt."

"You needed me. And look, not a scratch on me."

"Luck. Next time I give you an order, you follow it. Do you understand?" *Wow, Elwin is angry at me—very angry*. I watched him for a moment. He was white-knuckling the steering wheel.

"I'll listen next time. I promise. So what now? Are we still going to Tennessee?"

"No."

"So, where are we going?"

"There's a cairn in Irish Hills."

"What! I've lived here my whole life and I've never seen a cairn in Irish Hills. There's no way I missed a giant hill you walk around and into and end up in la-la land. How is that even possible?"

"Were you ever looking for a portal to la-la land?"

I shook my head no and looked at his bicep again. The bleeding had stopped, but it was a really nasty-looking cut. "We need to get that looked at, it could get infected."

"I know someone near the exit of the cairn who can remove the poison and seal the wound."

"Poison!?"

"The roushum's nails have venom in them, like a rattlesnake. Don't worry, we have plenty of time before the poison works its way to my heart."

"What happens if we don't have plenty of time?"

"Hide. Nora will find you."

"Elwin?"

"Uh huh."

"Drive faster."

"Will do, Princess." Elwin stepped on the gas, blew past the light and got onto US-12. Rounding that curve at breakneck speed, I realized my seatbelt was unbuckled when my side forcefully hit the car door. I blindly buckled myself in because I was too afraid to take my eyes off of Elwin. *Poisoned fingernails? What's next? Dandelions blow darts?*

Elwin had a slight grimace on his face when he slowed and turned into the Prehistoric Forest. It was once a busy tourist attraction, but it hadn't been open for years. All that remained was a run-down amusement park with creepy dinosaurs made of paper-mâché and plaster.

Elwin pulled into a carport so covered in vines and brush that I hadn't even realized it was there. He popped open the trunk and we got out. I looked into the trunk and I saw my sword. I still had no idea how to wear it, so I stuck it through the belt on my left hip.

Elwin grunted when he lifted his bag and said, "You're going to have to carry your own bag, Princess."

I gasped when I saw him. He already had dark rings under his eyes, like he hadn't slept in a week, and the cut on his bicep made me gag. Thick, green, tar-looking bubbles oozed out of it and dripped onto the ground. They hissed and disappeared, leaving burn marks on the pavement.

"I'll grab your bag, too."

"Prin—"

"I'm stronger than I look." I took his duffle bag out of the trunk and put it over both shoulders, then I grabbed my backpack and slung it over one shoulder. I put my other arm out and Elwin handed me the small backpack from Celine's. I slung it over the other shoulder. "Where to?"

Elwin tried to smile when he reached into the trunk for his sword. He looped it through his belt, which looked just like mine. Elwin shut the trunk and started walking past the first set of decaying plaster dinosaurs. He made a sharp left and walked into a small copse of trees to the right. I followed behind him, taking in the shadows, watching for movement and sagging dinosaurs.

I was using all my effort to carry the heavy bags. I didn't want Elwin to know I was struggling. *Sure, Sarette. Big strong Sarette. Maybe you should carry Elwin, too.* We quickened our pace and made our way into a small clearing. In the middle of this half-acre space was a giant hill. I didn't have time to pay attention too closely. Just then, Elwin started to trip. I dropped both backpacks and reached him before he fell. He looked at me but wasn't able to speak because of the swollen scratches on his face. I helped him stand. He took the duffle bag that was still on my back and started toward the cairn. I retrieved the backpacks and put them on as I caught up with him. We walked counterclockwise around the cairn and on the third loop, a shimmer appeared just ahead of us. Elwin took my hand and squeezed it as we walked into the cairn together.

EIGHTEEN

Inside the cairn, I felt like I was on a ride at the fair—the ride that swiftly spins around and causes your body to stick to the sides, and then the bottom falls out. I squeezed my eyes shut and anxiously rubbed my thumb back and forth on Elwin's hand. The spinning stopped abruptly and we fell in a heap on the ground.

Elwin didn't look good. His face had a green sheen, and sweat was beading on his forehead. The tar-looking substance was dripping bigger drops. A single drop landed on my arm as I tried to help Elwin stand up. It ate through the fabric of my sleeve, burning like battery acid on my skin. *If one drop did that to me, what must it be doing to Elwin?*

"Elwin, what do I do? Where do I go? Where does your friend live? Help me!" I was trying to physically pull him up by the front of his jacket, but he was just too heavy! *Oh God, his eyes are rolling backward in his head!* "Elwin! Please! You can't leave me!" His lips were moving, so I leaned down to hear him.

"Greee shutt."

"What?"

"Grreeeeen shut-ah."

"Green shutters?" Elwin barely nodded his head. I stood to look around. We were in the middle of a road that ended at the cairn behind us. I ran around the cairn to see if there was a house on the other side. There wasn't a house or even a road on the other side of it. I ran up the hill, and in the distance I could see a stream of smoke ascending from another smaller hill about half a mile away. *Hills do not smoke. That has to be it. There is nothing else around, and I can't see any other signs of life.* I half-ran and half-slipped down the cairn and knelt by Elwin. "The hill? Does your friend live in that hill?" He nodded once and I took off running toward the smoke.

I ran as fast as my legs could carry me. Even though I felt a pain in my side, I pushed myself even harder. *Hang on, Elwin,* I repeatedly chanted telepathically, sprinting so hard it felt like my insides were ripping in two. *I'm almost there!* A house built into the hill started to take shape as I came closer. There was a normal-sized door and a window to the side. *Green shutters! Yes!*

I was running so fast that I couldn't stop. I skidded into the door and banged it with my fists. The door opened and a middle-age woman was standing there.

"What's going on?"

I collapsed into her arms and tried to tell her what was wrong, but I the only noise coming out of my mouth were deep wheezes. "Hhh, hhhhh, hhh!"

"You have to calm down, sweetheart. I can't understand what you're saying. Philip! Help!" She yelled to the back of the house. A man came out from a hall.

I managed to say, "Elwin."

With clear recognition of the name, the man pulled a wand out of his belt and ran past me and the woman, who was still holding me. About two steps from the door, the stick burst with white light. The man leapt upward and took flight toward the cairn and Elwin.

"Let's get you inside, Sarette," the woman said as she tried to lead me into the house. *How does she know my name?* I broke away from her grip to see what was happening in the distance. She kept trying to take hold of my arm, but I wouldn't let her pull me away. I had to know what was happening to Elwin. The fear of losing him made my heart feel like it was being ripped in two. I was at the point of tears when I saw them coming. The flying man had Elwin in his arms, and our forgotten luggage was floating behind them as they approached. As I turned to the woman, I suddenly felt very lightheaded. Everything went dark as I heard her say, "Oh, dear." I was still semi-conscious, but I didn't have control over my limbs. I began to feel weightless, even though I hadn't felt any arms lifting me. "I'm going to put her in our room. Take him to the back. I'll be right there." I felt myself being lowered onto something soft before sleep overtook me.

"Sarette, Sarette!"

I sat straight up and turned to the female voice. It was the woman from earlier. "Is Elwin okay? Please tell me he's all right." Pretty, she was older than my mom, but around her same height. She had mostly brown hair with some gray mixed in throughout. Her blue eyes gazed at me with compassion.

"He's going to be just fine. We're going to let him sleep for now. Come, get some food, we have soup." She smiled and left the room. I followed her.

The house was incredibly bright and modern, especially for one built into a hill. It looked like an ordinary house on the inside, including drywall and a regular looking kitchen. If I didn't know better, I'd think I was back in Adrian. The woman was ladling a bowl of steaming soup and motioned for me to sit.

I took a seat opposite of the "flying guy" and asked, "How did you know my name?"

"Elwin told us about you on his last visit." She put the bowl of soup down in front of me. It smelled delicious. "Eat up."

"And, who are you?" I swallowed the first bite. I had no idea what I was eating, but it was yummy.

"Old friends of your father and Elwin's father, dear. My name is Marge. My husband's name is Phillip." She motioned to Phillip as she introduced him.

"You did good, half-blood." Phillip had a smirk on his face.

"Phillip! Her name is Sarette. Do I also need to remind you that she is a princess and one day will be Queen? Perhaps we should provide the same courtesy and respect that we provide Roland and Paige. You never know. . ." she paused for dramatic effect. "She might want to bring back the guillotine."

I looked from one to the other and they both burst out laughing.

"Sarette, you saved Elwin's life . . . Thank you. Just to be clear, even though you are a half-blood, I am giving you the same amount of respect I gave Roland well before he was king," Phillip said with a wink.

"Can I see Elwin now?"

Marge looked at my bowl and noticed it was empty. I would have licked it clean if I had been alone. "If you're full, he's in the room past the kitchen on the left."

I smiled and made my way to the bedroom door. I took a deep breath and went in the room. Elwin was in the middle of a gigantic bed with the sheets pulled up to his waist. His eyes were closed and he was shirtless. *Wow, even injured he's beautiful.* I walked over to his injured arm to take a closer look at the cut. It was stitched together with what looked to be a tiny transparent tube of rope lights, and it looked like it was already healing.

I sat carefully on the bed, making sure I didn't wake him and inspected the cuts on his face. The scratches were gone and his face was no longer red or swollen. I reached out my hand and traced where the scratches had been. Elwin started to stir a little. "Shhh, it's just me . . . sleep," I whispered.

Carefully, I crawled over him, avoiding his injured arm. I lifted his good arm and snuggled underneath. Elwin gave a contented sigh and pulled me closer. He kissed the top of my head as his injured arm crossed my chest and held my hand that I had placed over his heart. "Love you," I murmured into his chest, then I closed my eyes and fell asleep.

NINETEEN

I woke up to Elwin lightly tracing my hand with his. I was still tucked by his side with my head on his chest. I opened my eyes a sliver to watch his lazy exploration; it was like he was memorizing every detail of my hand. I turned to see his face. It felt so nice, lying there next to him.

Elwin shifted his gaze from my hand to my eyes. I found it hard to breathe under the weight of his stare.

"I'm supposed to be protecting you," he said quietly, "and by my count you've already saved me twice."

"Luck." I shrugged my shoulders. "I was so worried about you." I tried to stop the tears from coming, but a single drop escaped. Elwin brushed it away and rested his hand on my cheek. His gaze was filled with longing that he would not act upon. I lifted myself off his chest and looked into his eyes. His lips were perfect. Looking into eyes and hovering close enough to feel his breath on my lips, I felt powerful and confident. I waited another second and then lowered my lips to meet his.

Elwin growled as he moved one hand to the back of my head, lacing his fingers through my hair. His other arm pulled me on top of him, and my left thigh settled between his legs. Our kiss intensified, and I ran my fingers through his hair, teasing and pulling. With another growl, Elwin flipped us over so he was on top of me. He left my mouth and went to his favorite spot above my collarbone. He had just started to kiss the spot when there was a loud bang on the door. He lifted his head and we stared at each other, panting.

"You guys need to get out of here now!" Phillip screamed from behind the door. "Marianne just had a group of fey on horseback pass her house; they're coming! It's not safe here!"

Elwin jumped out of bed and jerked open the door to find Phillip and Marge looking frantic. In their hands was our stuff, which they had hurriedly gathered.

"Head straight into the Eitlean Forest. They are approaching from below the hill and shouldn't see you from that angle." Marge helped me throw my gear on as I hurried toward the back of the house.

Phillip threw open the door, then grabbed Elwin and hugged him. "Love you, boy."

Elwin nodded, then turned to Marge and hugged her. "Love you, Aunt Marge."

She had tears running down her face. "Love you too, Elwin. Don't stop until you get to Melinda's." He nodded and ran out the back door without a second look. Marge gave me a hug and said, "Godspeed, Child."

I nodded, then gave Phillip a quick hug. "Thanks. See you."

Phillip shook his head no and said, "Goddess, save the queen. Now *go!*"

I started running to catch up with Elwin.

The open space, about the length of a football field, left us vulnerable to attack. All I could do was pray. *Please, please, please, please, God and Goddess, let Marge and Phillip be right about the angle. We're sitting ducks out here.* I picked up the pace and concentrated on closing the gap between me and Elwin, who was at least fifty yards ahead.

We made it through the field and entered Eitlean Forest. I stopped to catch my breath just long enough to look back. There wasn't much daylight left and the trees were very close together, making the forest really dark. Elwin was getting farther and farther ahead of me, so I forged onward. Maneuvering over a huge fallen tree, I slipped off, my foot landing between the fallen tree and another one, still standing, that was almost as large. I tried to get my foot out of the tight space when a sharp stick punctured my calf. I looked up and saw Elwin far ahead. I started to panic.

"Elwin! Help!"

He turned and started running back to me. I was struggling to get my foot loose when a massive explosion shook the ground. I could see a giant plume of smoke rising from Phillip and Marge's house. *Oh, my God!* I was yanking and pulling at my leg, paying no attention to the pain. Elwin got to me and was somehow able to move the fallen tree enough for me to pull my foot free.

"Are they? . . . Did they?"

"We have to keep moving!" Elwin grabbed me by the hand and took off running, practically dragging me behind him. *If I get out of this alive, I'll have to thank Mathew for making me jog every day.* Carefully navigating the dense, spooky terrain, we came to a small creek. Without crossing the creek, Elwin turned right and led me by the hand along the bank. We reached a log that was lying across the creek. "Ready?" I nodded yes to his question. "Don't let go of my hand." He walked us onto the log and stood in the middle. The creek bed was only a foot below us.

"Ready for what? There's nowhere to go."

"Jump!" He pulled me with him, but instead of landing in the creek bed below, we continued to fall into a cavern filled with fireflies. As I noticed the ground approaching, I grasped Elwin's hand a little tighter, closed my eyes, and waited for the pain that would inevitably be encountered by hitting the earth as we fell. When there was no impact, I opened my eyes and looked down. We had stopped a foot above the ground on some invisible but solid platform. I looked at Elwin in shock. As if nothing unusual had happened, he removed his arms from around me and stepped off the invisible step. He reached for my hand, but I leapt into his arms, relieved but still frightened. I was enveloped in his bear hug with my feet suspended above the ground. He held me close and whispered, "Its okay, you're safe now." Elwin smiled as he lowered me to my feet and reached for my hand.

"Well, if it isn't Elwin Colin."

I looked around for who might have spoken. We were the only ones in the cavern, or so I thought.

"Melinda, I can't hug you when you are only an inch tall," said Elwin.

That's when I noticed the firefly three inches from his face. She moved back about three feet and started to glow even brighter. The radiance extended to the ground, shimmering as it took shape and transformed into one of the most beautiful women I have ever seen.

Melinda was even taller than Elwin and wearing a strapless black-sequined mini-dress. Her skin was golden and looked like it was glowing. Her long hair was the color of rose gold, and her see-through wings had black sparkles around the edges.

She looked me up and down and said to Elwin, "Who's she? And why are you crashing my party?"

I was too stunned to move. Elwin let go of my hand and took a small step away. He looked to the fireflies above us and around the cavern before he met the woman's gaze again. He said in a loud, regal voice, "Melinda of the Air Fey and her esteemed guests, I would like to introduce you to Princess Sarette of the Spirit Fey." He did the heart-fist-bow thing.

Melinda's eyes got really wide and she said, "Oh, my Goddess, it *is* true!" She did the heart-fist-bow. A loud buzzing mingled with barely audible voices began from the expanse above us. I looked up and watched as hundreds, maybe even thousands, of fireflies flew downward. Twinkling continuously, their light completely filled the large cavern. The shimmering glow transformed the fireflies into fey, and they all were doing the heart-fist-bow thing.

It was surreal. I had no idea what I was supposed to do next. I looked at Elwin. He raised his head and took my hand in his. He smiled at me and winked. "Melinda, we need—"

Melinda raised her head "You need a place to rest, supplies, yada, yada, yada." She turned and clapped her hands. Suddenly, and with a sudden burst of light that temporarily blinded me, all the fey turned back into fireflies. I buried my face in Elwin's chest, and he wrapped an arm around me. "This way," Melinda said in a singsong voice. Keeping my head nestled in his chest, Elwin took my backpack off and set it down, then he took off his own backpack. Fatigue had set in and I didn't have the energy to open my eyes. I tried to walk as Elwin led me, but my feet would hardly move. Finally, he stopped and lifted me into his arms, cradling me to his chest.

"I'm so tired. Why am I so tired?" My words sounded incoherent, even to me.

"Is she okay?" Melinda asked.

"She needs sleep."

Melinda led us to a room. "You're safe here, Elwin. You can lock the doors from inside the room. You don't have to worry, the alarm will go off if the perimeter is breached," she said.

"Thanks, Melinda."

"She's going to save us, isn't she?"

"Goodnight, Melinda." I heard a door close and lock. Elwin lowered me onto a soft bed and started taking my boots off.

I was able to open my eyes a little and ask, "Why am I so tired?"

"Daearen may look similar to your Earth, but the energy is quite different. It will take time for your body to acclimate to the changes. You need to sleep to recharge." He carefully removed the sword from my belt and untied my dagger, leaving it attached to the belt. He unbuckled the belt and slid it from beneath my body. He unzipped my jacket and dropped it on the floor beside the belt and dagger.

He turned and walked to other side of the room. I mustered the energy to sit up and take off the long john shirt. While his back was turned, I quickly and silently removed my bra and dropped it and the long john shirt on the floor. It was so much better to sleep wearing only a comfy tank top. Elwin had a blanket and pillow in his hands when he turned around. Underneath the sheets, I took off my pants and dropped them to the floor with a clunk. Elwin's eyes widened, then he dropped the pillow and the blanket right where he was standing and started to lie down on the floor.

"Don't be silly. Come and sleep here."

"That's not a good idea."

"I'm too tired to be anything but a perfectly behaved princess, I swear. I need you to hold me, okay? I'm so completely freaked out. I am in a crazy place. Please." I felt slightly embarrassed about begging, but not enough to stop. He walked over to the bed, carefully lifted the blanket and lay on top of the sheet that I was lying under. He still had his clothes on and was lying very stiffly next to me, staring. I rolled onto my side, away from him, and whispered, "I'm scared."

Elwin moved closer and tucked a strand of my hair behind my ear. "Sleep, Princess," he whispered.

"Sarette," I murmured.

"Sleep, Princess Sarette."

TWENTY

Tuesday, December 16

I woke up and saw that I was alone in the room, which, for the most part, looked like a hollowed-out cave. The walls curved up and inward to a chandelier glowing at the top; it lit the entire room. I was lying on a large cast iron bed positioned between two nightstands that matched the table and two chairs along the wall. A bookcase in the corner held linens and other various supplies.

I had swung my legs over the side of the bed and was stretching myself awake when there was a knock on the door. "Come in."

"Goooood morning, Princess!" Melinda sang in my direction as she walked in with a tray of food.

"Good morning. Where's Elwin?"

"No worries, Princess. He's been working on logistics. He's arranging the next couple of legs of your journey. He'll be back soon."

"How many 'legs' of this journey are there?"

Melinda gave me a strange look and said, "As many as you need—no more, no less." She put the tray down on the table.

"What is that supposed to mean?" I walked to the table and sat in the chair. Another delicious-smelling mystery dish sat in front of me and I dug in. "Seriously, in a matter of three days, I've gone from a geeky high school senior, looking at colleges with no real direction, to being a fairy princess. Most girls would think being a princess is a fantasy come true. If I wasn't running for my life at every turn, I might too. I've been acting out of trust. I'm exhausted and I just can't work on faith anymore. I have next to no knowledge and I would appreciate someone telling me what's happening."

"It's not my place to say anything, Princess," Melinda said.

"Not your place?" I countered, "I've heard so many versions of 'not my story to tell', 'in time you'll know', or other such nonsense, and… GRRRRR! Can I command you to tell me what I want to know because I'm a princess?"

"You could, but I don't really know anything. Everyone and everything on this mission is compartmentalized. Each of us only knows our personal role and what we need to know to do our part. Like me, most fey did not even know they were involved in this mission until you showed up. Besides, I left the room before Elwin started planning. That way, if we get raided or someone gets captured, none of us knows anything that could harm the rest of us."

"If I ask you something of a personal nature, can you keep it between us?" Melinda nodded. "Can you think of any way I can get out of mating someone with quote *strong magic* unquote?"

Melinda gave me a sad knowing look and shook her head no. "Because you're half human, you might not even have enough magic to accept the role of spirit queen, let alone the responsibilities. You may have to use some of your mate's magic to fulfill your duties. If you choose someone who is not strong enough, in turn, you will not be strong enough. We need a strong queen to lead us to peace and balance, or darkness will win."

"You know, when I was five I dreamed of being a fairy princess when I grew up, but this . . ." I stood up and started pacing, "this right here is *crap*."

"Princess, it is what it is and you are who you are. You have a great destiny ahead of you."

"What does all that matter if I'm miserable? Isn't it possible for me to save this world and the other one without entering some arranged marriage?"

"It is not arranged. Once they hear of you, all the best and most powerful families will send their sons. With the rumors circulating, I wouldn't doubt if some weren't already on their way. You will have your choice. Don't worry. There will be many fine options to choose from." She looked at me and smiled.

"I feel like a piece of jewelry being auctioned off. Have any fey raised a bid yet?" I shook my head in disgust and leaned on the table with my arms crossed. "The *fine* option I want will not be on the list of suitors."

I heard the door open. Elwin walked in and stopped in his tracks as he slowly scanned my body up and down. I looked down and realized I was still in my underwear and tank top. Thank goodness my panties were cute, dark-blue boy shorts with lace around the edges. I shrugged my shoulders and looked at Melinda. "Same amount of clothes as a Hooters girl and way more than some of the bikinis on South Beach. I'm fine." She cocked her head like a dog does when it is confused. I rolled my eyes and grabbed a piece of bread off the tray. "So what's the plan, Stan?" I asked with my mouth full. It didn't come out too clear, and I'm pretty sure I spit a few crumbs as I spoke. *Such a dainty queen I'll make.*

Elwin tilted his head in confusion. "Who's Stan?"

"No one. What's the plan, *Elwin*?"

"Today we train, tonight we train, and tomorrow we leave," he said matter-of-factly.

"Would you care to elaborate?"

"No."

"I don't understand how you expect me to train for twenty-four hours straight."

"Today we will use our pendants," he said. I reached up and felt my pendant under my tank top. I hadn't taken it off since Elwin gave it to me. "We can train in the physical plane today. Tonight, when we go to bed, we will train in the dream plane."

"That sounds exhausting."

"Tonight your body will rest, even as we train. You'll be okay to travel in the morning."

"Well, it sounds like you two kids need to get to work," Melinda said as she walked across the room. "Remember to lock the door behind me. I have a guard posted outside. And, Princess . . . ?"

"Yes?"

"Nothing that happens in the dream realm can affect your destiny in this one."

"So if I die, it's all good."

"Not exactly what I was referring to, but that is correct. Happy training." Melinda shut the door behind her.

I was confused and looked to Elwin for an explanation, but he had turned to lock the door and had his back to me. He turned around, leaned his back on the door, crossed his arms, and said, "You ready?"

"No, I haven't showered in two days. Could I do that first?"

"We could always go swimming."

"Sounds good. Let's go." I grabbed my necklace by the chain and opened the latch.

"We should take everything we need."

"We're safe here, right?"

"Yes."

"Since we are safe, we can take a break and just go swimming, and then come back for our gear. I want twenty minutes of fun." I pushed the two crystals together and in a blink I was at our spot. I didn't wait for Elwin but ran straight into the lake. I was about twenty feet from the shore, water reaching my mid-thigh when I turned around to see Elwin standing on the shore watching me.

"Are you coming in or not?" I turned and ran farther into the water, diving under when it got to my waist. I came up about thirty feet farther and had to tread water when I realized my feet no longer touched the bottom. I swam several strokes toward Elwin and stood up. The water reached just below the spot he loves above my collarbone. I didn't plan it that way; it just happened, I swear.

He was walking toward me, shirtless. I dove back under the water, swam to his right and came up te

91

TWENTY-ONE

Elwin was not there when I got back to the room. On the bed, next to a pile of clothes and a folded towel, was a note in Elwin's handwriting.

> *Princess,*
> *There's a shower in the next room to the right. You've got 30 minutes.*
> *Knight*

The clothes were not mine. I picked up the first item and shook it out to get a look at it. It was a completely see-through light blue top. My eyes got a bit wide and I looked at the pile. There was a dark blue tank top underneath. *Oh, thank God! Or is it 'Thanks Goddess' here?* I put it to the side. Next, was a pair of khaki utility pants that were sitting on top of a giant gold fluffy towel. *Not bad. I guess this is a five-star cave.* I went to my backpack and got my toiletry bag and underclothes. I grabbed everything in a big messy pile and went to find the shower room.

I opened the door, looked into the empty hall, and muttered, "Huh, I thought there was supposed to be a guard." As I walked out, a bright flash of light hurt my eyes. "I guess there *is* a guard. Is there any warning before you guys do that? You're going to burn my retinas." I blinked the dark spots away and opened my eyes. In front of me was a girl who looked younger than me. She had an Asian appearance, beautiful exotic dark brown eyes, and delicate features. At about five-feet tall, she was shorter than me. Her black hair was twisted up into a ton of tiny buns all over her head, kind of looked like a pin cushion. Her black leather dress looked like it was straight out of *Zena Warrior Princess* and she had a giant sword on each hip. When she caught my eye, she did the heart-fist-bow thing. *I don't think I'll ever get used to that.*

"You don't need to do that royal salute thingy. Where's the shower?"

She looked and gave me a strange look, "But you *are* royal."

"As far as I'm concerned, I don't turn into a princess until I am introduced or whatever to the court."

"You are what you are, Princess, with or without the pageantry of the court introduction."

"I command you to call me Sarette and to act like I am an ordinary girl," I said in my most queen-like voice. W*orth a try, right?* She started laughing and covered her mouth with her hand. "What? Too much? I must really I suck at this."

"Do you know what Sarette means?" She was still laughing.

"It doesn't mean anything."

"Actually, Sarette means princess. So, I *can* call you Sarette."

"Awesome. I wish I had Googled my name a long time ago. I'll have to use that little nugget of information to my advantage at some point. Shower?" She pointed to a door on my right. "Thanks. What's your name?"

"Lilly." She was smiling at me with a big toothy grin. Lilly looked so small and innocent.

"You seem a little young to be a guard. And with *those,* no less." I pointed at the swords she had on either side of her. I bent to get a closer look. The swords were three-feet long with a tapered blade that was thicker at the end than the hilt. It also had a spike coming out near the tip, which made the end look like an open mouth.

"I'm twenty, the same age as Elwin." She walked to the door and held it open. The shower room looked like a campground bathroom, but without the musty stench. It smelled like flowers.

"Do you have to guard me outside? Or can you come inside and continue this conversation? This is the most honest conversation I've had since all this started, and it would be nice to not feel so in the dark. Plus, I probably only have twenty minutes before I start training non-stop until we leave."

"Sure, Sarette."

I walked in past her and she followed, locking the door behind her. I went into one of the shower stalls and shut the door. I reached in and started the water before I undressed in the attached changing room.

"What kind of fey are you?" I asked through the wooden door.

"I am of the Air Fey."

"I didn't see you when I first arrived. Are you also a firefly and I just missed you?"

"No, when I change, I take the form of a fly. It's easier to travel; there is no need to bring food or a tent. I just stay in fly form and eat and sleep wherever I am."

"What do you do with your swords?"

"My *kampilans* are an extension of me; they also change when I become a fly."

"Am I going to change into anything?"

"No idea. We are all more than curious to see how you turn out. You are the first half-blood in Daearen in over 1,500 years and your magic will be weak. But, it's actually really rare for any fey, other than air, to be born with the ability of a changeling. It does happen, but there's no rhyme or reason to it.

I think your scientists would call it genetics; we call it being 'touched.' We will have to wait and see if you are in fact touched, but it's unlikely."

"How is this place so much like the human world?"

"Our world isn't all that different from yours. Imagine the human world in which science has been replaced by magic. The Earth realm would look like this. All things are made and held together by magic here. Things just are what they are and we accept it. We do love the human world though; you folks are so ingenious. We take the technology we need or like from your world and convert it to magic in ours. Does that make any sense?"

"Yes, it does. So my iPad will work here. Do you have the Internet?"

"We don't *need* the internet. We *are* the Internet. We can communicate telepathically to any fey we have ever met in person. We can recall their knowledge, ask a question, and get a response as quickly as your machines process zeroes and ones. Besides, we are in the middle of a war, so IP addresses, status updates, and geo-location check-ins are a really bad idea."

"That makes sense. I'm going to miss my Words with Friends, though."

"Huh?"

"Never mind, just rambling. So what's your take on all this? You're here, so I'm assuming you're on my side, but what about the other fey?"

"Of course I'm on your side. But, I'm not sure I should be the one to explain the rest to you. You should be concentrating on getting to Meanmna. Worry about the rest later."

"Lilly, please? I feel unprepared. I've got a good vibe from you. You already feel like a friend that I can trust." I cracked open the door a couple of inches and looked at her.

Lilly was leaning back on the door with her hands on the hilts of her swords. "You trust me?"

"Good vibes."

"I don't understand what that means. But if I were in your situation, I'd want all the dirty details. A lot of fey are afraid of you. They've forgotten what's it's like when there's a half-human around, and there has *never* been a half-blood queen. Uncertainty, fear—the fact that you're an outsider and a half-blood—and so many unknown issues exist that those who have turned dark can use in their favor. A fey that loses faith will be more susceptible to becoming dark. Your other opposition honestly does not care what kind of queen you will become. They want the power for themselves and will try everything to stop you from ascending to the throne. With you dead and gone, they will take over." Lilly shrugged and looked sad. "Issues with the ruling family have always existed, but when the rumor of you became more of a truth…" She took a deep breath. "…it stepped up the unrest and gave the dark ones all the ammunition they needed to stage a coup."

"I'm doomed," I said as I shut the door and got in the shower.

"If you're doomed, we are all doomed. A little more positive energy if you could, or we will lose and you know what will happen then."

"Got it, the fate of the world is in my hands. Thanks for explaining, Lilly. I actually appreciate the bluntness," I shouted above the water.

After my shower, I resumed chatting with Lilly through the door. "So, what I remember about changelings is that you can change into whatever you want. Is that right?"

"No," she replied, "our forms choose us. It's one of our first clues as to what our part will be."

"What the heck does that mean?" I asked as I opened the door a crack, stuck my hand out and reached around for my towel. She handed it to me.

"We all play our parts in the big scheme of things. Melinda offers direction and shelter for travelers."

"Lightning bugs—or fireflies, as some call them—seem to light the way. What about all the thousands of lightning bugs that were here last night?" I stepped out of the shower. Lilly was standing in the exact same place as before.

"Melinda is their leader. Last night was just a party. That's why so many were here."

"So, what's your part in the scheme of things? Why are you a fly?"

"Where do you think the phrase 'fly on the wall' comes from? I'm a spy."

"That's hysterical. So why are you doing something as menial as guard duty?"

"Menial? Sarette, you don't understand, do you? You are the most important part in everything. Without you, all would be lost. It's the greatest honor to guard you and forfeit my life for yours, if necessary."

"I'm sorry. I didn't mean to insult you. So, then . . . you're a total badass, aren't you?" I tried to lighten the mood.

Blushing, Lilly responded, "I guess you could say that. Ready to go back to your room?" Lilly held the door for me, then followed me into the hallway.

"Thanks for treating me like I'm normal for a little while."

"Anytime, Sarette."

We headed to my room and I gave her a quick hug. Lilly had a surprised look on her face as she opened the door to my room, but she smiled when she shut it behind me. *Great! Another faux pas on my part. Hugging a woman who majored in bad-assery? Not a good idea.*

TWENTY-TWO

"Ready?" Elwin asked as I walked through the door.

I locked the door behind me and turned around to lean my back on it. "So what are you going to train me to do first?"

"First, Melinda is going to show you how turn your stick into a proper wand."

"Why can't you show me?"

"My magic isn't strong enough. Melinda's is very strong and she will give you some of her own magic once the stick becomes your wand."

Great, one more example of my magical shortcomings and my predetermined crappy destiny. Move on, Sarette. "And then what?"

"Then I'm going to teach you basics of magic." Elwin grabbed his spirit blade and wand from the desk.

"And tonight, when we go back to the dream realm?" I said without moving.

"I will begin your combat training. Whatever happens there will not hurt you here and your safety is paramount. Also, when you awaken, you will be able to do whatever we learned without any of the pain of the mistakes."

I walked over, grabbed my stick, and said, "Where's Melinda?"

The fact that Melinda was not the Queen of the Air Fey did not mean she was not royal. She was the youngest unmated sister of Sampson, the ruler of the Air Fey. Their family bloodline was powerful and Melinda's air magic was unparalleled. She had left Eitlean Castle long ago, but I had not yet learned any of the dirtier details.

The process to turn the stick into a wand was much like how we bonded the Lavakite crystals. After I had used my spirit blade to prick the middle finger on my right hand, I dropped a bead of blood on the wood. The blood soaked into the stick and the rod let out a small burst of purple light.

Melinda then used her own spirit blade and pricked her ring finger on her left hand. "Princess Sarette of the Spirit Fey," she said, "I give you the gift of my blood and, with it, the magic of the Air Fey." Melinda let a drop of blood gather on the tip of her finger before she released it onto the wand. The blood was absorbed into the wood and the rod began to shimmer. The shimmer surged out of the wand with a burst of bright white light. Melinda's knees weakened and a guard was at her side before she fell. "I gave you a lot, so you need to be careful. Now, if you will excuse me, I think I need to lie down to recharge for a little bit. I'll leave you to your training." The guard helped Melinda cross the room with her head held proud and high. When they thought they were out of sight, the guard swept her off her feet and carried her down the hall.

Elwin and I went to our amazonite spot after my stick became my wand. It was an intense day of spell training. Elwin didn't say it, but I think I impressed him. I was a quick study. Nothing I learned took more than two tries, most only took one. There was a ton of information to take in, and casting spells was draining. I was exhausted when we got back to Melinda's for lunch. I lay on the bed and went over everything I had learned so far: protection, flying, defense, and a couple of magic ninja combat spells. My brain was full and I was on information overload. I groaned and closed my eyes. I kept my eyes closed when I heard the door open and shut.

"You need to eat. It will help restore your energy." Elwin said.

I opened my eyes and sat up. "So, how long will it take my body to charge up correctly? When will I be able to stay awake for a reasonable length of time?" I joined him at the table.

"Not sure. Hopefully soon, but this is new to all of us, not just you," he said. "Maybe you should rest for a couple of hours before we continue. We'll eat, you nap, I'll plan, and in two hours we get back to work."

"Three hours," I bartered.

"Three hours is fine. Melinda will have dinner ready about then; so, we can eat, then practice magic, then start combat training after we fall asleep."

"Can't wait!" I said with fake enthusiasm. "I just want to sleep. No training, or thinking, or planning for me for the next three hours. My brain needs a break."

"Whatever you wish, Princess." He started eating.

Whatever I wish? Really, well that's a load of bull! If I got my wish, I would choose you, dumb ass. I made sure to think these thoughts in a way that he could not hear them telepathically. That was something I had learned to do in my training. Thoughts and ideas can betray you if you don't guard yourself appropriately. Elwin didn't react at all to my thoughts, so I'm pretty sure he didn't hear me.

After lunch, I headed to bed and Elwin started for the door.

"Elwin."

"Yes, Sarette."

"Could you wait until I fall asleep before you leave?" I asked as I was getting under the covers.

"Sure," Elwin walked over. He lay down on top of the covers and tucked me under his arm with my head on his chest. I sighed and breathed deeply. If I could have, I would have stayed awake and to enjoy the moment. But, like always, I felt safe with Elwin and fell right to sleep.

After my nap and dinner, Elwin and I used our amazonite crystals to practice all the spells and magic I had learned earlier that morning. He wanted to see if any elementals would listen to me. They obviously heard me and responded, but they had difficulty understanding my intentions.

"Holy crap," I said as I stared at the surf. Well, it would have been the surf if I hadn't made all the water form into a giant column. It reached up so far into the sky that I couldn't see where it ended. I looked down at my wand. *I can't believe I just did that!* I looked at Elwin and he was gaping at the column.

"So, how was that?" I was a little proud of myself.

"How was *that*? I've never seen anything like that! You didn't say anything out loud— not in the ancient language or in English! As far as I know, no one can do that."

"All I did was think *water* and give a little flick of my wrist with the wand. Is that a good thing or a bad thing?"

"I don't know yet. Let's try something else!" He sounded really excited.

Over the next two hours, we tried everything we could think of. I thought *rain cloud* and a little rain cloud formed. I thought *fire* and a fire sprang up out of nowhere—no wood, no charcoal, just a blue flame rising out of the sand. I had gone through about ten different wind speeds before I stopped. I thought about the White House in D.C. and sand at the same time, and a six-foot model of the White House made entirely of sand and probably to scale, appeared in front of me.

"This is so cool!" I exclaimed as I sat down on the sand. "So what's your magic like?"

"I'm a Water Fey, so I can only do things involving water, like standing on it, moving it, et cetera. Lilly's magic involves air—wind, flying, floating. Mathew's dad was a Fire Fey, so that's what Mathew will be."

"Won't he be a Spirit Fey?"

"Technically? Yes, he will be a Spirit Fey. But only the king and queen have spirit magic. It comes with a lot of responsibility, mostly your ability to hurt the fey with magic."

"What do you mean?"

"There's a catch to our magic: we can never use it against any other fey. The only exception to the rule is the spirit queen and king. They alone wield enough power to affect a fey directly..." Elwin cleared his throat and looked uncomfortable, "...usually justice related. They are essentially the final law of the realm, like the US Supreme Court, but with the most severe punishments at their disposal."

"If all this power and crazy amount of responsibility that I don't even want to think about right now comes with the job, why can't I make my own decisions about things?"

"First, it takes an incredible about of magic to pass the crown itself. We still don't know how strong you are. Parlor tricks aside…?"

"*Parlor tricks*? The look on your face didn't read parlor tricks to me!"

"I don't know what you want me to say. It is what it is."

"I'm starting to get really annoyed with that phrase. Why do *you* think I can do all this magic stuff—especially if I'm such a weak 'half-blood'? Which, by the way, is the other phrase that's really starting to piss me off. If I'm such a weak half-blood, how can I do all this magic?" I waved my arms over my creation. The sand that formed the Whitehouse started to vibrate until a spark occurred somewhere in the middle of it and the whole thing burst into a blue flame. Once the structure was entirely consumed by fire, a nimbus cloud appeared over it and rain began to fall, putting out the fire and leaving a cloud of blue smoke behind. I heard something that sounded like an approaching freight train. It was so loud that Elwin and I both had to cover our ears. As the sound came closer, the smoke gathered and shot toward Elwin, dissipating as it passed over his face. His mouth hung open in surprise, then he began sputtering.

I started laughing so hard at his expression that I fell backward, holding my stomach. "I'm beginning to think I'm not so weak. Maybe I *am* powerful enough to save the world." *And if I am powerful enough, maybe I can choose whoever I want to be king. Don't get your hopes up, Sarette, stick to the task at hand.* "What do you think?"

"I really don't know what to think yet. I don't believe that we should tell anyone about how strong you *could* be, though—at least not yet."

"I guess I understand," I said and closed my eyes to enjoy the sun on my face. This place was odd; it was always the same, every time we visited. "Quick question: I keep forgetting to ask you how come the sun never moves when we are here. And why aren't there aren't any birds or animals of any kind? It changes in the dream plane, but not here."

"This is our place, a place frozen in time just for us. Where we are right now is more like a snapshot of the exact moment the amazonite was found. Our crystal came from here and that moment is our backdrop. In the dream plane, it will change according to the time and we can manipulate it because it's not a real tangible location, it's a dream," he answered. "We should have enough time to shower and clean up before dessert is ready if you want to."

I didn't wait or say anything; I just separated my crystals and left.

TWENTY-THREE

Later that night, Elwin and I climbed into bed fully dressed in our gear.

"This is super uncomfortable. How am I supposed to fall asleep like this? And with someone watching me?" I nodded toward the guard inside the room. "Also, how do we know that we're not going to stab ourselves while sleeping with this sharp stuff? I have a long and storied tradition of being accident prone."

"The guard will remain inside as we sleep because this is when we are most vulnerable. We won't stab ourselves because we won't move at all once we're in the dream plane." Elwin slid into the bed next to me and tucked me under his arm.

"At least I get to fall asleep like this, it's my favorite way," I whispered.

"It's mine, too." Elwin kissed the top of my head and we drifted off to sleep.

In the dream plane, Elwin ran through a series of lessons and tactics, one right after another. Combat training was a lot harder than magic training. *This sucks!* I telepathically yelled at Elwin as I ducked behind a fallen tree. We were playing what amounted to a tenacious version of hide-n-seek involving weaponry. The goal was not simply to find someone, but to beat them in combat, and at the moment he was "it" and clearly winning. I heard a sound to my left and took off away from it, running smack into Elwin's hard chest.

"Ow! What did I do wrong that time? What did I hear over there?" I readjusted my sword and belt that had gotten knocked sideways on my hip.

"That time I could still hear you from way over there." Elwin pointed to a small stand of trees "That noise was the stick I threw to distract you. It's one of the oldest tricks in the book. The bad guys will be cleverer than that. You need to try harder and focus. Use all your senses. Don't just depend on one sensory input like sound to make a decision. Use all of your senses, and then analyze your next move before taking action."

"I *am* trying hard and focusing! I have never worked harder at anything. What I really don't understand is why can't I use my magic? This whole physical attack stuff seems pointless if I can just grab my wand, say 'invisible', and sneak away."

Elwin's eyes got really wide. "Sarette! Where'd you go?" He turned in a circle and his hands were groping the empty air. "How did you do that?"

I brought my hand in front of my face and realized that I couldn't see it. "Holy crap! I'm invisible! I didn't even touch my wand! How do I come back to the land of the visible?" Elwin's eyes widened again. "Can you see me now?"

"Yes!" Elwin said. "You are amazing! I've never seen that type of magic before. I've never even *heard* of magic that strong."

"So, what's next?"

"I think we try this again, but this time you use your magic."

"Really? What should I use?"

"You decide. I'm in unchartered waters here." He turned and walked away. "You have two minutes before I turn around and start looking for you."

I ran in the opposite direction, but I could hear every step I was making as I crashed through the leaves and sticks on the ground. *This is ridiculous. Be quiet, Sarette.* I picked up the pace and could no longer hear my footsteps. I continued toward the lake and paused at the tree line. I quickly surveyed my surroundings and looked up. *I'm light as air.* I started levitating so fast I let out an audible squeak. *Darn it! I hope Elwin didn't hear that.* I waited until I was high enough to be hidden by the branches and leaves. *Stop.* I grabbed a nearby branch and lightly sat upon it. I could see Elwin below me, looking around.

"I know you are over here! I heard that cute squeak of yours!" Elwin yelled from below me.

"You think I'm cute?" I shouted.

He looked up. "I think you're beautiful. Come on, let's see what you can come up with by the water."

"Sounds good." I hopped off the branch. *Down gently.* Elwin watched in astonishment as I floated toward earth. I looked up to where I had been and shrugged. "I really didn't do much, I just thought light as air, stop, and then down gently. Not that I'm complaining, but shouldn't it be a lot harder?"

"It is a lot harder than this, for *every other* fey. There isn't even a legend about a fey that can create magic in their heads without using a wand. You could be the first fey ever who can do that, so for now this needs to be our secret. When we are around other fey, you need to pull your wand and look like everyone else."

"Shouldn't this prove that I'm strong enough to take care of myself? Or at least scare away the fey that want to kill me?"

"I wish it would, but I suspect this information will make you even more of a target. And before you ask, I don't think it changes your mating issue either. We need to get back to your training, come on." Elwin turned and jogged to the shoreline like he couldn't wait to get away from me.

101

I watched him, unable to move yet. I couldn't understand why Elwin would think this wouldn't change my mating issues. What reason did he have to say that? I certainly seemed powerful enough; he said himself that no fey could do what I could do. Maybe I was reading too much into his feelings for me. Maybe he really didn't want me. Maybe, he just couldn't say no when I threw myself at him. *Oh my God! That's exactly what I have been doing, throwing myself at him.* My heart literally began to hurt as I walked to Elwin.

"What's wrong, Sarette?" Elwin asked.

"Nothing."

"It's not like I like the situation any more than you do. It is what it—"

"Don't say it."

". . . is."

I pointed my finger at him, "You can be a real jerk sometimes." Elwin jerked up about five feet into the air. "Holy crap! I'm not supposed to be able to do that." I spun my finger around and Elwin's body spun, too. I moved my finger over the water. Elwin swung out and hovered over the water.

"Sarette!" Elwin screamed.

"Oh sorry!" I brought him back to the sand and gently set him down. "I'm not supposed to be able to do that yet, right? That power only comes after I become spirit queen. How could I do that?"

"I have no idea. You shouldn't have enough power to do anything like that. It's dangerous to use that much magic, Sarette."

I smiled at him, "I feel fine. This is a good thing . . . Ooooooow!" I screamed and doubled over in pain.

"Sarette!" Elwin raced over. I couldn't support my weight and fell to my knees. I started dry- heaving so hard I couldn't get any oxygen into my lungs. The world looked fuzzy and I was beginning to have tunnel vision. Elwin picked me up and walked with me. I was suffocating.

"Sarette, you need to fall asleep. Whatever happens in this realm will not follow you to the other. Please, love." I was lowered to the blanket and could feel the warmth of the fire on my back. Elwin was holding me tight to his chest. I held onto his shirt but couldn't look in his eyes. I could not watch him as he watched me die. I was still gasping for air and it was becoming harder and harder to breathe. I could hear the death wheeze coming. I heard Elwin beg, "Please, just fall asleep. You don't have to die for this to stop. Just please, oh God!"

I exhaled my last breath.

TWENTY-FOUR

Wednesday, December 17

I woke with a start the next morning. I started hyperventilating all over again as the memories of my death rushed through my mind. Elwin's strong arms wrapped around me and I felt an instant sense of calm. We both sighed loudly and I said, "Well, I guess I won't do that again."

Elwin chuckled and said, 'Please don't."

"Let's shake a leg." I kissed his cheek and bounced out of bed.

"You say the strangest things."

We quickly packed our bags and were finally able to drink some coffee. Yes! They have coffee here! Caffeine is the best way to start a day—the *only way to start a day*. No matter how easily I awake or how much energy I have, I just don't feel right without my morning joe. With our bags packed and all of our gear on, we set out to see what else needed to happen before we left.

In true form, Melinda was rushing around, barking orders at her firefly follower people, fey, bugs, whatever. Lilly had gone to the top of the cavern to watch for our ride. I assumed it was a car, but I hadn't seen a car yet in Daearen. Elwin headed to the exit while I took one last look around to make sure I had not forgotten anything.

As I was rushing down the hall to leave, the silent guard from last night stopped me. "Princess," he said.

"Yes." I stopped quickly, almost losing my balance.

"Godspeed! And, Goddess save the queen." Of course he did the heart-fist-bow thing. I was still uncomfortable with the royal salute, but I realized that it "is what it is". I needed to accept it as readily as a head nod from a passerby on the sidewalk or a smile in a hallway at school. I was still clueless as to the right response, but I decided to go with my gut. I gave him a quick hug. He raised his head and gave me a strange look. *Wrong again, Sarette. Say something to not look like a fool.* "Do the fey not hug? Because where I come from, a hug passes strength from one to another. It is a sign of sincere appreciation and kindness."

He looked at me for a second, a debate raging behind his eyes. He smiled and swept me into a bear hug—a too-tight bear hug, but it was a start.

"Can't . . . breathe. . ." I managed to speak and he set me down. I smiled at him and turned to find a receiving line of fey to the exit. All had their arms out; all had a smile on their face. *Did I just do that? Wow.* I took the time to hug each and every fey on my way out. Lilly, Melinda, and Elwin were at the end of the line.

I grabbed Lilly into a big hug and said in her ear, "Thank you! Thank you for helping me feel normal. That helped more than you can ever realize."

"Until we meet again, Sarette," she whispered.

I moved to Melinda and gave her a hug. She pulled back and said, "Godspeed, and may the Goddess keep you safe, Sarette." She pulled me close for another hug. I saw her wipe her eyes as we parted.

I looked at Elwin. "Ready?"

He looked at me with a proud look on his face and lifted my feet off the ground in a hug. "You are going to be the most amazing queen."

You know I made that whole hug thing up, right?

I don't know, Princess; I think you just gave them a lot of strength. You should look around. He set me down and I looked at everyone. The fey were smiling. A couple of them were crying, a few were doing the heart-fist-bow thing. There was a different feeling in the room—a charged and exciting vibe that hadn't been there before. I honestly didn't understand what I did, so I looked at Elwin.

He smiled and said, "You have given them hope, Princess. Hope is a very powerful thing." He took my hand and we stepped onto the invisible step. I turned around and waved as we went upward into the forest portal.

As soon as we broke the surface, Elwin took off running with me in tow alongside the creek bed. A firefly ahead of us started blinking. Elwin noticed it and jumped to the other side of the creek. Ahead, I saw another firefly flash and Elwin ran straight for it. We kept running for another ten minutes and the trees started to thin out. I could see another firefly ahead of us. Elwin and I slowed down and he still had my hand in his. I was walking with my head down so I didn't trip.

We kept moving toward the break in the trees. We stopped at the edge of the forest and I looked across the vista.

Oh my God, this is our spot, isn't it? I spoke telepathically to Elwin.

Yes, this is where our crystal was found. We'll have to come back again when we can enjoy it. Elwin started scanning the lakeshore. *There they are. Remember, do not show your abilities.*

I nodded and we walked toward the shore of the lake, hand in hand. I didn't see anyone. *Where are we going?* Elwin nodded and kept walking toward the water. I followed his gaze and saw two male fey standing on the water thirty feet out.

"Get your wand out," Elwin mumbled an incantation as he pulled out his own wand.

How about I just do it right? God and Goddess please, I need help. I took a deep breath and we both walked onto the water. *Thank you, God and Goddess.* When we got close to the fey, I could tell that they were brothers because their features were so similar. Both had curly bleached-blond hair, one wore his shaggy hair to the top of his ears; the other man's hair reached his chin. Their eyes were the same shape, the one with the shorter hair had dark brown eyes and the other had bright blue eyes. They were both barefooted and wearing board shorts and swim shirts but in different colors. They were shorter than Elwin's six-foot-three inches, but with their broad shoulders, thick-strong arms, and strong muscular legs, they looked like a couple of California surfers. When we reached them, they did the heart-fist-bow thing.

"Hi," I called out, wasting no time with formalities." Is there an invisible boat or something? You *are* our ride, right?"

They both looked at me, straightened and, in unison, looked at their feet. I followed their gazes downward and saw four giant seahorses below the surface of the lake. Seahorses the size of real horses—only in la-la land.

"You have got to be kidding me," I said under my breath as the two fey started waving their wands and murmuring something I couldn't understand. The four of us began to sink underwater. We mounted the seahorses like cowboys mounting their steeds in an old Western. I was holding my breath as my head went underwater. My oxygen was running out and I started freaking. I looked around nervously to see what I should do. The twins and Elwin were talking and laughing like nothing was unusual.

"Huh?" I exclaimed and a bubble leaked from my mouth.

One of the twins said, "Breathe normally."

I can't breathe underwater; that's how people drown. My lungs were burning and I couldn't see the surface anymore because my vision was starting to get spotty. I was panicking, but I had no choice. Prepared to die, I took a breath and expected water to fill my lungs. But it didn't. It felt normal, just like breathing air. "How is this possible? I'm underwater, riding on a seahorse. How am I breathing?"

Elwin said, "Princess Sarette of the Spirit Fey, I would like you to meet Ray..." He pointed to the fey with the shorter hair, "...and, Mike Jones of the Water Fey."

"Jones? That's not a very fey-sounding name."

"And what does a fey-sounding name sound like?" Mike asked.

105

"I have no idea," I said. "I'm new here." Mike laughed and Ray looked a little annoyed. "So how am I able to breathe underwater like a fish? I can see schools of fish over there—how are they breathing air?"

"Everything works differently here than where you're from. This water is magic. It feels and acts like air to us, but it works and feels like water to fish. The water magic also provides something akin to gravity. You wouldn't be able to get off the seahorse and start swimming now. You'd drop and hit the ground with as much force as you would on dry land. The plants are aquatic so they are sustained. Only the Water Fey can stay here indefinitely. Our bodies adjust automatically, but everyone else needs a Water Fey to spell them so they can stay under water for longer periods. When you are in a building under here, it will be air filled and everything will be completely normal," Mike explained.

I watched as a school of a thousand silver fish swam by. "I feel like I'm a Bubble Guppy. Maybe Angela Lansbury is going to fly by on a bed with a knob and a broomstick any second."

"I have no idea what you are talking about, but we have to go. Father is waiting to meet you." Ray took off on his seahorse.

"How do I get this thing to work?" I asked. "Whoa!" The seahorse took off after Ray. I heard Elwin and Mike laugh behind me. Elwin caught up and rode next to me on my right side and Mike caught up with his brother.

I think we were about one hundred feet from the bottom and about forty feet below the surface. Instead of talking, I looked around to take in everything and was amazed at what I saw. I could see large solitary fish and schools of small fish whisking around. The seascape was dotted with brightly colored plants at the bottom and small reefs and boulders. They all had so many colors, elegant off-shades of the rainbow that appeared to glimmer.

It didn't feel like we were descending, but I noticed we were getting closer to the bottom. We leveled out about fifty feet above the lake floor. The closer we got to the bottom, the more clearly I could see the life below. *Wow, I can actually see fey down there. This is so crazy.* If it wasn't for the fish swimming by, I would have thought we were above the surface. Next was a farm and someone tending a flower garden. There was a field filled with vegetation I didn't recognize, and a guy was using an old-fashioned plow attached to a cow-sized fish with legs. To me, the creature looked like a scientific rendering of what a dinosaur fish would have looked like.

We passed over the undersea farm and I could see a mountain of coral a mile ahead of us. The road below us continued on and was cut through the giant coral reef. About one hundred feet from the coral mountain, Ray and Mike stopped and then dropped down like an elevator. I looked at Elwin just as my seahorse started falling. I let out a squeak.

"That squeak is so cute," I heard Elwin say, and then down I went. I felt like I was on the Demon Drop ride at Cedar Point, my favorite amusement park. We came to a jarring stop at the bottom of the lake. The four of us closed the distance to the mountain and I looked up. The reef was at least eighty feet tall and I couldn't see how far it reached the sides. The four of us entered the road that was cut through the reef ahead of us. We were probably on it for a mile or so when Ray and Mike stopped their seahorses and got off. The seahorses swam past us, back the way we came. Elwin and I dismounted as well.

"Thank you," I said as I got off.

It was my honor, Princess, I heard in my head before my seahorse swam away.

When I looked back at the brothers, I noticed that Ray had a strange look on his face. He quickly masked it and said, "We have to go by foot the rest of the way into the city. Tonight, you guys will stay with us. Tomorrow, we will escort you to the other side of the lake for the next part of your journey. What are your arrangements for the next leg, Elwin? Do you need us for anything?"

"No, we don't need anything, thank you." Elwin had his poker face on and I wondered what he was thinking. The brothers turned toward the side of the canyon with their wands raised. I couldn't hear what they said, but a giant boulder rolled to the side, revealing a hidden path. We followed them in and I heard the boulder roll back in place.

The space looked like the canyon at the end of *Indiana Jones and the Last Crusade*. The cavern was only four feet wide, requiring us to walk single file. Ray had the lead, followed by Mike, and Elwin was behind me.

I don't like this, Elwin. We could get trapped here very easily. A boulder could fall. We could get attacked from above. Maybe I'm just being paranoid, but something doesn't feel right.

Trust your instincts, Sarette. There is nothing wrong with being cautious. Be ready for anything. I've never come this way before. Something is off.

Lights up ahead revealed the end of the cavern, then our path opened up and we exited onto a ledge overlooking a large space. We continued down a steep incline and approached a road. I followed it with my gaze and saw a small city in the distance. Mike smiled at me and I thought to Elwin, *Nothing happened, I guess there was nothing to worry about.*

Keep your guard up. Elwin took my hand and we kept walking.

107

TWENTY-FIVE

We continued to walk toward the city ahead. Ray took the lead and was twenty yards ahead of us when Elwin asked Mike, "How has it been lately?"

Mike frowned and said, "Not good. We're safe here for now, but many other areas have been attacked. Eascanns have burned entire fields and livestock has gone missing."

"What is an Eascann?" I asked.

"An Eascann is a fifty-foot-long eel. They can control fire under water. It's the same as the fire you have in your world, but it works underwater, much in the same way you can breathe underwater. Oxygen acts differently in our realm, which is why your breathing—as well as fire—can happen underwater. It's the magic. With the hard times we are experiencing, the fey have tough choices to make. If the choice is to let your children starve or let darkness into your heart, what would you choose? Desperate times, difficult choices and desperate measures. That's what I mean when I say lose them," Mike explained.

"So if all your crops and livestock are being destroyed, how are the fey surviving down here? Do you import goods?" I asked.

"Lake Hasani might be the hardest hit, but we are not the only ones. We import what we can, but a lot of fey just pick up and leave. It's not that straightforward; it's far more devious and hard to figure out. Over time, however, we have seen a pattern emerge that indicates how deeply the darkness has taken root. Our first clue in figuring out who is dark is the condition of a particular family. Down here, everyone knows everyone—it's really just like any small town anywhere. If one fey family never gets attacked like everyone else around them, it's safe to assume they have been turned. Or, if one child in a class is never hungry, then they too are probably turned. When we see something like that, we investigate. But usually by the time we have real proof, rather than just suspicions, they are gone—vanished. We find empty houses every day now." Mike looked toward the town.

"Where do they go?" Elwin chimed in.

"We don't know. Entire families, and even a few of the smaller outposts have just vanished. We're still trying to piece it all together."

"Why did you guys lead us in from that direction?" Elwin asked.

"Last week Ray was attacked near the main entrance. It is now too risky to use that one. The tight cavern we went through is a secret. I never knew it was there. Dad showed us after the attack," Mike said.

As we got closer to the underwater settlement, I was again reminded of the Old West; that is if a town in the Old West could be made out of sand and seashells. There was one main street, with stores lining either side. There weren't any real roads, so to speak, but little well-worn paths to small, sand castle-looking houses spread out from the center in a haphazard way. It was clearly a busy place, with fey going about their business. I did notice a couple of sideways glances in my direction. Mike looked at me and caught my eye.

We kept your identity a secret, Princess, Mike said telepathically, *Visitors are rare down here, so my father had to come up with something. Your name is Mandy. You were in the queen's court when you met Elwin. He's escorting you home to Beinn-Theine.*

Okay. Two questions. Where and what is Beinn-Theine?

Beinn-Theine is the Fire Fey castle. It's carved out of the middle of a volcano.

Got it—inside of a volcano. That would have been my third, maybe fourth, guess. I smiled at Mike, but he was looking at his brother.

We followed Ray into a store called Jones Mercantile. It looked like a modern convenience mart, like a 7-Eleven or QuikTrip. Ray walked straight through the store and went behind a curtain along the back wall. Mike glanced at the curtain for a moment before he turned to the girl standing behind the counter. He got a "come hither" look on his face and sauntered, no *swaggered*, to the girl and said, "Good morning, Tessa." He placed his forearms on the counter, lifted himself over and gave her an intimate kiss on the lips.

She turned bright red. "Stop that," she said with a smile. Tessa was stunning; I was beginning to think all the fey were gorgeous. She was my height—five-feet-six—with long, straight, blonde hair that reached her small waist. She had dark, cobalt-blue eyes, high cheekbones, and full lips. And if I guessed correctly, she was in her early twenties.

"Tessa, do you remember me talking about my old friend, Elwin?" Mike asked, "Well, Elwin, Tessa. Tessa, Elwin."

Elwin shook Tessa's hand.

"It's so nice to finally meet you, Elwin."

"This is Mandy," Mike said and nodded at me without taking his eyes off Tessa.

I walked over and shook her hand. "It's very nice to meet you, Tessa," I said with a smile.

"I've got to go, sweetheart. See you later," Mike said and kissed her again. Tessa nodded, and Mike spread the curtain and went through the opening to join Ray. We followed, went up a set of stairs, and walked into a modern and reasonably sized apartment. A middle-aged version of Mike and Ray walked out of a hallway with a giant smile on his face. He also looked like a beach bum with board shorts, a swim shirt, and the weathered face you might expect from a surfer.

"Paul Jones of the Water Fey, may I introduce Princess Sarette of the Spirit Fey," Elwin did the heart-fist-bow and Paul and Mike followed suit.

"Princess, it is an honor. Welcome to my home." Paul swept his hand like Vanna White does after turning a tile on the *Wheel of Fortune*.

"Please call me Sarette—oh wait, Mandy. Shoot, is it safe here to call me Sarette? Or did I already blow my cover?"

"You are completely safe here, dear. Do not worry; your cover is not blown." He chuckled, then turned to Elwin. "Elwin! It's been too long." Paul walked over and gave Elwin a man-hug. They shook with one arm and used the other arm to hug and pat each other's backs.

"You two must be exhausted. Come, let me show you to your room." Paul turned and disappeared down the hall. Mike followed his dad and we followed Mike. We all turned into a room on the far end. This bedroom had a king-sized bed, desk, and two nightstands. "There's a bathroom through that door." Paul pointed to a door in the right wall. "I have invited some loyal friends for dinner at five. Do you guys need anything else?"

"No, Paul. This is perfect. Thank you," Elwin said and shook Paul's hand again, this time in gratitude. Mike smiled at me and walked out after his father, closing the door behind him.

"Finally, we're alone," Elwin said. "Maybe we can relax and rest a little."

"Can I shower first?" I asked.

"Sure."

I dropped my bag and walked into the bathroom without saying anything else. I locked the door, turned on the water, and waited for it to warm up before stepping in. I stood in the shower, thinking about the inevitable heartbreak that was looming. I knew I needed to come up with a plan—not to avoid the pain, but to be prepared for it and, hopefully, quickly move on from it. *What's the bigger picture, Sarette? I have to save my world. I have to save my mom's world. It is all in my hands. I feel like Atlas with the weight of the world on my shoulders. It's time to get real, get ready, and get to work.*

I turned off the shower and got out. *No towels in here. Just awesome.* One thing was for sure: being alone and naked with Elwin in a bedroom was not the best idea. I did not want to ask Elwin for help. I needed to keep my distance, no matter how insignificant our situation. *Maybe I can make a break for it, grab my bag, find a towel, and get back in the bathroom without Elwin knowing.* I cracked the door open to peek out. I didn't see Elwin; however, I did see a towel on the bed. Eye on the prize, I opened the door to make a mad dash to the bed and back. I made it about halfway across the room when Elwin walked in and shut the door behind him.

Elwin looked up from the papers he was carrying and froze in place, his mouth gaping open.

"Oh, my God!" I turned and ran back into the bathroom without the towel.

"Princess, I'm sorry. I should have knocked. Are you okay?" Elwin asked through the door.

"It's okay. Grab me a towel." I opened the door and stuck my hand out to it. Once I had it in the bathroom and the door was shut, I blurted, "I think it's time for a come-to-Jesus meeting."

"A what?"

"I think it's time to lay all the cards on the table."

"Huh?"

Clearly, clichés were not working. I wrapped the towel around my body, opened the door and leaned on the jam. "Elwin, I need all the info now. I can't make sense of this with one tiny bit of information at a time. For me to be ready for this, I have to know where and what we are going to do. I do not understand my enemy. I don't even know how large la-la land is! And it's my kingdom, right? This is all my responsibility. I'm done with just going along for the ride. Be prepared to start talking after your shower." I walked to my bag by the door.

"I'm not sure if that's a good idea. At this moment we have one thing to do, get you to the castle safely. That is my mission from the king and queen and that was my promise to you. I think we should just focus on staying alive long enough to fulfill your destiny." Elwin used a forceful tone I hadn't heard before.

I turned around so fast my towel's twirl gave him a peep show. "I am fully prepared to play my 'do-you-know-who-I-am?' card, Elwin. Don't make me go there with you. You will tell me what I want to know, and I'm not going to continue on my journey until you do." I had a definite tone to my voice too.

Elwin stalked over to me and grabbed his bag, then headed for the bathroom. He turned to me and said, "My orders do not come from you. I have authorization to get you to the castle, by any means necessary, Princess, so don't make *me* play *that* card." Elwin said through clenched teeth and a furrowed brow. He shut the door before I could respond.

TWENTY-SIX

I was fuming as I got dressed. The nerve of Elwin, and whoever gives the orders around here (i.e. Grandma and Dad). *Any means necessary?* I don't think so. I heard the shower turn on as I was shoving my dirty clothes into one of the empty compartments in my backpack. Looking up at the ceiling, I wished I could look up at the glow-in-the-dark stars on my bedroom ceiling back home. I used to be able to sort out my thoughts while watching them. Feeling alone and overwhelmed, I missed my stars, my mom, Peggy and Mathew. I missed the times when I wasn't fighting for my life and when I had the ability to choose whom I could love. I wished my new reality wasn't real; I wished it was just another dream from which I could wake up and not remember the details. Even if it meant I had never met Elwin, at least my heart wouldn't break a little more each day. I felt so confused and lost. I rolled over with my back to the bathroom door and drifted off to sleep.

I woke up some time later to a flutter across my forehead. I opened my eyes a little and saw Elwin lying next to me with his head on the same pillow as mine.

"Hi," Elwin said. "I'm sorry, but I do have my reasons for not explaining everything to you. I need you focused on what's ahead of you, not what's lurking behind. But you are right. You do need to learn about your kingdom. I got you a map of la-la land. You can start learning about your realm whenever you want."

"Thank you for the map, Elwin. You know, I do understand you have your reasons for not telling me everything, but this is my life. I will be better prepared to be queen if I actually know what is happening."

"Yes, and you will at some point. I promise."

"That doesn't help me feel better now."

"I'll make you a deal. Let's get through dinner and finish training. Then, after you become comfortable with your sword, we can go over some, but not all, of what is happening."

"Doesn't sound like a great deal to me . . . but I'll take what I can get. I need a better understanding of the enemy. That is what I want to be explained tonight. Deal?" I asked.

"Yes, Princess," Elwin said as he tucked a loose curl behind my ear.

"Elwin, unless you would like me to start calling you Sir Dickhead, please call me by my name. I'm not ready to be a princess."

"Yes, Sarette," he replied, with a flicker of a smile.

We spent the next few moments just looking into each other's eyes. I started getting that longing inside, but I resisted. I couldn't let myself go there right now. I took a deep breath, closed my eyes, and started to sit up.

Elwin caught my arm. "Sarette . . ." His choked voice made my heart hurt worse than the thought of leaving him. I let him pull me back and we were looking into each other's eyes again. Elwin cupped my face in his hand and swept his thumb over my lips. He started to move his lips closer to mine and I closed my eyes in anticipation. I felt a soft chaste kiss on my lips. We both made a noise like a growl and started to deepen the kiss when there was a soft knock on the door. My eyes flew open and met Elwin's hungry-angry-dissatisfied eyes.

"Oh, for the love of all that is holy," Elwin muttered as he sprang from the bed and opened the door. "*What?*" he snapped. I couldn't help it. I giggled at the annoyed tone in his voice. Elwin cleared his throat and said, "Sorry, Paul. I'm . . . um . . . sorry."

"Oh, my boy," Paul chuckled behind the door. "I'm sorry to interrupt, but our guests will be arriving shortly."

"Thanks, Paul," I answered between giggles. "We will be right out." I sat up with my legs hanging over the side of the bed. I was in the middle of a good cat stretch when Elwin's arms encircled my waist. He was behind me with his legs on either side of me. I leaned back and enjoyed the feeling of his arms around me. He tightened them into a hug.

"Come on. Let's go," he whispered in my ear and nibbled my earlobe. After my involuntary shudder, I turned and kissed him on the cheek. I stood up and put my hand out for him. He took it and stood, looking at me. He kissed me on the forehead and we walked hand in hand out of the bedroom and down the hallway.

There was something yummy smelling when we walked into the kitchen. Paul was wearing a "Kiss the Cook" apron and humming as he stirred something in a pot on the stove.

"Paul, that smells so good. Maybe if I make it safely to the castle, you can give me a cooking lesson or two." I walked to him and looked into the pot. None of the food here looked the same as at home, and this was no exception. It was a blue sauce, the consistency of marinara, with brightly colored chunks of *something* floating in it. Looked weird, but smelled delicious.

"It would be my pleasure, Princess! But, of course you will make it to the castle safely. Elwin would never let anything happen to you."

"I know that. I trust him completely." I felt Elwin squeeze my hand, and when I looked at him, he was smiling.

"Did you rest well, Princess?" Ray looked upset as he walked into the apartment.

"Yes, I did. Thank you." I thought I might have been seeing things because Ray looked cool as a cucumber by the time he made it across the room.

Paul snagged my attention from Ray. "Sarette, tonight we have two very good friends coming over, McConnel and Michealla. They are going to impart some of their water magic to you. You will need your wand. They are in charge of the second part of your journey tomorrow. My boys and I are taking care of the first leg. Please be ready to go at 8 a.m." Paul checked on something he had warming in the oven.

Mike slammed the door as he came stomping in. He looked pissed off.

"Are you okay?" I asked.

Mike looked at me and then zeroed in on his brother. "Why did you tell Tessa who Sarette really is?" He stopped two feet away from Ray. Mike was clenching his fist.

Everyone in the room looked at Ray. He shrugged his shoulders and crossed his arms. "Tessa is going to be your mazon. I assumed you told her."

"Tessa's furious," Mike fumed. "She thinks that I don't trust her, and that's not it at all. She wouldn't even let me explain why. Tessa said that no matter what my reasons were there is never a valid excuse for lying to her. 'Valid excuse' is a phrase you use all the time. What else did you say to her?"

Ray almost smiled, smirked really and took a deep breath. "When I mentioned dinner tonight with the princess and the royal family of the Water Fey, she was shocked and assumed that you didn't tell her because you don't trust her. Maybe you don't. Why else wouldn't you tell her the truth?"

"I was protecting her! Knowing who Sarette *is* makes Tessa a target and you know that! And you also know what the mission is—this is need-to-know information and she *didn't* need to know." Mike stormed out of the room and slammed a door down the hallway.

Elwin let go of my hand and said, "I'll go talk to him." He walked down the hall and went into a room on the left. Ray looked at me with no apparent emotion, yet something in his eyes made me cringe.

"Dad, I'll go wait downstairs for McConnel and Michealla," Ray said as he left.

Change of plans, Princess. Be ready at 6 a.m., Mike communicated telepathically.

Paul changed his frown to a smile when we heard greetings exchanged downstairs. There wasn't time to discuss what had just happened. It was time to be a princess. I took a deep breath, planted a smile on my face, and turned to greet two more fey who were willing to risk their lives for me. It was a humbling thought.

The two sets of footsteps on the stairs belonged to a set of Hawaiian beach bums. Both were five-nine, had light mocha-colored skin, almond-shaped eyes, dimpled cheeks, and heart-shaped lips. Their only difference was the length of their curly dark-brown hair. Hers fell to her waist and his was trimmed to his jaw.

"McConnel and Michealla of the Water Fey, I would like to introduce Princess Sarette of the Spirit Fey." Paul did the fist-heart-bow thing and the Twins did the same.

"Please call us Mick and Mica," McConnel said.

"Only if you call me Sarette."

"I think I like you already," Mica said and linked her arm with mine "Paul, Ray said he would be up as soon as he locked up downstairs."

"Why don't you three go check on Mike and Elwin and imbue Sarette's wand now. Dinner will be ready when you are done with that." Paul shooed us out of the room with a dishtowel.

Having Mike and Elwin as witnesses, Mick and Mica blessed me with some of their magic. And then, we went back to the kitchen where Paul had just put the last plate on the table. Ray had returned and was lighting the candles on the table.

While I was shoving my face full of one of the most delicious meals of my life, I learned that Mick and Mica were the unmated fraternal twin rulers of the Water Fey. Their parents had been killed last year when Mick and Mica were away at the Spirit Fey castle, Meanmna. It happened when the farm of one of the royal family's servants—the chef at Castle Hasani—was under attack. Mick and Mica's parents personally rode out to help him, but they were ambushed on the way. The twins had to stop their training with my father, Roland, who prepared all future knights in this realm to step in and rule. Mick and Mica had to sneak out of their own castle because ensuring the future queen's safe passage through their realm was their duty.

"Why aren't you expected to find your mates?" I asked.

"Because we represent the male and female entities for the throne, there's no need for us to search for our mates right now," Mica snuck a glance at Ray and then back at me. She registered a shock at being caught with her feelings exposed. I smiled, nodded, and mouthed, "It's okay" before anyone else noticed.

"What happens when you do find your mate?"

"We will rule together until that happens and then the mated pair will have to take over and rule." Mick glanced at Mica. "Not it!" they said at the same time. I had just taken a drink, so naturally I laughed and swallowed it down the wrong way. Elwin patted my back to help me stop coughing.

Mick and Mica were thoroughly entertaining with their well-played humor. Well, actually, everyone at the table played off each other. Elwin, Ray, Mike, Mick and Mica had been friends their whole lives. Mick and Mica's parents were busy ruling and Elwin's mom was always working, so Paul became the group's surrogate father. That's the way it worked here, a community in which everyone does their part.

It all felt so normal. I let myself pretend for the night that I was just a girl, meeting her boyfriend's friends for the first time. Everyone had a different embarrassing story to tell about someone else in the group, all in good nature and fun. The evening ended entirely too soon.

"Thank you all. Tonight has been wonderful," I picked up my glass to toast. "To new friends."

Everyone picked up their glass and said, "To new friends." We all took a drink.

Then everyone but me said, "Godspeed and Goddess save the queen."

After Mick and Mica left, Elwin and I excused ourselves. I was able to talk him into not training that night. I gave him the excuse of being mentally exhausted and I was, but really I just wanted to hold onto that *normal* feeling a little longer.

We were soon ready for bed. I got in and laid my head on Elwin's chest. He put his arms around me and kissed the top of my head. I fell asleep with him running his fingers through my hair.

TWENTY-SEVEN

Thursday, December 18

I set my internal alarm for 4:30 and woke up on time the next morning. It made me feel like my usual self. I left Elwin asleep when I went to take a quick shower and brush my teeth. When I returned to our room, I found Elwin lying with his hands behind his head and his ankles crossed. He grinned when he saw me.

"Good morning," I said as I walked across the room to grab my brush off the desk.

"Good morning. You're up early," Elwin said, watching me brush my hair.

I set the brush down and grabbed the rolled up map. "I want to look at the map and get my bearings before we leave." I unrolled the map. "Do Mike and Ray share a room?"

"No. Why?"

"If there's a way to sneak out of here even earlier than six, I think we should. I just don't want Ray to know. He gives me a bad feeling." I straightened the map on the table and began scanning it from left to right. I ran my finger slowly from top to bottom, taking special note of major topographical landmarks like rivers, mountains, and Lake Hasani. The lake actually looked to be about the size of the Indian Ocean. I looked for the town of Caldea, where we were supposed to get out of the lake and back onto land. Elwin interrupted my studies by putting his arms around me. I sighed and leaned back. It really was amazing how safe I felt in his arms. I allowed myself to enjoy the feeling for a moment, then I squeezed Elwin's arms and unwrapped them from my waist. "Go shower. I want to leave in half an hour if possible." I gave him a little shove toward the bathroom.

"Yes, Princess," Elwin said with a laugh. He grabbed his bag from the door and walked back to the desk. "Do you want me to point anything out to you?"

"No, I'll memorize it better if I discover it myself. I am going to prove myself a worthy ruler to the fey of Daearen. Go. I can't study if I'm distracted." I pointed to the bathroom.

Elwin looked proud of me. One look from him could make me feel such joy. I was going to make this happen. Not only would I prove myself a worthy ruler, but I would also prove that I am powerful enough to make my own decisions. I nodded to myself and my newfound resolve. Elwin gave me a brief, but knee-weakening, kiss before striding into the bathroom. I think he was humming. I went back to trying to locate Caldea.

At 5:20 a.m., Elwin and I left our room armed with our battle gear and ready to go. He had his spirit blade in hand and I held my wand. I still had to be careful not to accidentally stab myself, or anyone else for that matter.

Mike, decked out in gear similar to ours, was waiting for us in the hall. His utility camo pants had even more colors than ours. He was wearing a black wife beater and had a machete on his right hip and a spirit blade in his left hand. Mike looked at my wand, then his spirit blade, and gave me a strange look. "What's with the wand?" he said.

"It's one of my weapons," I said. "You'll see."

I wondered if I could talk telepathically to more than one fey at a time. I reached out to both Elwin and Mike, *I'm better at magic than combat. I'll be less of a liability if I use my wand.* I raised my wand.

Both Elwin and Mike nodded at the same time, then turned to look at each other, mouths gaping and eyes wide. Then they turned to me with the same shocked expression. They both started talking in my head at the same time.

How did you do that?

Holy crap! That was incredible.

Let's get out of here now. We can talk one at a time, out loud, when we get out of town. I walked down the stairs and through the shop to the street. Tessa was waiting outside with three seahorses. She smiled and did the heart-fist-bow thing so quickly I would have missed it if I had blinked. I walked up and gave her a hug.

You honor me with your strength, Princess Sarette, she said mentally.

Well, that got around fast. I thought to myself as I walked to my seahorse.

I got on the seahorse and took off behind Elwin. I looked back in time to see Mike give Tessa a kiss. *Good. All is forgiven.* The seahorses were very fast and we made it back to the canyon in no time. We dismounted, thanked our ride, and walked into the cramped space in the same order as we rode: Elwin in the lead, me in the middle, and Mike bringing up the rear.

Mike broke the silence. "So how did you talk to us at the same time? No one can do that."

I thought about it for a second and decided to go with my gut. *I'm going to show Mike my magic*, I warned Elwin. I turned around and put my wand in its pocket.

"Can I show you something, Mike?" I didn't wait for an answer before I put my right hand up like I was holding a serving tray. *Fire*—a small flame appeared in the middle of my palm. Mike's eyes got bigger. *Water*—a miniature raincloud appeared and put the fire out. Mike's jaw dropped. *Air*—a tiny tornado came down from the cloud, sucking all the manufactured elements and weather events off my hand. Mike was leaning against the cavern wall for support.

I smiled a small, devious smile, then flipped my hands like a magician showing that my hands were empty. I flexed and spread my fingers like a jazz hand, then wiggled them. Below, a rock shook and then rose into my hand. I looked at Elwin, expecting him to be angry. Instead, he looked as shocked as Mike did. *I should play this cool. Of course I can do that—I'm Sarette, Princess of the Spirit Fey, for goodness sake. Yeah, right. Just shrug it off like it was no big deal.*

Mike came back to reality first and said, "That was incredible! You might be the most powerful fey ever born even with a human half. Let's go. We need to get you to safety."

We all took off at a jog through the canyon.

119

TWENTY-EIGHT

There wasn't much talking as we walked through the tight cavern. When we came to the end, Mike used his magic to roll the boulder out of the way. After we had walked into the first crevice that we had passed through the day before, we turned left to exit into an open area I recognized. I was good at remembering directions, distance and spaces. I knew we only had one more bend to go before we reached a one-hundred-foot stretch to the entrance of the reef mountain. When we got within five feet of the bend, Elwin surreptitiously hugged the corner and glanced down the corridor.

Elwin glanced at us and whispered, "Someone is blocking the exit."

Mike squeezed by us to take a look. His face was grim when he slunk down the wall.

"There's no point in hiding. I know you're there," Ray shouted from outside the cavern.

"Why are you here, Ray?" Mike yelled from his seated position. I could see heartbreak written on Mike's face. He shook his head and stood. "Ray, what are you doing here?"

"I'm hurt, Mike! I thought you'd be happy to see me."

"You didn't answer my question, Ray. What are you doing here?"

"Wasn't I supposed to be here? Weren't we supposed to do this together? Imagine my surprise when I discovered the three of you had already left when I woke up this morning." Ray's mocking hurt was starting to piss me off.

A woman screamed.

"Who is that, Ray? What are you doing? Why are you here?" I had a feeling I already knew the answers to my questions.

"Oh, Princess, only yesterday you were but a footnote in my plan. But then Tessa forgave Mike for being a liar! Unfortunately, Tessa has proven she is not smart enough to be my queen."

"Leave me and get the princess out of here!" Tessa screamed. A loud smack echoed down the cavern. Mike broke from our grasp and ran around the corner. Elwin and I were right behind him.

Ray was outside the entrance looking at us. Tessa was unconscious. Ray was holding her up by her long blonde hair, gripping it near the scalp and wrapping it around his arm. From the look of her battered face, she had been used as his punching bag. Ray pointed his wand at us, a black sphere of light gathering at the end. He flicked his wrist and the ball flew toward us, gathering mass as it accelerated. Elwin grabbed me, pushing me and Mike behind the corner. Elwin followed, pushing us even further out of harm's way. The sphere of black light hit the cavern wall so hard the sonic boom knocked all three of us down.

"You said that no one can use magic against another fey here."

Both Elwin and Mike answered, "You can't."

"I don't think Ray got the memo."

"I'll tell you what, Brother. I'll let you have Tessa if you give me the princess. What do you say? A trade? Sounds like a great deal to me. It's definitely a good deal for Tessa."

A noise sounded in the cavern. Elwin, Mike, and I all raised our heads to look. A fifty-foot eel-looking creature with black scaly skin, beady red eyes, and jaws that could literally bite a man's head off blocked the path. With every wheezy inhale it took, a puff smoke out came out of its gills. Elwin and Mike released me; Mike picked me up and set me on my feet.

Ray laughed like an insane evil clown, "Do you like my new pet? I don't know why eascaans have such a bad rap. She's actually really handy to have around and has done such great job convincing other fey to join with me. She eats whoever doesn't want to side with me. It's a win-win—I get followers or she gets breakfast."

My eyes were locked on the giant sea creature as it slowly glided through the water.

Mike pulled his sword. "Elwin, you have to get Sarette out of here!"

Elwin looked around the corner and then looked up, "I think the only way out of here is up. You have to fly us."

"We can't leave Tessa and Mike." I panicked.

"Yes, you are leaving, Sarette! You are more important than all of us. I will keep the eascann busy so it doesn't go after you. Now go!" Mike charged the eascann.

I grabbed Elwin's hand and said, "Light as air." Elwin and I rose to the top of the cavern where we could see what was happening below. *I can't leave Mike down there.* I dropped off Elwin on the top of the reef and jumped back down before he could stop me.

I looked at Elwin and he yelled, "Sarette, no!" I put my finger to my lips to shush him simply because I had no idea what else to do.

I landed, gave Elwin a "thumbs up" sign, and then peeked around the corner. Tessa was lying in a heap behind Ray, who was pacing back and forth, not actually paying attention to our whereabouts. He probably assumed we were dead, or would be soon.

Think! Think, Sarette! What would Katniss Everdeen do? She would kill the eascann and look like a badass doing it. The fight on my other side was not going well. Mike couldn't get close enough to strike because the eel kept shooting streams of fire at him. Mike had avoided disaster so far by jumping, ducking, and weaving. He was getting tired and the last blast almost got him.

I pulled my sword. "Up!" I raised ten feet in the crevice. "Over!" I moved to the left until I was above the eascann's monstrous head. I held my sword with two hands and pointed it down, "Down!" I dropped, burying my sword all the way through the eascann's head and drove it into the ground below. The creature let out a high-pitched whine as it died. I braced my feet and tried to yank my sword free. It was stuck, so I tried again; this time it came loose with a hard tug and I fell ass over tea kettle and into Mike's arms.

"I owe you my life, Princess Sarette of the Spirit Fey. I pledge my life to you." Mike set me down and did the heart-fist-bow.

"Let's get Tessa so you can pledge your life to *her*, okay?" I said and peeked around the corner. When I saw that Ray was still pacing and distracted, I came up with an instant plan. I telepathically spoke to Mike and Elwin simultaneously. *Elwin, move to where Ray is. When I distract Ray, climb down behind him. Mike, you get Tessa out of here.* Mike and Elwin nodded in agreement and Elwin took off along the top of the reef mountain.

Sarette, I'm in position, Elwin spoke silently. I took a deep breath and started screaming at the top of my lungs as I ran down the tiny space. Ray looked at me with an evil grin. Elwin dropped behind Ray and was in position to strike when my concerned glance at Elwin betrayed us. Ray pulled his sword from its sheath, turned swiftly, and started attacking Elwin. I ran out of the crevice, leaving the clanking of battle behind. I ran past Elwin and Ray to Tessa. I was trying to get her to wake up when Mike emerged from the crevice and ran to us.

"Oh, baby, I'm so sorry. Please be okay." Mike sat down and pulled her into his lap.

Tessa groaned and opened her eyes a little. She reached up and wiped the tears off Mike's face. "I'm okay. You need to get Sarette out of here."

"No! Mike, get Tessa out of here. I'll be fine," I insisted.

A seahorse swam to us. Mike got up with Tessa in his arms and climbed onto the animal. "Godspeed and Goddess save the queen," they said in unison and took off into the crevice toward home.

I went back into the cavern to check on Elwin's battle with Ray. I watched as the two expert swordsmen circled each other, the clang of their swords echoing off the reef. Ray said something that I couldn't make out. Elwin was thrown backward fifteen feet up the reef by some unseen force, losing his sword as he slammed into the coral. He fell in a heap but tried to find his footing and get up. With his back to Ray, Elwin stumbled into the wall and one of his hands went into the reef. He tried frantically to get it loose but was stuck.

Ray laughed and put his wand in his pants pocket. He raised his sword with both hands as he walked toward Elwin.

"No!" I screamed and ran toward Ray. I pointed at him and then mimicked a baseball pitch. Ray was thrown into the air and crashed thirty feet up the reef. He began to slide down the wall, seemingly lifeless. Halfway down, his pants caught on a small outcrop and he hung there like a marionette. I ran to Elwin and pulled on his stuck arm. No luck. I waved my hand over the reef and it spread apart, giving Elwin the room he needed to get free.

Princess, we are coming! I heard in my head. Two seahorses were swimming toward us. Elwin and I jumped on their backs and took off along the lake floor. There was no time to talk as we focused on putting as much distance as possible between us and Ray. We had gone several miles when Mica approached from the left and joined us. We nodded to each other and kept moving. We zigged and zagged with no rhythm or rhyme until Mica took the lead position. She made a hard right and we followed her into an area that was desolate and lifeless. A burned-out ghost town of a village came into focus on the horizon. I had a strange sense of déjà vu as we reached the outskirts of town. We followed the edge of a building, dismounted the seahorses, and sent them on their way. Mica led us around the building and moved a sheet of plywood, exposing a hidden door. Elwin walked in first and we followed him down a set of stairs into what looked like a root cellar.

"I heard from Mike." Mica was wringing her hands as she looked around our space. "Tessa is safe and will be okay—awful bruises and a couple of stitches," she said. "Ray must have survived because Paul took some fey to retrieve his body, but it was gone. The backup plan definitely isn't as nice as the original. Sorry. You won't be here very long. Mick should be here soon with your ride. I don't know what to say about Ray . . . I didn't see this coming. I'm going to go look for Mick." Mica walked up the stairs without a second look.

"She's been in love with Ray for as long as I've known her, and I've known her all my life," Elwin said.

I took off my backpack and walked over to him as he took off his own. He wrapped me up in his arms and said, "When you dove down . . . I have never been more scared in my entire life. You can't put your life in danger like that. I don't know what I would do if I lost you." Elwin lifted me up and kissed me, hard. I felt weightless. Not just because I was a foot off the ground, but because I felt completely free, completely whole, and completely loved at that moment. I breathed him in and held him tight.

"Cough! Cough!!" I heard and reluctantly pulled away from Elwin. Mick was at the foot of the stairs with a rather amused expression.

Elwin continued to hold me up like a rag doll. "Are we ready?" he asked Mick.

"Yes, your chariot awaits. I would say to take five, but we really don't have time," Mick said with a grin. "I'll give you one minute, though. Make it count!"

Mick wasn't even finished talking before I snaked my fingers in Elwin's hair and pulled his mouth to mine. I didn't need soft. I didn't need gentle. I just needed to feel alive. I turned every ounce of fear I had in my body into a passionate kiss. I rubbed my chest against his, trying to get closer to him. I was so wrapped up in what was happening, I hadn't noticed we had moved and the next thing I knew my back was against the wall. I used the wall as leverage and lifted my legs to wrap around his waist. Elwin made his sexy growling noise, but it turned into a regretful moan and he pulled back from the kiss.

"I think our time is up," Elwin said breathlessly.

"I think we deserve another minute, don't you?" I whispered into his ear and nibbled his lobe.

Elwin moved his head just a little and kissed a trail down my neck to his favorite spot above my collarbone. "Maybe one more minute," Elwin lightly blew along the route his mouth had just taken. It sent a shiver down my spine and through my entire body. I moaned and kissed him one more time before he let me down.

"Let's go."

Elwin and I went upstairs.

TWENTY-NINE

"Holy crap!" I said as we exited the building. I had forgotten that we were in the water and the last things I expected to see were three blue whales. The babies were the size of a mini-van and the mom was the size of a stretch Hummer limousine.

"Your chariots," Mick said as he swept his arm to the whales and bowed.

"Is our ride hiding behind the whales? Reenacting Pinocchio isn't on my bucket list."

"You'll love them, Sarette. I've been working on these babies for a year." Mick tapped on one of the little ones and I heard a clang of metal. Mick took out his wand, said an incantation, and a blue spark came off the end. The two smaller whales stopped swimming and I could see they were tiny submarines.

"Wow! You built these? They're amazing!" I walked over and took a closer look. "Are you an inventor? Or are mechanics and welding your thing?" I ran my hand along the perfectly welded seams. "Just wow, Mick! I've never seen anything so fantastic." Mick stared at me with surprise. I waited for an answer, and waited, and waited.

"Since Mick has lost the ability to speak," Mica said as she walked over and put her arm around Mick, "I can answer. He's an inventor. He has an entire wing filled with completed, unseen, brilliant projects."

"Why in the world are they unseen?" I asked.

"I have other responsibilities that take precedence and I never thought they were good enough." Mick shrugged.

"Now you're preaching to the choir. Would you show them to me some time? If you have anything else half as awesome as this, who knows what we could utilize it for in the kingdom."

"Thank you. You are always welcome at Hasani Castle, Princess Sarette," Mick said.

"I also think that once I ascend to the throne, you should consider being part of my war counsel." I seemed to be slipping into royal mode more often lately.

Mica gasped and Mick dropped to one knee in front of me. "It would be my greatest honor, Princess."

All my regal feelings seeped away and I was once again lost as to how to react. I had spent so much time trying to think of how to act, I was sick of it. "All righty then, that's settled." Clap, clap. "I think you should show us how these babies work and we should get out of here. But first, I need a hug. I'm a hugger and having you down there on your knee is just plain awkward." Everyone laughed and Mick stood up and gave me a hug. Mica wiped away a tear and hugged me too.

Mike pointed and gave orders. "Elwin, you will take the rear. I made it the lookout post; there aren't any blind spots there. Sarette, I outfitted yours with a bed so you can sleep. You must be exhausted after using so much magic." Mick opened the mouth of the middle whale so I could peer in. The inside was the size of a one-person tent with a mattress on the floor.

"I love it. Thank you. I can't wait to see what else you have." I gave him another hug. Mick smiled and walked over to Elwin's whale sub. I joined Mica in front of the biggest whale.

"Princess, this is Maggie. She will be dragging the smaller subs and be the first line of defense," Mica said without looking at me. The whale she was petting looked at me and blinked.

"Wow! May I?" When Mica nodded, I began to pet the whale. "I'm so sorry about Ray. You liked him, didn't you?"

"I've been in love with him since we were kids. I always knew he didn't feel the same for me, but I always hoped that would change one day. I am so sorry. I should have seen this coming, and I can't believe I didn't see him for what he really was."

"I don't think anybody who loved him saw him for what he really was. Don't blame yourself, Mica. It's not your fault." I stopped petting Maggie and gave Mica a hug. "Besides, you are way too good for him, even if he hadn't turned out to be a sociopathic maniac."

Mica laughed and said, "Godspeed, Princess, and Goddess save the queen." She ended our hug and walked to her brother. Mick put his arm around her shoulders and kissed her temple.

Elwin walked over and picked me up in a hug. "I'm going to miss you on this journey," he whispered into my ear.

I nuzzled into his neck and mumbled, "I'm going to miss you, too."

Elwin walked to my whale with me still suspended in his arms. "I'll see you in five hours." He began to lower me. I lifted my head, looked into his eyes and pulled him to me for a quick, yet spine-tingling, erotic kiss. He set me down and I waved at Mick and Mica before I crawled into my whale sub where I had just enough room to sit up. I smiled as Elwin closed the whale's mouth. A small light came on near the head of my bed. I got myself and my stuff settled into the small space, then lay back on the bed.

A few minutes later, I heard a bang on the side of the sub and Mick said, "Godspeed and Goddess save the queen, Princess." *You better get used to hearing that,* I thought, *'cause they certainly like to say it.*

I felt the sub move. My mind was racing as I thought about this morning's revelations. I now knew who one of my enemies was, but how to proceed with that information still eluded me. I needed to rest, so, I counted backward from one hundred and fell asleep around seventy-five.

THIRTY

I had wished for dreamless sleep to help me get some much-needed rest, but the God and Goddess had a different plan. I had the town square speech dream again, but it was different this time. Instead of being blurry and out of focus, I could see that the dream was taking place in the village we had just left. It must have been how the town looked before it was burned and abandoned. I could tell who was speaking in the square now—it was Ray.

In the dream, it looked like Ray had amassed the entire town as his subjects in darkness. He told the town he would claim the Spirit crown and the Spirit magic that comes with it, by force if necessary. He said that if they followed him they would never want for anything. He never said that he would allow darkness to rule the realm, but as he was speaking a black aura formed around him like a shadow. I looked through the crowd during the speech and could see a change whenever a fey chose to follow Ray. The black aura around Ray would start snaking out like octopus tentacles and touch the fey in the chest. The fey would shimmer, and his or her aura would turn black.

I stretched myself awake. I had no idea how long I had been asleep, but I think I slept most of the whale sub journey. I decided to study my new realm for the rest of the ride. I got the map out of my backpack and found our destination, Brough. It was on the northwestern edge of the lake. I spent the next half an hour memorizing my kingdom. It was getting easier to think of this as my kingdom, my realm, my fey. It was all my responsibility.

I felt the whale sub slow its motion and come to a stop. I didn't feel us move, but my ears were popping and I could tell that we were rising to the surface of the lake. I waited because I had forgotten to ask how to get out of the whale. There was a knock on the sub, followed by a clicking noise, and then the mouth opened to reveal Elwin standing on the lake surface with his hand out for me. I took his hand and crawled out. He reached in and grabbed my backpack as I put my weapons belt on.

We were about fifty yards out from land and I couldn't see a town from where we were—just miles and miles of rocky shoreline. It looked like the beach at the end of the *Goonies* movie. Elwin took my hand and we stepped away from the subs. The whales went under the water. I saw a spout of water about twenty yards away and heard Maggie, the lead whale say, *Godspeed, Princess, and Goddess save the queen. If you need me again, you only need to ask. I am always at your service.* I saw two more spouts of water and I knew that Maggie was dragging the two baby whale subs behind her.

We walked to the shore and climbed a hidden stone staircase cut into the side of a small cliff. We reached the top, and from this perspective I could see Brough in the distance. We started walking a path that led to a bigger road. It wasn't paved, and there were deep grooves that carts had cut into it. We had walked about a half mile when we saw a firefly blinking on top of a boulder on the side of the road.

Elwin bent down and listened. The firefly blinked several times and then flew away. "Melinda sent something to help us blend in." Elwin walked around the boulder and stuck his hand right into it. He pulled out a large, dark-gray bundle. He shook and unfolded the bundle to reveal two capes. He handed me one and I put it over my shoulders and on top of my backpack. "You need to keep your hood up while we are in this area. Brough is like Switzerland, entirely neutral for the most part, but there are plenty of fey here who would sell their own mother for a price." Elwin grabbed both sides of my hood and pulled it up. He held onto it and looked into my eyes before he slowly moved in for a tender kiss. He let go of my hood and asked, "Ready?"

"Just a minute." I took the front of his cape and pulled him down so we were face to face. I looked at him for a second, then pulled him to my lips, hard and fast. I heard him gasp in surprise, but he quickly deepened the kiss. With a herculean effort, I broke the kiss and gasped, "Let's go." I let go of Elwin's hood and put my hand out for him. We walked hand in hand toward the town.

Brough was a typical fishing port. Ships lined the harbor. Bars and hotels lined the street we walked down. There were several streets that led down to the harbor, but we stayed on the main road as Elwin led us to the Brough Wayfarer Inn. On the outside, it resembled a European hotel or an Old West boarding house.

"We need to check into the hotel," he said. "I need to find someone tonight, but it shouldn't take too long." We walked up a set of stairs into the lobby that held a couple of beat up chairs and a check-in desk.

"We have a reservation under the name of Hill," Elwin flashed a wad of cash and the clerk took it and put it into his pocket.

"I see it right here, Mister Hill," the weasel-eyed man said as he wrote "Hill" in a huge leather-bound reservation book on the desk.

When the clerk looked at me, I turned my back to him and ran my hand up Elwin's chest. "Is there food here? I think we need to eat before we continue our honeymoon . . . Don't you think?" I then communicated

129

telepathically to Elwin, *This guy is giving me the creeps. Let's get out of here now, please.*

"We don't have room service, but the place next door will deliver." He handed Elwin the menu and a large metal key that had a tag with "Room 210" written on it. "Your room is upstairs and to the right at the end of the hall."

I kept my face partially blocked as we walked upstairs and found our room.

The room looked like one you'd find at any Holiday Inn. One queen-sized bed with a sag in the middle, a small desk, a table, and a couple of chairs. The bathroom was off to our left, with a wall separating the bedroom from the bathroom and open closet. I set my backpack against the wall by the bathroom door so it was ready for my shower. I lay down on the bed and stretched my aching muscles. I felt Elwin looking at me from across the room. I raised my head. "What?"

"Nothing. I need a shower. Do you mind if I go first?" I shook my head no. "I can eat anything. Order whatever you want. Food shouldn't take too long to get here, so go ahead and eat if I'm not out when it arrives." He walked into the bathroom.

I looked at the menu and decided on the one word I recognized, pizza. I called the number and ordered by asking for "whatever is your most popular pie." I passed the time looking out the window. Even from this angle, Brough looked like a regular seaside town except for the occasional use of magic. I watched a woman sweep her porch; not with a broom, but she passed her wand over the area and . . . *poof!* All of the dirt flew off the porch. A man with a large cart, filled with who knows what, was walking down the road. Nothing was pulling the cart; it was moving along on its own.

Elwin was taking a long time in the shower so I moved back to the bed and closed my eyes. I was almost asleep when I heard a knock on the door.

"Pizza."

"I'll get it," Elwin said as he walked out from behind the wall. "You stay back." I couldn't stop staring at him with only a towel wrapped around his waist. His back was sexy and I was mesmerized by the way his muscles moved as he reached the door and handed money to the delivery guy. Elwin shut the door, crossed the room, and put the box on the table. I stared at his naked torso. My goodness! He was so beautiful. Elwin cleared his throat and I had to blink a couple of times before I could focus on his face. He looked amused. "Go ahead and eat. I'll be right out."

He walked behind the wall. Once he was out of sight and I was able to break free from my trance, I got up to inspect dinner. I had no idea what the pizza toppings were. Vegetables I think, but I had never seen neon polka-dotted vegetables before, so I had no idea. I grabbed a slice and inhaled it before Elwin walked out, fully dressed.

"Do you like it?" Elwin grabbed a slice and started eating.

"It's delicious!" I took another piece. "So, I had a dream during the trip here. I think there might be a way to recognize whether or not a fey has turned dark."

"I'm not sure if that's possible."

"Do you think of darkness as a tangible object or more of an idea?"

"I've always thought of darkness as an idea, the philosophical approach to decision making and one's life path."

"What Ray was doing was not philosophical."

"True. I'm not sure how much unrest was here before your father left, or if that was the catalyst to what has been happening for the last seventeen years. When there was no king on the throne, fighting began and it hasn't stopped since. That's what the darkness is."

"Sounds like the fey are becoming more like humans," I said and shrugged my shoulders.

"What? That doesn't make sense."

"What doesn't make sense is that everyone has been consistently happy for thousands of years. Think about Ray," I offered. "I'm sure he was happy with what he got for a while, but when Tessa came into the picture, everything changed. Once that jealous, no-fair-she's-mine attitude became part of him, darkness took root in his heart." I looked at Elwin, who was wearing a rather confused expression. "Maybe if everyone stopped blaming the boogie man, i.e. darkness, and started acknowledging that these issues are typical, and dealt with them as such, we could get more accomplished."

"Ray aside, that's the way it's always been though." Elwin took another bite of pizza. "Everything has had a natural evolution. Families merged, marriages happened, names changed, rulers changed—it just always worked out. There has always been a natural progression to determine who is in charge of the other four elements. There has never been fighting to decide who rules. In fact, the only fey family that has remained in power for our entire existence has been the Keltoi family. Your family is the only family whose name never changes. Whoever marries a Keltoi, becomes a Keltoi, no matter the sex. What were you saying about a way to see if a fey is dark? What was your dream?"

"I'm not going into the dream; but, I think a fey's aura might change if they are dark. I'll try to see if I'm right when we walk out of town tomorrow. There's no point in explaining if it was just a dream and not a clue."

"You look at things from a different perspective than any fey I've ever known." Elwin embraced me and whispered in my ear, "I think we have a real chance at winning with you, Sarette. Never doubt yourself."

"I think the jury is still out on that one. I need to take a shower." With that, I squeezed Elwin, grabbed my bag, and went into the bathroom.

After my shower, I found Elwin sound asleep on top of the bed. Poor guy, he didn't get any sleep on the trip to Brough. I cleaned up the pizza mess and set the trash outside the door. I looked for my map in my bag and couldn't find it where I put it. Then I saw that Elwin had it rolled up in his hand. I very carefully pried it out of his fingers and spread it out on the desk.

I spent the next two hours studying my realm. I was feeling confident that I had all the main elemental castle locations down, and most of the major cities. Satisfied with my progress, I left the map and got my iPad out of my backpack. I grabbed an extra blanket out of the closet, snuggled up to Elwin on the bed and spread the blanket over both of us.

I hadn't used my iPad since I got here, so the battery was still nearly full. *I need to figure out how to get this converted to magic.* That sentence would have seemed weird a week ago. I had only read a chapter when I fell asleep.

THIRTY-ONE

Friday, December 19

When I woke up, Elwin was sitting in one of the kitchen-type chairs, looking over my notes on the map. I walked over to him and gave him a peck on the cheek.

"Morning."

"Good morning." Elwin looked me up and down, swallowed, and said, "Maybe we should get you a pair of pajamas on the way out of town."

"Why would we do that?"

"Because that is um . . . *distracting*?" he wouldn't look me in the eye. Feeling a bit confident because of my very noticeable effect on him, I pulled his chair out from the table so he would face me. He looked surprised when his eyes met mine.

"So, I'm distracting?" Elwin nodded in response and started to look away. I put my hand on his cheek so he couldn't turn his head. Feeling even bolder, I took a step forward and lowered myself slowly onto his lap, straddling his legs. "Is this distracting?" Elwin barely nodded once. He seemed to be completely paralyzed. I was so happy to know that I had the same effect on him as he did on me. I put my hands on his shoulders and ran them down the entire length of his arms. I took his hands in mine and pushed his arms back toward his shoulders. I held his hands in place, shifted my weight, and whispered in his ear, "I think I like being distracting."

Elwin took a sharp inhale and I shifted my weight back to see his face. His sharp inhale turned into a full groan, so I rocked my hips a little harder this time and his groan turned into a moan. I sat back and looked into his eyes as I did it again. Elwin's eyes rolled back and his grip on my waist tightened slightly. I began moving my hips in a steady rhythm and then my body started to react.

I let go of his hands and grasped his shoulders, pressing my chest against his. Elwin moved one hand to the small of my back and moved down to squeeze my ass. He yanked me to him—hard—and I let out a gasp of pleasure as the pressure increased. Elwin's other hand moved to the top my thigh.

133

Kneading it, he started to draw small circles downward to my inner thigh. He slowly inched his way with slow circles until he reached between my legs and touched me with the least amount of pressure. I exploded with sensations and screamed, "Elwin!" I couldn't breathe. I couldn't see. Every nerve in my body was yelling, "Holy crap!" and "Woo hoo," and "Oh, my Goddess," all at the same time. I shuddered as Elwin wrapped both of his arms around me. He held my shaking body tightly to his, stroked my back, and ran his fingers through my hair. I whimpered into his neck. It was several moments before I could lift my head to look at him.

"You are so beautiful." Elwin brushed my hair behind my ear and gave me a very soft kiss. He inched his body away from mine and took my hands from around him and held them in between us. He cleared his throat to regain his composure. "I located my contact when I woke up late last night. We have to meet him in a couple of hours."

"So we have time then." I leaned in to kiss him and tried to remove my hands from his to run up his chest.

Elwin held my hands tight, moved his head back, and cleared his throat again. "I . . . uh," Elwin swallowed hard. "You should get dressed. I need to take a cold shower."

"What if I said you didn't need to?" I leaned in and he moved away again.

"I'd still go take one." The pain of rejection ripped through my chest and caused my eyes to fill with tears. "You don't understand." Elwin sighed and looked away.

"I think I do. It's fine that you don't want to be with me, but you need to stop going along as if you do, only to reject me in the end. This rejection afterward hurts much worse than if you would just tell me the truth beforehand. Maybe you should try to remember that." I quickly got up and turned to escape. As much as I wanted to, I couldn't let myself cry in front of him. Elwin caught me and pulled me back down to his lap. I wasn't facing him, and I couldn't get up.

Elwin snaked his arms around my waist and I was unable to resist letting him pull me back to his chest. He sighed and I felt him put his forehead on my back. "This has nothing to do with you; it's all me. My God, I want to be with you. Don't think that I stopped because I don't *want* you. The connection I *already* have to you is so strong that when you have to break our bond, it could kill me."

"What?" I shifted my body so I was across his lap. I turned his head so I could look in his eyes, "Not literally, right?"

"Yes, literary. That risk was always there. Our bond will be broken during the mating ceremony with your chosen your mate. It's the way it will work; it's the way it will be."

"If that's the way it will work, why would the risk of death be there? You are my knight, my bodyguard. You can't be the first one of those here. Has any other bodyguard died when their charge was mated with another? Why would anyone ever take on a mission that would kill them?"

"It's not the same for everyone else."

"Why not?"

"Not everyone has been in love with their charge for their entire life." Elwin looked down, "You were so cute in that frilly-pink tutu. It's only been you ever since."

"Frilly-pink tutu? Huh? I haven't worn a frilly-pink tutu since ballet when I was four . . ." I couldn't believe my ears. *Did he just say he was in love with me?*

"That was the first picture your father ever showed me of you. That was when I knew I would do whatever it took to always see to your safety. I also knew my feelings would grow and only become more dangerous to me over time. I should have gone to the king and queen and explained what was happening. Yet I trusted no one else to take care of you as I could. I want to make love with you so bad it hurts—literally, and in several locations. If you and I make love, whatever chance of survival I have would be gone. Half of *me* would be gone, I just . . . I don't know if I would *want* to exist like that."

"I'm done with this crap!" I said, causing Elwin to look at me in surprise. "You should go take your shower now, because the sooner we get to Meanmna, the sooner I can inform my father, grandmother, and every fey else that I do not give a rat's ass about the political benefit of an arranged marriage or how weak I am as a half-blood, I love you so much! You are the only one for me, period space space." I hopped off his lap and took a step away from him. *Holy crap, I just told him I loved him.*

Elwin grabbed my elbow and turned me to face him. He lifted me up so we were face to face; then he looked into my eyes and asked, "You love me?"

"More than I ever knew was possible." I cupped his cheek in my hand and moved within a hair's breadth of his lips.

"I love you too," Elwin said softly before kissing me. Soft and sweet and filled with love, this kiss made me feel whole. He set me down gently and tucked a loose hair behind my ear. "We should go. I think the sooner we make that announcement, the better off we will be." He walked to our bags and looked back at me. I put my hands on my hips and he looked me up and down. "Yeah, I still need a cold shower." Elwin picked up his bag and walked into the bathroom.

THIRTY-TWO

When we left the hotel, Elwin and I went to a store across the street. The store reminded me of REI, but on a much smaller scale. We picked up some basic camping supplies: a small tent, a sleeping mat, a blanket, some non-perishable food, and enough water for two days. The next stop was to procure our transportation. The stable was a block from the town's small square and main street.

A charming older gentleman greeted us. "Welcome friends, I'm Denby. How can I help you? There's one thing you can't ask for, though . . . a filly as beautiful as you, my dear." Denby winked and extended his hand to me. I put my hand in his and he kissed it but didn't release it.

"Excuse me, Denby. I believe you should have something ready for us under the name of Hill." Elwin crossed his arms over his chest, raised an eyebrow, and looked at our hands.

"Oh, my Goddess," Denby said breathlessly as he dropped my hand. His eyes got wide and he looked as though he might kneel. Elwin wasn't having any of that. He grabbed Denby by the elbow and held him aloft until he could stand on his own. "I have your things ready, Mister Hill. Everything is waiting for you. Let me lock up first." Denby shut the doors and locked them. He took a deep breath and then turned to me and did the heart-fist-bow and said, "Please forgive me, Princess. I meant no disrespect."

"*Disrespect*? Don't be silly. I find you charming." I went to him and put my hand on his fist that was over his heart. He looked up and smiled.

"Let's go to the back. I have them waiting for you." Denby gave me his arm and I allowed him to lead me. I looked at Elwin and wiggled my eyebrows as we passed by him. He chuckled and followed.

Denby led us through the stable and out the back barn door. Two of the most beautiful horses I had ever seen stood before me. I knew very little about horses, but I could see they were truly magnificent creatures. The black one was enormous and sleek. She neighed in our direction and bowed her head. I was instantly drawn to the deep reddish brown one. The top of his back was as high as the top of my head. The sun made his coat shine like it was on fire. He lowered his head and I placed my hand on his nose.

"You are the most beautiful horse I have ever seen," I said and looked into his eyes.

You honor me, Princess. Goddess save the queen, he telepathically replied.

I walked to his side, took my backpack off, and held it blindly out to Elwin as I studied the saddle and the impossibly high foot strap.

"Let me give you a hand, Princess." Denby stepped forward and held out his hand.

"Thank you, but no. I need to be able to do this on my own. We might need to make a quick getaway at some point." I smiled and looked at the plain, brown but beautiful saddle. I could barely reach the horn, so I turned instead to face the rear of the horse and stuck my left foot into the stirrup. Like the stunt riders I had seen at the state fair, I pushed off with my feet and twisted the stirrup simultaneously to lift my weight and get airborne enough to swing up and turn 180 degrees in the air. I landed on the back of the horse, facing the right direction. I looked to Denby and Elwin in triumph. Their mouths were open in disbelief. "I always wanted to do that." I took my foot out of the left stirrup, untwisted it and put my foot in the right way. "Do you want to hand me my bag?"

"I got it," Elwin said as he attached my backpack to the back of the saddle. "'Always wanted to do that,'" Elwin mimicked me. He squeezed my thigh and walked back to his horse, strapped his pack to his saddle, and climbed on.

"Thank you, Denby," I said.

"It was my honor." Denby walked over and opened a gate. Elwin and I nodded to Denby again, then we took off.

We had been traveling on a narrow road for an hour when Elwin telepathically said, *We're meeting over there in that wooded area. Lunch should be ready when we get there.* Elwin veered his horse left and slowed down as he entered a small wooded area.

We only had to go about one hundred yards in when the space opened up to reveal a campsite. There was a fire in the middle and I could smell food cooking. A string between two trees held up a heavy canvas tent. It looked like an old school military tent with new school materials. There was an absolute giant of a man braiding the mane of a golden mare; he was not just braiding, but making art. It was beautiful. *I wonder, would he do my hair?*

"Will?" Elwin called to the man.

"Holy hell!" the guy yelled as he jerked around. "Elwin, sometimes it's okay to make noise upon approaching. You don't always need to be in stealth mode. A little warning is not too much to ask."

Elwin dismounted, laughing, walked over to Will and hugged him. He had the size and look of a professional basketball player: seven feet tall, broad

137

shoulders, and muscular frame. He had sage green eyes, a pleasant smile, and dark reddish brown hair the same color as the horse I was riding. Elwin was a big guy, but Will was huge.

Elwin looked toward me as they talked. Then they both started walking toward me, looking a little upset. I swung off my horse and approached them.

"Will Sherwood of the Earth Fey, I would like to introduce you to Princess Sarette of the Spirit Fey," Elwin said.

"Princess Sarette, it is an honor." Will did the heart-fist-bow thing and looked into my eyes.

"I am the one who is honored." I closed the space between us and gave him a hug.

"You honor me with your strength, Princess."

"Please call me Sarette."

"Hope you're hungry; lunch is ready." Will walked over to the food that he had cooking on the fire.

Once lunch was served and we had settled by the fire, I asked Will, "Are you okay? You look upset. You do too, Elwin. What is it you're not telling me?"

"I just got back from Marge and Phillip's house and gave them a proper fey funeral pyre," Will said. "It was the least I could do for the only real parental figures I have ever known. They took me in when my uncle tried to have me killed."

"Oh, my Goddess," I said as I covered my mouth. "I am so sorry. I wish I could have been there to honor them, too. They saved our lives, twice."

"You claiming the Spirit crown and restoring the balance will be thanks enough, Princess." Will cleared his throat. "It wasn't just me. Marge and Phillip were always selfless, and many fey came to honor them."

"Why did your uncle try to have you killed?"

"I was the rightful heir of the Earth Fey. My uncle held the throne in trust for me since my birth because my mother died while having me and my father died of grief shortly thereafter. Five years ago, when I was seventeen, I was to be mated on my birthday and would then ascend the throne. The night before my birthday and the ceremony, I was kidnaped from my room."

"Um, how? You're huge."

"I was knocked out from behind. I woke up at Marge and Phillip's."

"Why would your enemy take you somewhere safe?"

"I wasn't kidnaped by the enemy. I was abducted by the good guys who knew I would never leave my subjects by choice. They also knew I would never believe what had been overheard, the entire reason why I needed to leave that night—my life was in danger. Cynthia, to whom I was to be mated the next morning, had been overheard saying, 'It will hurt to kill him, but as long as I become queen it will be worth it.' Subjects and servants loyal to my family were able to knock me out and get me out of Pozzolana Castle to save my life. They tried to save my aunt as well, but they were too late; she had been drowned in her tub."

"That's horrible."

"I was presumed dead. The throne couldn't be without a queen. Cynthia and my uncle were mated before dawn before I even woke up and knew what was happening. I didn't even want to be king, but it was my duty. I wasn't in love with Cynthia, but bonding with her was also my duty. If they were doing a half-way decent job, I might have just gone with it, counted it as a blessing in disguise. But Cynthia and my uncle only care about themselves and power. My subjects have done nothing but suffer for the last five years under their reign."

"Once I ascend the throne, I'd like to start putting together a plan for you to take back your rule. It will be one of my top priorities."

"While I appreciate you saying that, you are going to have many issues that will demand your attention. I should not be your top priority."

"And that's exactly why you should be. The fey of Daearen has suffered long enough. If you get your throne back, the Earth Fey will be able to rebuild. You will take care of your subjects and you will always put their needs first. Also, restoring the balance to Daearen is going to take more than me. Every fey needs to play their part, and yours is ruling Pozzolana. Until then . . ."

"I am at your service, my queen," Will said with the heart-fist bow.

"Any word on how far the word been spread?" Elwin asked.

"What word?" I asked.

"You were right. It was time to let our enemies and allies alike know just who they are fighting for or going up against—" Elwin answered.

"He started spreading the word last night," Will interrupted. "He told me, and I told the other Earth Fey at Marge and Phillip's about you. I went to Melinda's after the funeral. When Elwin got word to her, she had her fey fly to all major cities and let them know the Spirit Fey princess of rumor is real. That you are not the weak half-blood that the fey believed you would be. You are, in fact, the most powerful fey ever born."

"Holy crap," I muttered.

Will continued, "Melinda will not be coming to Meanmna, but has her fey in place to guide you on the rest of the journey. She's also gathering intelligence from every fey that enters her forest. Lilly is out there doing her thing and gathering information. She will meet you in Meanmna."

"And I heard from Mike," Elwin continued. "He heard that a large group of fey had settled into an abandoned ghost town on the east side of Lake Hasani. He thinks that might be where Ray and his followers are. Mick and Mica are going check it out, then they will also meet us in Meanmna. Mike, Tessa, and Paul are headed there too and are checking out the settlements along the east bank of the lake on the way."

"I'm headed further east to the Pozzolana Earth Realm and will work my way to Meanmna from there," said Will.

I un-focused my eyes and tried to check out Will's aura. Attempting to see someone's aura is a lot like those hidden pixilated pictures. You un-focus your gaze and—*boom*—there's a sailboat. Will's aura was made of dark hunter green and a mix of gold and orange. It looked like a tree in the middle of changing colors for fall. I looked over at Elwin and his was a mixture of blues. It actually moved around him like water.

"Have either of you ever read auras?" I asked and they both shook their heads no. "Un-focus or cross your eyes and look at each other, look just outside of the body. What do you see?" Elwin and Will did as I asked and, in less than a minute, their expressions changed.

"Elwin's looks like he has the ocean around him."

"Will's looks like a tree in early fall."

"What does mine look like?" Both turned to face me.

"It's beautiful," Will said.

"It is a brilliant and bright purple next to you, then a ring of white, a ring of blue and the outside it has the same purple as the inside." Elwin refocused his eyes on me. "I wonder what it will look like after Will gives you some of his magic."

Will removed his spirit blade from his belt and stepped over to me. I took my wand out and held it out to him. "Princess Sarette of the Spirit Fey, I wish to bestow upon you the magic of the earth fey."

"I would be honored to accept your gift."

Will pricked the thumb of his right hand and squeezed the tip so a big drop gathered. He turned his finger over and dropped the blood on my wand. The wand absorbed the blood and a small burst of green light was emitted. Both Elwin and Will crossed their eyes and looked at me.

"That is so cool," they both said in unison. "Your aura now has green."

"I haven't seen a dark fey since I thought of this idea. But I think their auras might be black. Do you think you can do that visual exercise for every fey you meet and let us know if you see anyone with a black aura or if the colors match the magic they represent?"

"I will. Maybe I can get close enough to see my uncle. If anyone has a black aura, it's him."

"Stay safe. We need you," I said.

"Sarette, I think you and I need to make a detour to Beinn-Theine. You should get some fire magic from the royal family there."

"Is that who I think it is? Am I going to meet Mathew's family?" Elwin nodded and I jumped into his arms for a hug. "Thank you! That sounds like a fantastic detour." Elwin set me down and the three of us walked to our horses.

I gave Will a hug; he almost had to bend in half to reach me. "Godspeed and Goddess save the queen." He released me and did the heart-fist-bow as I did my fancy horse mount. "Until we meet again, Princess."

Will walked over to Elwin and they hugged. Elwin mounted his horse and our horses walked slowly out of the camp. We took off at a full gallop the moment we got out of the woods. *I'm going to meet Mathew's grandparents! I can't wait.*

THIRTY-THREE

We rode hard all afternoon to Bienn-Theine Forest. There was two older fey waiting inside along the tree line when we approached. They stepped out into the sunlight as Elwin and I slowed our mounts.

Oh, my Goddess! I was looking at Mathew in fifty years. This couple had to be his grandparents. Mathew looked exactly like his grandfather: same build, same hair, and same face. I'm not sure what came over me—perhaps I hadn't realized how much I missed Mathew—but I didn't even wait until the horse completely stopped before I jumped off and ran into their outstretched arms and said, "You're Mathew's grandparents!" They both nodded, but they were so swept up they couldn't speak.

Elwin spoke. "Ethan and Meghan Conner of the Fire Fey, I would like to present Princess Sarette of the Spirit Fey!" The three of us pulled away from each other. "It's nice to see you again, sir," Elwin looked to the man. Then he nodded toward the woman and said while bowing, "Ma'am."

"Son, how many times do I need to tell you to call me Ethan?" the gentleman said.

Meghan walked to Elwin and gave him a hug. "And how many times do I need to tell you calling me ma'am makes me feel old." She looked up—way up—at him. "You're huge!"

"Hi, Meghan," Elwin looked down into her charming face with such love that I could tell he considered her like a mother to him.

"You never told me you knew Mathew's grandparents."

"It never came up," he said with a smile. I met his eyes and absentmindedly touched my necklace and smiled back.

"I see you've already chosen your mate, Sarette. I'm so happy for you, Elwin," Meghan said with a toothy grin.

Elwin and I looked at Meghan and simultaneously said, "What?"

"Your mazon necklace, Sarette. Elwin, what beautiful work; it is truly lovely."

"I did make the necklace, but it was for this mission. It wasn't intended for a mating bond."

"The amazonite crystal is used *only* for mates," Ethan chimed in.

"The only reason why Sarette and I are using the amazonite crystal is because *that* particular crystal would give us the bond we needed to get Sarette safely to Meanmna. Queen Paige herself brought the crystal to me on the other side."

"I see Paige hasn't given up playing matchmaker. She hasn't changed in fifty years," Ethan said as he walked up and kissed Meghan on the forehead.

Meghan wrapped her arms around Ethan's waist and looked up adoringly at him. "Paige has been doing this her whole life and she's never been wrong. She hasn't even changed her method much." Meghan chuckled.

"I, too, was a knight with a protection mission, only mine was for the Fire Fey heir," Ethan responded with a smile.

I was speechless. Elwin looked shocked as well. Ethan and Meghan looked at us, then shared a knowing look with each other. Meghan walked over to me and put her arm around my shoulders. "Come. We were able to have a camp set up for you. We have guards patrolling the outside perimeter and someone is already taking care of your horses." Meghan started to lead me through the trees. "You know, Sarette, if you leave at sunrise you could make it to the sky train around sunset. You'd arrive at Meanmna just after midnight. You could be home for your birthday on Sunday."

"Is today Friday? I've totally lost track of time." We walked another fifty feet to a clearing with a blazing fire in the middle and a small cabin.

"We only had an hour to prepare. Sorry, we didn't have enough time for anything other than quaint."

"You did this in an hour? Wow, that's amazing!" I went to inspect the cabin. Looking in a window, I saw a bed and a table with five chairs. There was a door that probably led to a bathroom. "This is lovely! Thank you so much."

Just then, a girl about my age burst through the trees with what looked like a reusable shopping bag. She had pale skin, dark eyes, and fiery red hair in a spiky pixie haircut. She was running as fast as her small five-foot frame could carry her. She stopped in front of Meghan and doubled over, wheezing.

"Grandma . . . I got dinner . . . wheeze. . . Sorry I'm late . . . wheeze . . . Did I miss him? . . . cough." Meghan looked at Elwin and grabbed the shopping bag just as the girl took off running toward him. Without stopping, she punched him in the stomach and said, "Dude! I've missed you." Then she gave him a hug.

Elwin must have expected that because he didn't even flinch. "Nessa, I would like you to meet Sarette." Elwin nodded toward me.

She looked at me, smiled and said, "So you know my cousin, huh? What's he like?"

"He's my best friend. We grew up together. I brought a photo album. You guys want to see it?" Everyone nodded and drew near as I opened my bags.

"Let's get the official stuff done first. Grab your wand, Sarette." Nessa pulled her spirit blade and walked over.

After Nessa gifted me with the magic of the Fire Fey, we spent the rest of the evening eating and looking through the album and learning about each other.

At seventeen, Nessa was the most powerful Fire Fey in Daearen, and a genius to boot. The magic in her was a mix of the most potent Fire Fey bloodlines. I instantly liked her.

"You don't give yourself enough credit," Elwin said and bumped Nessa's shoulder with his own. "Don't let her fool you, Sarette. Nessa is smart as a whip. We all have a core curriculum to complete before moving on in our studies. The fey finish this primary education at age thirteen. Nessa finished it at age six and she hasn't stopped taking courses and earning specialties since." Elwin turned to Nessa and asked, "How many specialties are you up to now?"

Nessa looked at me. "Specialties here are the equivalent of human college degrees where you're from. I just finished my fourth specialty; I haven't decided what to do next, though."

"Geeze, you are only seventeen. Why do you need to decide anything yet?" I asked.

"I just can't decide on one thing."

"So do them all and whatever else you want to do, too."

"A lot of fey think I should have decided by now. They think that I should have stuck to one thing."

"Who gives a crap what anybody else thinks?" The whole table looked at me. "I'm so over the negative opinion of others. It'll only bring you down. It is what it is and you are who you are, right? So who are you, Nessa?"

"A librarian, historian, geographer, geologist, and I'm a pretty decent party planner too."

"If you're interested, I'd like for you to be on a council I'm putting together," I stated more than asked.

"I'd be honored," Nessa looked stunned.

"If you're a geologist, can you teach me about these?" I took the pouch of crystals out of my belt and handed it to Nessa.

"Sure, I'd be happy to." Nessa was looking into the pouch.

"Good, I don't want you coming to Meanmna until it's safe, though," I said. Nessa nodded in agreement.

It was just before sunset, so I excused myself from the table and rose to set up our protection circle. I began setting up the four protection candles that Celine had packed for us. Ethan and Meghan were smiling and hugging Nessa. Elwin was looking proudly at his old friend and Nessa was beaming. I was starting to enjoy all the good that I could do as a royal. I got back to work and spaced the candles around the fire at the compass points: north, east, south, and west, about eight feet out from the fire.

Soon everyone started drawing closer and all eyes were watching me. Several curious guards stepped just inside the tree line. My audience made me a bit nervous so I quickly finished the set-up.

"Sarette, shouldn't you put those candles out a little, no, perhaps *a lot*, further apart?" Nessa said with her hands on her hips shaking her head. "I don't think that protection circle will even reach the cabin."

"This is about the size of my room back home. That circle spread past my house by five feet."

"That's impossible. No fey can do that!"

"Pot, meet Kettle," I said.

"What?" Nessa looked confused.

"It's true, Nessa. I tried to break through her protection circles for a week. All I accomplished was burning up her water candle faster than normal," Elwin said as he put an arm around Nessa's shoulders and led her backward and away from the candles.

"Okay, I think I'm ready." I raised my hands.

"Where's your wand?" Nessa asked.

I lowered my arms. "Don't need it." I raised my hands again and said, "I call upon the—"

"What? This is never going to work. I guess I'm a pot. Whatever that means. You are not even using the ancient language, Sarette," Nessa said.

Elwin put his hand over Nessa's mouth. "Proceed, Princess," he said with a wink and a grin.

"I call upon the five elements: spirit, water, fire, air, and earth to protect this space and all those who enter with peace and love in their hearts." Nothing happened, and Nessa started shaking her head. "Maybe I need a real spell in Daearen," I said. I took a step toward the fire. *BOOM!* A ten-foot multicolored flame shot out of the bonfire and threw me airborne. Elwin caught me as I flew backward, knocking us both to the ground, where we landed with me between his legs. We both sat up and watched as a one-foot-diameter column of purple light burst upward out of this ten-foot flame and spread outward into a dome— not just around our camp, but farther than we could see.

"Holy shit!" I looked up to see Ethan, Meghan, Nessa, and the guards staring at me with their mouths open. "Excuse my language."

"That was the coolest thing I have ever seen! Oh, my Goddess! Oh, my God! Did you see that! Holy shit!" Nessa was yelling and jumping around.

"Okie dokie, then. So, standing inside the circle of candles is too close. Before I do this again, I need to figure out how far away to stand." I looked at Elwin. "Not that I don't love landing in your arms, but it's not very regal."

145

Nessa was still jumping around and screaming. "A column of light shooting up. Oh, my God. Everyone needs to hear about this! That was the most amazing shit I've ever seen."

Ethan looked around the clearing and spoke to the guards, "One of you will walk us home. The rest of you, go and find out how far this protection circle extends." Ethan gave Elwin and me a hand to get up from where we were still sprawled on the ground.

"That was truly amazing, Sarette. You are going to make the most wonderful queen," Meghan said as she gave me a hug. Then she turned and looked at her granddaughter. "Time to go, Nessa. And, please watch your language."

"Yes, Grandma." Nessa gave me a hug and punched Elwin in the stomach. "Later, dude."

"I'll let you know when we find out how big this circle extends. Goodnight." Ethan hugged me and Elwin, then took Nessa's hand and led her out. Meghan hugged us both and all three walked out of the space.

"You are amazing." Elwin took my hand and led me into the cabin.

Sometime later, I walked out of the bathroom after my shower, my long johns on over my tank and shorts. "I am willing to wear this hot and ridiculous thing for now, but I refuse to sleep in it," I said as I set my backpack down. "Do you really think my grandma did this on purpose? You know, matched us up, you and me? If she believed that I needed to choose a mate based on power, why would she have brought this crystal?" I looked down and held my necklace.

"I've been thinking about that too," Elwin said, walking over to me. "You know, she can be linked to my parents getting together. Dad became a steward in the castle kitchen specifically to help my mom. He never knew why he was selected; I guess I do now. Plus Mathew's dad, Liam, was Penelope's hand-to-hand combat instructor by order of the queen. I think Paige has had a part in the matching of every couple I know. So no, I don't think she would have brought me this crystal if she thought your mazon should be anyone else but me." Elwin put his hand over the hand I had holding the necklaces. He lifted my chin with his other and kissed me.

Elwin went to take a shower and I took off my hot and sweaty long johns. I grabbed my iPad and climbed into bed. I was on the last chapter of my book when Elwin walked out of the bathroom. He was only wearing a pair of jockey shorts that came to his mid-thigh.

"Seriously?" I put my iPad down and sat up.

"What?"

"If I have to wear more clothing around you, then you should wear more too because that . . . ." I pointed at him up and down . . . "is distracting."

"Are you saying you find me distracting?" Elwin had a mischievous smile on his face. "Maybe I *like* being distracting." He reached into his bag and took out a shirt and a pair of pants.

"New rule: no scratchy, stiff, uncomfortable pants in bed. We can behave. You had better put the shirt on, though."

Elwin laughed and pulled the shirt over his head when I asked, "Do we have to behave?"

"Yes, we have to behave."

"Aren't we technically already mates with the mazon crystal?" I asked as he slid into bed.

"No, we haven't had the ceremony. While most fey do the ceremony alone, you are the next spirit queen. Your grandmother needs to conduct our ceremony."

"Do you want to?"

"Want to what?"

"Be my mate. Since it's supposed to be my choice, I assume I need to be the one who asks. Do you, Elwin, want to be my mate?"

"Yes!" Elwin pulled me into an earth-shattering kiss, tucked me under his arm, and kissed the top of my head. I laid my head on his chest and felt the world melting away. I had to do something to distract us from our passion, so I reached behind me and grabbed my iPad.

"You're going to read?"

I pulled out of Elwin's embrace "Yes, we still have to be good, right?" I unlocked the iPad. "I'm on the last chapter anyhow. Love you."

"Love you, too." Elwin kissed the top of my head and got into bed.

Before I finished reading the chapter, my mate was asleep.

THIRTY-FOUR

Saturday, December 20

Elwin and I had awoken before the sun came up. We packed our things while we ate some rolls left from last night's meal and some jerky-type meat that we had bought in Brough. When we walked out, a guard was waiting outside for us with our horses ready.

"Princess," the guard said as he did the heart-fist-bow. "I was one of the guards last night who went to find the edge of the protective circle you cast. I rode out twenty miles from here and didn't reach the edge of it. The other guards are still riding. A truly amazing feat. You will change everything, I know it. Please, if you are ever in need of me, I am at your service." The guard knelt in front of me and I put my hand on his shoulder.

"If Ethan and Meghan will let you, I would be honored to have you serve as one of my guards in Meanmna. What is your name?"

"Darrius."

"Please rise, Darrius." He did and I gave him a quick hug, then mounted my steed. With a final nod of thanks to the guard, Elwin and I were on our way.

Elwin and I rode in a northern route until we reached the outskirts of the Meanmna realm and then we turned east. Meanmna sat at the northern most edge of Daearen, completely blocked from the rest of the realm by a small mountain range. My father and grandmother planned to send the royal guard to meet us at the base of the mountains. The guard would then transfer us over the mountains by sky train. At the pace we had set, we expected to reach the guard by sunset, and would arrive at Meanmna castle by midnight.

I couldn't believe it. I was going to be in my castle for my eighteenth birthday. I was going meet my dad and grandmother on my eighteenth birthday. If all went according to plan, I would also become Elwin's mazon on my eighteenth birthday.

We stopped for lunch around noon and Elwin updated me on everything he had heard from our allies. Mick and Mica had found the abandoned town that Mick had heard about on the west side of Lake Hasani. It seemed that every fey there had recently dropped what they were doing and left all at once. Mick and Mica followed the trail of the townspeople, who were obviously on their way to Meanmna. Mick and Mica doubled back and should arrive shortly after us. Mike and Tessa found a similar scene in a small recently abandoned settlement along the eastern shore of Lake Hasani. Mike and Tessa were taking the most direct route to Meanmna, but they were on foot and would not arrive until Monday. Lilly went to Eitlean, the Air Fey castle, to inspect auras. She reported that Phillip, heir to the Air Fey throne, had a black aura. He was still in the realm—only those loyal to my family had left Eitlean. Lilly was flying and spying on the fey along the way to Meanmna and would report any dark auras to Darrius, who had been released with honor from Ethan and Meghan's service and was on his way to join the Meanmna castle guard. Will was able to get close enough to see his uncle. He had a dark black aura but had stayed at his castle, Pozzolana. Will was on his way to meet us and hopefully would make it in time to meet the sky train and journey with us.

Elwin and I finished lunch and were soon on our way. I pushed my stallion a little bit harder as the sun's descent approached the horizon. I was very anxious and wanted to arrive before dark. We were earlier than expected and made it to our meeting point before the royal guard. We dismounted and took our gear off the horses. I placed my hand on my stallion's nose and telepathically said, *Thank you.*

It was my honor, Princess. It would please me if you continued to use me. I would love too. Can you come with us on the sky train?

No, I need to take a different route, but I shall arrive tomorrow.

I'm so terribly rude. I've never asked your name.

I belong to you, you shall name me.

Your coat looks like fire when the sun shines on it. I think Ember would be perfect.

Thank you, Princess. That is perfect. Until tomorrow.

Until tomorrow, Ember.

Ember galloped away with Elwin's black mare. I could feel Elwin looking at me. I shifted my gaze to meet his. "I named him Ember," I said.

"I named her Max. Is he coming too?" Elwin asked.

"Yes. Where is this sky train thing? What is a sky train anyway? I'm starting to get nervous. Oh my Goddess, what am I about to walk into? Holy crap!" The weight of the world had officially landed on my shoulders. My breath started coming faster, my vision was blurry, and I sat down so I wouldn't fall over.

Elwin dropped his bag and rushed over to me. He sat down and took my backpack off. Then, he picked me up, sat me on his lap, and began stroking my hair. "Breathe. Just breathe, Sarette. I've got you and I'm never letting you go."

"Promise?" I asked into his chest.

"Promise." Elwin kissed my forehead.

I took a deep breath, lifted my head from his chest, and said, "Sorry. I felt completely overwhelmed there for a minute. I think I'm okay. I can do this. *We* can do this, right?" He nodded and I kissed his cheek. I took a deep breath and looked into his eyes. "I love you." I gave him a quick peck on the lips and stood. "Where's the sky train?" I put my arm out to give him a hand up.

Elwin chuckled and took the help. "The sky train will be here soon. We should put on our winter gear. It will get very cold on the way and it's snowing up there."

"I thought you said the weather was always beautiful in Daearen. I hate snow."

"The only place it snows in Daearen is on top of these mountains. Your castle Meanmna sits on the other side. Going over the top by sky train is the fastest and easiest route to take. I can't wait to see your face when you see Meanmna from that direction for the first time. It helluva a sight."

I dug into my backpack and found the space bag with my winter gear. I pulled out the cape and shook it out. After I put it on and buttoned it, I took my pants off from underneath. I grabbed the snow pants and put them on underneath the cape. I met Elwin's amused expression. "What?"

"The future queen changing her clothes in the middle of the road. Tsk, tsk, tsk. Well, I never," Elwin said and shook his head in mock indignation.

I walked to him and snuggled into his arms. "You like it and you know it."

"As a matter of fact, I love it." Elwin was leaning in to kiss me when we heard a train whistle. Then came a thunderous sound more intimidating than a train, but I couldn't see anything.

"Look up, Sarette," Elwin said in my ear. A train appeared out of nowhere, only three hundred meters from where we were standing. It looked like an old-timey steam engine with a single passenger car being pulled behind it. It was red with gold trim and surrounded by windows. I could see several royal guards in front and others rode on the sides on a tiny plank that went around the car.

"Wow," I mumbled when I saw the train. Elwin handed me a pair of white boots to put on. "Thanks." I put the boots on as the train came closer.

"Let's go," Elwin said and slung my backpack over his shoulder. He picked up his bag, slung it over the other shoulder, and put his hand out for me. I took it and we started walking to meet the train.

The train stopped near where we were standing, but when we walked closer, Elwin stiffened. I asked telepathically, *What's wrong?*

I don't recognize any of the guards. Stay with me and stay alert.

A guard stepped out of the engine room and said, "Welcome, Princess Sarette." All of the guards did the heart-fist-bow.

"Thank you all for coming," I said with a smile.

"This way, Princess. The entrance is around back," a guard near the back of the train said. Elwin and I began walking and someone else said, "Let me get those bags from you." I let go of Elwin's hand as he took the bags off his shoulders.

"Princess, this way please," the guard at the back said again. I began walking to the back when I heard a grunt from Elwin. I quickly spun around to see that one of the guards had Elwin in a choke hold; the other had a blade pressed into his chest. Elwin looked behind me and yelled, "No!" I felt a cold metal band tighten around my throat and my body was being yanked skyward.

It was hard to breath and I was trying to get my fingers in between the band and my throat. Kicking, yelping, gasping for air, clawing, and doing anything I could to get free. Then I looked down. My heart felt like it stopped. Elwin had freed himself from the chokehold and was fighting five guards. There were too many of them. I watched as two men successfully grabbed Elwin's arms and pulled him backward. The other three were taking turns punching and kicking him.

I heard laughter coming from my left. Ray was walking around the corner of the train, wand in hand. "Not much of a personal knight are you, Elwin? Princess, so lovely to see you again," He said with a bow. "You owe me a new pet, Sarette. I've been debating for the last couple of days between you and Elwin as a pet. I came to a decision. I think you will be much more *fun* to play with." Ray gave me a diabolical smile and moved his wand. I moved in unison with the wand, over and down and toward him.

I could still hear Elwin behind me, grunting each time he got punched or kicked. Tears were rolling down my face and I was still trying to claw this thing off my neck.

"Princess, you can't get that off; it's made from magic. You see, after you demonstrated how strong your magic is, I got right to work," Ray said while touching the neck band. "With it, I have bound your magic to you. If you try any magic to get it off—or use magic for any other reason—it will only affect you. Bounce back. Return to sender. It's the magical equivalent of 'I'm rubber, you're glue.' Whatever spells you cast bounces off me and sticks to you, very, very painfully. You didn't actually think you were going to live happily ever after, did you?" He turned his wand and I turned to face Elwin.

Elwin was bloody and still trying to fight the guards off. "He's going to die attempting to save you. Isn't that sweet, Princess? Well, good news is, it's better to not kill him yet." Ray nodded at one of the guards. The guard pulled out his spirit blade and hit Elwin over the head with the hilt, knocking him unconscious.

"So much better this way. When you and I get your grandma to bond us, it will break your bond with Elwin and kill him. He'll need to suffer for several more hours and then you will kill him. Then you will live with the guilt of that for the rest of your life, however long *I* decide that will be." Ray laughed behind me as I watched the guards take Elwin's weapons and cloak. They each took a turn kicking him as they walked by to board the train. Elwin was just lying there in a lifeless heap. My heart breaking, I stopped struggling. Then I was turned to face Ray again.

"Done fighting already, Princess? That's okay. Save your strength for the wedding night." Ray turned and walked ahead of me, whistling. My magical prison dragged me along behind him.

THIRTY-FIVE

I sat at the front of the passenger car for most of the trip, everything happening around me in a blur. I had a physical pain in my chest. My tears wouldn't stop flowing and I did nothing to try to stop them. The guards occasionally attempted to get my attention by making rude remarks, but I just stared out the window and wouldn't respond to anyone. I had given up.

"Princess, would you like to see your castle? You'll be able to see it soon," Ray said from behind me and put his hand on my shoulder. "Come with me. I'll show you." I refused to respond or move a muscle at his command.

"You're so mopey. Get over it already. Today is your bonding day. Look! You're even wearing white, like in a traditional human wedding. How sweet and sentimental. You're a mess, get up." Ray tightened his grip on my shoulder, but I just continued to stare out the window. "Fine, Princess, I don't need your cooperation to get what I want." He must have lifted and twisted his wand, because I rose above my seat and was turned to face him. I hung like dead weight when he magically dragged me across the train car to a window on the opposite side. "Take a look, Princess. This will all be ours." Ray pointed out the window.

I squeezed my eyes shut and said, "No!"

"Open your eyes, Sarette." I kept them shut. "You are acting like a child." Ray's voice was getting terse. "I. Said. Open. Your. Eyes. *Now.*"

"No. Elwin wanted to see my face the first time I saw Meanmna. I am not opening my eyes for anyone but him!"

"Elwin is as good as dead, Sarette," Ray said with contempt in his voice.

"Well, he is *not* dead yet, I am *not* opening my eyes, but, you *can* take a long walk off a short pier, asshole!" Ray spun me around so I was facing him. My eyes were still shut, it may have been childish, but it really ticked Ray off, so I kept it up.

"Have it your way, Princess. I will quite enjoy teaching you your place." Ray slapped me so hard that my suspended body flew into the window, cracking the glass. When I felt something drip down the right side of my face, I opened my eyes. There was blood on the cracked window and from the gash on my cheek onto my white cape. "Go clean yourself up. It's our wedding day and you look a mess." Ray walked over and opened a door, then pointed his wand at me. He used it to magically drag me into the bathroom. He slammed the door and locked it from the outside.

"When you are ready to be more pleasant, I will let you out. If you are not ready when we get to Meanmna, I will have no problem dragging you—in whatever state you are in—to meet your family. They will give me whatever I want to save your life."

"You will never really get what you want. Tessa doesn't love you and never will," I screamed at the shut door. Ray punched it.

I looked around the small windowless bathroom. It had a toilet, sink, mirror and a stool. I should have watched more *MacGyver* episodes; he would have been able to make a bomb out of this stuff. I walked to the mirror. *What the hell!* It was the first time I saw that thing around my neck. It was a two-inch silver metal strip etched with Celtic knot pattern. It went around my neck and rose from the back two feet up. *That asshole put a dog collar on me! Are you freaking kidding me?* I washed the blood off my face, staring at my collar as I did so. The more I looked at it, the angrier I became.

There had to be a way to get it off. Ray had said that any magic I did would come back to me. He was so caught up with his personal issues I doubted the contraption was foolproof. I took off my cape and looked at what else I had on me. Ray's guards had removed my weapons belt, spirit dagger, and wand. But they left my necklace. Elwin did say he wanted to teach me tricks with it. We ended up making out that night, instead of learning what else my necklace and pendant could do. I looked closer and saw that my necklace chain had very similar knot work to the band around my neck. I picked up the pendant and rubbed my thumb across its surface.

"What the hell am I going to do?" I said out loud to no one and felt a slight buzz under my thumb. The knot work that circled the crystals began to glow and the glow spread up the length of the chain. I picked up the chain and touched my "dog collar" with it. I heard a hiss and there was a small area that had melted and burned where I had touched it. I twisted the dog collar around, bringing the part that was joined was in front. I took a deep breath and pressed the chain to the collar. The entire collar heated up, my skin underneath where the two pieces met was literary burning. I clenched my teeth and pushed the chain harder into the choker. There was a click and the collar disengaged. I couldn't believe that actually worked. I checked the damage in the mirror. My neck was really red and some ugly nasty blisters were forming where the collar was broken. But I was free of my restraint!

I hated to do it, but I needed to get the collar back on so Ray would not notice. I ripped a small piece of lining out of my cape, folded it, and I put it on the blisters. It hurt so bad that I had to bite my other hand so I wouldn't scream. I looked at the leash and thought, *Do whatever Ray says to do, except hurt me.* The collar lifted out of my hands, wrapped itself around my neck and stretched up behind me. *Shoot! I should have asked for it to bounce Ray's spells back to him.*

I needed to get word to Meanmna about what was happening, but I had never met anyone from there in person—only my grandmother, and it wasn't really her, just a projection of her five-year-old self. I wondered if that would be enough to establish a connection with her. It was worth a shot.

Grandma Paige, Queen of the Spirit Fey, please tell me you can hear me.
Sarette? Sweetheart, is that you?

Yes, Grandma, um, I don't want to be rude or anything, but there's no time to chat. Listen, Ray Jones of the Water Fey is a bad guy. He probably had all of your guards on the sky train killed; he showed up with his own followers on it. They hurt Elwin and left him to die. They kidnaped me and I'm on the sky train to you now. Ray thinks that I'm under his control and I'm going to let him continue to believe that until I come up with a better plan. You have to send help for Elwin. Will of the Earth Fey was supposed to arrive at the base when we did, but I didn't see him. You have to do something. Elwin is my chosen mate. Please, save him.

Are you hurt? Grandma asked.

Don't worry about me. I've got this. You have to help Elwin.

I will send help and prepare for your arrival. I know you can handle this situation. I'm so proud of you and love you so much. My grandma ended our connection before I could tell her I loved her too.

"Knock, knock, Princess!" Ray shouted through the door, "We will be arriving at *our* castle in the next couple of minutes." He unlocked the door.

"Just a minute!"

"I'm dragging you out in thirty seconds!" He yelled, but he didn't open the door.

I put my cape back on, adjusted my collar in the mirror, and walked out.

THIRTY-SIX

"My queen," Ray said with an elaborate bow. I stopped just outside of the bathroom and glared at him at the other end of the car. Ray gave me a diabolical smile; he looked overly confident and smug. It took every bit of restraint I had to not wipe that dastardly smile from his face.

"I am not your Queen."

Ray pointed his wand at me. *Please God and Goddess, let my spell work.* Ray moved his wand up, my collar followed his command and I was lifted several inches off the ground. Ray moved me through the train car to him. The sudden pressure on my blisters made me grimace and brought tears to my eyes. Ray's smile grew even larger when he saw my tears.

"Now, now, my queen, don't cry. It'll all be over soon." Ray grabbed my cape and pulled me to him. I grunted in surprise and nearly gagged when he thrust his tongue into my mouth. I bit down on it so hard it I drew blood.

"*Bitch*!" screamed Ray. He slapped me across the face. My body jerked and the collar dug into my blisters, bringing another set of tears streaming down my face. Ray spit blood on the floor and looked at me. My eyes were already unfocused from the slap, and I could see the black, smoky aura around his body. There was an overwhelming feeling of evil emanating from it.

Ray began straightening my hair and clothes. "First impressions are the most important, my dear."

"You're certifiably crazy."

Ray yanked me closer to him. "I am *so* going to enjoy breaking you." He stared at me. His blue irises now had a black ring around them. His aura touching me felt like a million no-see-ums biting me at once. I was filled with such a sense of dread that I started gasping for breath. Ray was pure evil and if he succeeded, I would wish I was dead.

"Oh, Goddess," I choked out of pure fear. I closed my eyes and took several deep breaths to stave off the imminent panic attack. The train stopped. I took one more calming breath and opened my eyes.

Ray smiled. "All better? I am certainly ready to meet the in-laws. Are you ready to meet the family for the first time?" He opened the door, walked out, down the steps, and out of sight.

I heard a powerful male voice. "Ray? Where is my daughter? Where are Elwin and the royal guard?"

"All indisposed at the moment, I'm afraid," Ray responded.

"Where is Sarette, Ray?" It was my grandmother's voice.

"I guess you *would* be anxious to see her, wouldn't you?"

"Why are you here, Ray?" The male had to be my father. Who else would it be?

"I suppose you've waited long enough for the long lost heir." Ray walked into my field of vision and said, "Come, pet!" Ray moved his wand and I floated out the door and down the stairs. "King Roland and Queen Paige, I would like you to meet your daughter, granddaughter, and my future mate, Sarette." I was turned to face them and saw my family for the first time. I couldn't believe how much my features resembled my dad's. We had the same hair color, same nose, same mouth and chin. He was dressed like Elwin always did: camo utility pants, black tee shirt, boots, and a weapon belt around his hips. He looked more warrior-like than regal and as soon as he saw me, he took his sword out of his belt and glared at Ray. "What have you done to my daughter?"

Ray adjusted my clothes and touched my face. "Perhaps if you hadn't abandoned Sarette to the humans, she would be more gentile and lady-like. As she is right now, though, she needs to be trained into her place. No worries, Roland, I will take great pleasure in breaking her." Ray grabbed me by the chin and yanked me into a hard kiss. I was pushing and hitting him until he grabbed me by my hair and yanked my head back. "Paige, I think it's time to bond us, don't you?"

"I think it's time for you to let my granddaughter go, don't you?" My grandma raised her wand and pointed it at Ray. She was stunning; five-foot-nine and slender, with strawberry-blond hair streaked with white and high cheekbones. Her hazel eyes were wide with shock and looked like they were glowing. She had the same silver band across her forehead—I guess it was a crown—and the same wand that I saw her with at Vision's, crystal clear with an amethyst spirit crystal at the end. She was dressed in a floor-length royal blue dress.

Ray let go of my hair and pointed his wand at my father. "I will be king, one way or another," he said to Paige. "You can mate your granddaughter and me and *then* we will ascend the throne. *Or,* I kill the king *and* you, take the throne, and still keep Sarette as my pet. Your choice. Tick, tock." Ray looked away from my grandmother for a moment and she caught my eye.

Sarette, it's time for you to become queen.

What? Wait! Without thinking, I moved my hand in a "stop" motion. Unfortunately, that was the moment Ray looked back to me and noticed that my grandmother and I were communicating with one another. "You stupid bitch! Tighten!" Ray flicked his wand at me. I felt nothing, but he started clawing at his throat like something had tightened around it. His eyes were bulging from the lack of oxygen. Ray pointed his wand at me again and croaked out, "Release."

A black light flashed from the end of his wand and my collar and I clattered to the ground. With my bounce-back spell, Ray's invisible collar released him too. He pointed his wand at my grandmother and a giant black plume of smoke came out of the end. It hit my grandmother and she went flying some twenty feet and landed in a heap. I got up and ran toward her. Ray ran in the opposite direction, with my father in close pursuit. I reached my grandma and rolled her over; she was knocked out. I sat down and put her head on my lap.

"Grandma, I'm not ready to be queen," I whispered as I shook her gently, trying to wake her. Just then, a bright flash of black light filled the courtyard and when it faded, the courtyard was filled with fey. I checked everyone's aura and they all were black and smoky. "Oh crap," I muttered and looked down.

My grandmother's eyes were open and she had a slight smile. "Help me sit," she said. She looked at me and touched the side of my face with her free hand. Then she put her hand down, gave me a toothy grin, and said, "How did you put it? No worries, I've got this?" She held out her wand and started speaking under her breath. The spirit crystal at the end began to glow brightly. A purple light burst out of the crystal, spreading in all directions and filling the courtyard and beyond. As the light faded, good and loyal fey appeared. No one moved. All was silent for what seemed like forever, and then all hell broke loose.

THIRTY-SEVEN

As a single unit, every dark fey attacked my loyal fey at once. There was an instant cacophony of fighting sounds and I scanned the crowd to see if I recognized anyone. Then my grandmother—still lying in my lap—grunted. When I looked down, I saw that the spot on her chest that Ray's smoke had hit was starting to sizzle and shimmer. She moaned and her eyes rolled to the back of her head as she fainted. I laid her on the ground, took off my cape, and put it under her head. Movement caught my eye and I saw one of Ray's dark fey running for us, swinging a battleax above his head.

I stood up and blocked my grandma from the battleax fey. I raised my hands to magically throw his butt elsewhere when out of nowhere a blurred figure with dark reddish-brown hair tackled the fey from the side. The battleax was let go and landed with a thump. The two fey landed and skidded. The fighting was so swift I couldn't tell who was involved, but the fey with reddish-brown hair twisted and grabbed the battleax by the handle, using it as leverage to swing himself to his feet. In one fell swoop, he swung the ax over his head and into the face of the other fey. He then dropped the battleax and turned to face me.

"Will! Can you get the queen somewhere safe?" I shouted as he ran toward me. Behind Will, I spotted Elwin trying to break through the throng of fighters. Will scooped my grandma in his arms and ran into the castle. When they safely made it through the door, I turned to where I had last seen Elwin. He hadn't made it much closer and was in the middle of a sword fight with another fey.

I was running toward Elwin when I was grabbed from behind. The force of two beefy arms wrapping around my arms and chest knocked the wind out of me. As I was lifted off the ground, I kicked my legs frantically, trying to will my lungs to inhale. I had grown slightly fuzzy as I sucked in my first breath and channeled my inner Harry Potter. On my exhale, I wheezed out, "Stupefy!" The fey released his grip on me and collapsed. I ran toward Elwin and was within five feet of him when he ran his sword all the way through his opponent. He yanked the sword out of the fey's chest and let him drop. I jumped over the fallen fey and grabbed Elwin's shirt. I yanked him down and looked into his eyes for only a second before I gave him a hard, fast kiss on the lips.

"Come on." I turned and ran toward the castle door that Will had gone through. Elwin followed me. I mentally flicked a couple of dark fey out of the way. I wasn't interested in fighting or the ramifications of using magic against a dark fey. I had to get to my grandmother. I ran through the open door and immediately zeroed in on her; she was lying on a chaise lounge along the left wall of what looked to be a grand ballroom. There were two marble winding staircases with landings, and another single stairway that led to a grand entrance at the top. I ran to my grandma. The black shimmer was gone and her eyes were open, but she was ghostly pale. I could tell by the rasp that she was having difficulty breathing. Will was standing behind the chaise, crying. He looked at me with such sadness that I choked up.

"Grandma," I said as I sunk to my knees and took her hand. "Is there anything that I can do? Please tell me what I can do!"

"It's your time, Sarette. This was always meant to be. This was always *who* you were meant to be. You are going to be the most wonderful queen Daearen has ever had." Grandma squeezed my hand.

"I'm not ready for this. Please, tell me what I need to do."

"You need to fight to save your fey and your kingdom now. Elwin?" Grandma put her other hand out to him. He took it and knelt next to me. "To conquer this enemy and the ones that will follow, you should be made whole." Elwin's mouth opened and shut. He looked at me and reached for my free hand with his. He brought our hands up to kiss my knuckle and kept them next to his lips. "Is he your chosen?" My grandma asked.

"What?" I broke eye contact with Elwin and looked at her.

Elwin whispered in my ear, "Do you want to be mine forever?"

My grandma smiled and nodded. I turned to look in Elwin's eyes. "I do! And, do you want to be mine, forever?"

"And so much more!" Elwin started to kiss me when my grandma squeezed our hands and interrupted us.

"Will, please move to where I can see you so you can bear witness." I had forgotten Will was even there. I looked at him and he was smiling with tears running down his face. It was quite a sight seeing a giant of a man weep. He nodded at me and walked around the chaise to be at my grandma's feet. "Please take out your amazonite crystals."

Elwin and I let go of our hands and reached into our shirts. We both took out our necklaces and clasped one another's hands. "Are you ready?" Grandma asked and we nodded. Grandma closed her eyes and took a deep breath. Elwin's and my amazonite pendants began to glow brightly and heat up. It wasn't the same heat or pain I felt when I cut through my collar on the train. The heat felt warm and inviting, like an electric blanket on a cold Michigan winter night. I was at peace. I was content; it felt like my soul became bigger. A tingle and a rush went through my body and forced me to close my eyes from the overwhelming feeling that was encompassing me.

Elwin squeezed my hand and I squeezed his. "Forever," he whispered. "Forever," I replied.

The sensation faded and I opened my eyes to find the room bathed in purple light. The light grew in brightness, blinked once, and then faded. My grandmother and Will were smiling. Elwin and I leaned in and were about to kiss when a giant rock broke through a stained glass panel above the door. As the glass shattered, it rained down on the dark fey that were streaming in and running toward us. On the other side of the room, the castle guard came to intercept.

My grandmother let go of our hands, "You have to go, now."

I looked at Will and then nodded to the door that was tucked under the stairs on the other side of the room away from the vicious battle ensuing in the ballroom. Will scooped my grandmother up and ran in the direction that I had indicated. I looked at Elwin, "All of our weapons are on the train. I saw where Ray's guys threw them."

"Okay, follow me. You do whatever it takes. Do you understand? You have a higher purpose."

"Yes, I do have a higher purpose and for now it's about killing Ray. Let's go." I took off running before he could argue. Elwin quickly took over the lead. With our backs hugging the wall, we made it to an exit without being engaged in the interior fighting. Outside the door, a dead dark fey was pinned to the wall with a sword run through his chest. I stepped past Elwin and yanked the sword out. The fey dropped to the ground. I nodded toward the train and Elwin instantly complied.

Elwin led us around as much of the fighting as possible. He used his borrowed sword when necessary, cutting through any dark fey that got too close. I scanned the area and realized that without even un-focusing my eyes, I could see every fey's aura. I was shocked. I didn't know when it happened. I stopped when I saw an Earth Fey and a Water Fey fighting each other. They had no idea they were allies. *God and Goddess, please give my loyal fey my own sight.* I ran again but kept my eye on the fighting allies. I saw as they stopped and looked at each other confused. Then they nodded to each other, went back to back, and began fighting as a unit. It was awesome!

Elwin had reached the train car and was making sure the coast was clear from the door when a dark fey broadsided me. The force knocked my shins against the train steps, and I fell forward on top of them. The heavy sword I was carrying flew out of my hand when my elbow hit the platform. I flipped over and made a motion like I was pushing him away with my hands, and an invisible force sent him flying. I scrambled to my feet and practically fell into the car. I shut the door and locked it.

Elwin looked to make sure I was okay, then continued checking all the nooks and crannies for the enemy. My backpack was right by the door and my weapons belt was probably still under the cushioned bench it had been flung under about halfway down the car. Elwin's was in the same general area. I went to my backpack, unhooked my boots from their D-ring and took out camo pants and a tank top. I was kicking off my boots and taking off my long john shirt when Elwin asked, "What the hell are you doing?" He was next to the bathroom door with his mouth gaping open.

"Uh, hubby, no reason to be shy," I said as I unzipped my pants and pushed them to my ankles.

Elwin sputtered until he could form words, "I'm just, uh, um,"

"Oh, for goodness sakes, Elwin. That crap I was wearing is hot and confining. Plus, I have never trained wearing it. I'd rather fight for life and death in something I'm comfortable in and understand how it moves." I grabbed my camo pants and started putting them on.

Suddenly, the bathroom door flew open and one of Ray's train guards knocked into Elwin. They both crashed into a table. Maintaining his balance, the guard punched Elwin on the side of the head, rendering him unconscious.

"Oh crap," I muttered as I ran to my belt and dropped to my knees to grab it from under the seat. I couldn't reach it in the position I was in so I got on my belly and reached my arm underneath. I touched leather with the tips of my fingers and was able to scoot it closer. I grabbed the hilt of my spirit blade as my attacker fell to his knees next to me.

The guard jerked me by my hair and pulled me backward, causing me to land on top of him. He forced my head to his body and held me by my hair with my face near his crotch. "I like it rough," he said.

I managed to get onto my hands and knees with my hair still anchored as I flipped over in one fluid motion and stabbed him in the heart. His eyes widened. I tried a couple of times to pull my hair out of his hand, but part of it was knotted up and wrapped around through his fingers and around his hand. My twisting had caused it to get stuck around the brace where the train seat fastened to the floor. So, I yanked my spirit blade out of his heart and cut my hair loose to free myself.

"I like the new look." Elwin was standing up, rubbing the side of his head. I got up and ran to him so fast I knocked him slightly off balance. He caught himself by grabbing my arms. He slipped his arms around my torso and picked me up. I kissed him hard. Elwin broke the kiss and asked, "I don't suppose I could talk you into staying here, could I?"

"Nope." I jumped down and went to get my weapons. I pushed the dead guy out of the way and grabbed my belt from under the seat. I stood and put it on. "We need to find Ray." I picked up my spirit blade, put it in its sheath and tied it to my leg. I looked at Elwin and said, "You ready?"

"Aren't you forgetting something?"

I looked at my weapons belt and everything including my sword was there. "No."

Elwin had an amused expression as he walked past me to the door. He picked up my shirt and handed it to me. I looked and realized I was only wearing my sports bra.

"Oops!" I put my shirt on and as my head came through the hole, I saw a black light flash beyond the courtyard near the foothills of the mountains in the distance. "Look." I pointed to another flash; this one was purple. "There they are."

Elwin found his weapons belt and was putting it on as we walked to the door. We took our swords and spirit daggers out. Elwin moved and unlocked the door. He gave me a quick kiss and said, "I love you. Try to save your magic; we have no idea what Ray has planned. Stay behind me." He opened the door and we ran.

THIRTY-EIGHT

I ran out of the train after Elwin. The sights and sounds of battle were all around. Screams and wails were mixed with metal swords clashing together. We were crossing the courtyard, going toward the area where we had seen the flashes of light. I was close behind Elwin as he ran through the least congested areas and cleared a path with wide swings of his sword. I followed picking off the few fey Elwin missed. I swung my sword low and to the right, and took a dark fey out at the knees. I swung it back to the left and clipped one in the shoulder, knocking him from my path. As I kept running, I sensed a fey was coming from behind me on the right. In my peripheral vision, I saw him swing his sword. I dropped into a crouch to avoid decapitation. The dark fey couldn't stop in time and tripped over me, landing face first on the other side. I dropped my sword and grabbed my spirit blade with both hands. I swung the dagger and planted it in the dark fey's back. I pulled it out, grabbed my sword, jumped to my feet, and ran after Elwin in one fluid, graceful move.

Elwin doubled back and was only a couple yards away when I saw a dark fey approaching him from behind with a spirit blade poised to strike. I reached Elwin, pushed him out of the way, and stabbed the dark fey through the chest with my sword. I pushed the fey off my sword and held my hand out to Elwin. We heard a scream to our left. A young man with the red Fire Fey aura had lost his weapon and a dark fey had pushed him to his knees and was holding his sword to the kid's neck.

"Go help him! I'll catch up," Elwin said.

I sprinted as hard as I could to the young fey. The Fire Fey was on his knees, looking bravely defiant as he waited for his enemy to deliver the deathblow. The dark fey was enjoying torturing the lad. I swung my sword and released it toward the would-be executioner. It made two complete rotations before planting itself in the back of my enemy. I got to the Fire Fey and helped him to his feet. He couldn't have been more than fourteen. He was too young to be fighting.

"What's your name?"

"Reece."

"Reece, I want you to try to get inside and check on my grandmother. Can you do that? Can you go check on the queen for me? Will is with her. Please help with whatever he needs." He nodded, wide-eyed. "Okay, be fast and safe." I gave him a quick embrace and he hugged me back before he took off running to the castle.

Elwin had Mike Jones with him when he arrived at the scene. Mike took my sword from the dark fey's back and handed it to me. A dozen fighting fey spilled into our immediate area and blocked us from every direction. I grabbed Elwin and Mike by their shirts and said, "Up." We started rising above the crowd just as a pair of fighters crashed into the space we had just occupied.

"Look for Ray and my dad!" I scanned the hills past us, hoping to see a flash of black or purple.

"There!" Mike pointed to our left. We didn't see anything for a second or two and then we saw a purple flash followed by a black one that lit up a hill more than a mile away.

"Over," I said and we flew in the direction of the flashes. As I looked down on the scene, I could see that those loyal to me were grossly outnumbered. I brought us down just past the imminent slaughter. "I'm going after Ray and my dad. You both are needed here." I let go of Mike's shirt and pulled Elwin to me. "I love you. I can do this." I kissed him. "They are using a lot of magic. I won't use a lot of my magical power getting to them. I'll have enough strength left to do what needs to be done. I have to do this." I kissed him again and released his shirt. One last smile and I flew.

I was still half a mile away from where the flashes were occurring when they began to move all over the hills instead of staying in one location. *Stop and float.* I watched the flashing light display. They were moving miles in split seconds. There was no rhyme or reason to their movements. If I flew all over the mountains tracking them, I would end up completely exhausting my magic like they were doing to themselves now. I still didn't have a full battery life, and I had this gut feeling that I needed to conserve it. I needed to get back to the castle. If my dad was successful, he would come back to the castle in victory. If Ray bested my father, he would still want to destroy me. As morbid a thought as that was, the only thing that mattered was stopping Ray. However, I needed to make it through a kabillion fighting fey to get there.

I turned and started flying back through the empty space but felt my magic weaken, so I set myself down and ran the rest of the way. When I neared the edge of the fighting where I had left Elwin and Mike, I spotted them instantly. More of my fey had joined them and they were all working together as a team. They had the upper hand with their foes and didn't need my help. The path to the castle from there was filled with fighting, but I couldn't spare any more magic to fly over the mess. I ran along the edge of the fight, praying for a safe route through.

As I ran, I recognized Lilly by her hairstyle—little buns that looked like pincushions. She was fighting off three dark fey. "Lilly behind," I yelled as I neared her. Lilly nodded without taking her eyes off the fey. I joined her and we became our own deadly duo fighting side by side. Lilly wielded her kampilans like she was dancing—swaying and moving. Each move she made was well executed to deliver a death sentence. I held my own with my sword and dagger. I fell into a rhythm that allowed me to hit two blows in succession, one to incapacitate and one to kill.

A shrill scream sounded from my left. I looked past Lilly to see Tessa being carried over the shoulder of some big oaf as if she was some spoil of war.

"Lilly," I said as I nodded to Tessa. Lilly flew off to help Tessa. I kept my eye on them as I killed the last of the three enemies near me. Lilly dropped and slid like she was stealing a base, past the fey and cut off both of his legs at the knee. Tessa dropped off the oaf and sprang to her feet. Lilly and Tessa looked to me. I nodded and took off running toward the castle.

I ran as fast as I could through the fighting. I couldn't believe I hadn't fallen yet. Somehow, my body just knew what to do. I didn't question it; I just went with it, ducking under swords and jumping over dead bodies. I twisted and turned my way until I was back in the courtyard. A flash of black lit up the courtyard. It was coming from the roof of the castle and I could see Ray there. I ran through the same door we used earlier and sprinted to the large white marble staircase in the back of the room. There were a few dead fey on the ground, but no active fighting. The ballroom's walls were lined with gold-edged mirrors and golden wall sconces blazed between each one. While walking, I looked up and gasped when I saw the ceiling. I lost my footing and rolled my ankle. I sat down in pain but couldn't help looking up again. The ceiling was about the size of a basketball court and had a chandelier that spanned the entire area. The ornate, round center was about five feet in diameter and looked like an upside-down wedding cake with hundreds of strands of glowing crystals that spread to the walls. It was so beautiful.

I moved my ankle in a circle a couple of times to make sure it wasn't broken, then I ran to the stairs. I had only made it up the first ten steps when something yanked me from behind and threw me upward. I crashed into the center of the chandelier near the ceiling. On my descent, I reached out and grabbed onto a strand of crystal lights. It broke loose from the center and I swung across the room, hitting the wall with my feet and bouncing off a couple times before I felt the strand giving away. When it broke, I fell the last five feet, but that was better than the forty-foot drop I would have had if I had fallen from the center. I stood and turned to run, promptly tripping over the chaise that my grandma had laid in earlier that evening. I sat up and heard a laugh as I was hit with black smoke and lost consciousness.

THIRTY-NINE

I woke up to a hard smack across the right side of my face and my left temple hit a solid surface behind me. I hadn't even opened my eyes when another blow landed on the left side of my face. I tried to move my arms and legs, but my entire body was immobile except for my head. Opening my eyes a little, I looked at my extremities. My arms and legs were stuck to a white, slightly curved stone wall. I was held in place by magic; nothing visible was holding me. My head was pounding and my ears were ringing. I focused on the fey standing in front of me.

"You bastard," I said.

Ray's smile grew wider. "Tsk, Tsk, Princess. Is that any way to talk to your soon-to-be mate?" He closed the distance between us and pressed his body against mine and nuzzled my neck.

"Too late," I declared and Ray grabbed me by the hair, wrenched my head to the side and bit the skin where my neck and shoulder met, hard enough to draw blood.

"Ow! What? Are you a freaking vampire, too? What the hell is wrong with you? Never mind, too much to go into and you'd need a real shrink to deal with your issues."

Ray grabbed my chin and ground his groin into me. I nearly gagged with repulsion. He whispered in my ear, "Just think about how *fun* those issues are going to make the loss of your virginity." I opened my mouth to scream for help and Ray clamped his hand over my mouth. "You better stop that or I'm going to do with your feet what I did with your hands."

What? I looked to my right and left, my heart seizing with panic. My arms were extended out, but they ended at my wrists. There were bloody stumps with stringy tendons hanging out. I screamed the loudest scream I have ever screamed and just kept screaming behind Ray's hand.

"Shut up." Ray moved his hand from my mouth. I tried to scream, but no sound came out. Ray ground into me again. "Couldn't have you doing any magic. No hands and no voice means no spells. The devil is in the details, my dear." Ray licked up the side of my neck and said in my ear, "I'll let you scream tonight. I can't wait to hear you scream." I silently whimpered and he

167

pushed off me. He winked and walked to the edge of the roof and gazed upon the fighting below.

Ray raised his wand and lit up the sky with a bright black light. The fighting below us stopped and Ray's booming voice filled the void. "Put down your weapons. The Queen is dead and the king has fallen. I have the princess. She is mine. Bow and I may let you live. Bow to the new king!"

Oh no! My grandmother and father are dead? I stopped worrying about how I might escape or survive this. I was about to lose my virginity to a sadist who planned to kill anyone who refused to bow to him. Not to mention the eventual end of the world would be my fault. The weight of it all began to overwhelm me and all I could do was cry.

"You can't have her." Elwin was walking slowly across the roof like a giant cat stalking its prey. I tried to think of a plan, but I couldn't think. The pounding in my head was so bad that I couldn't get a single thought to form completely.

Ray was angry, poised, and ready to fight. "You lost her again, Elwin. I can't believe you were the king's favorite. What a waste of his time and energy." In his anger, Ray let the hold on my voice go.

"Geeze, Ray. How many issues do you have? Don't you guys get *Dr. Phil* here? 'Cause you, dude, you are in some desperate need of sentences with verbs in them." I shook my head and rolled my eyes at him.

Confused, Ray looked at me in disbelief. "I told you to shut up!"

I had succeeded in distracting Ray long enough for Elwin to close the distance between them. Elwin swung his sword, but Ray dodged just in time. The clang of the first hit echoed around us. They jumped back from each other and the fight was on—ducking and diving around the roof trying to kill each other. Ray landed the first strike and a dark red line of blood appeared on Elwin's thigh and began running down his leg. It steeled his resolve, though, and he began raining sword swings and thrusts with such strength that he soon backed Ray behind whatever wall I was stuck to. I could not see them, so I strained my ears for any clue as to who was winning. Suddenly, I heard my grandmother telepathically say, *Sarette, your hands are an illusion.*

I looked at my right hand; it was still a stringy stump. If it was an illusion, I needed to see reality. I focused on where my hand should be. I zeroed in so tightly that I went crossed eyed, but through the haze, my hand began to take shape. I could also see Ray's magical bond and envisioned it opening. Soon my hand was whole and the bond faded into nothing. I repeated the process with my left hand and then quickly removed the bonds from my ankles. I slid to the ground but was unable to stand. It took a minute of shaking my limbs before the feeling came back to them.

As soon as I was able, I got to my feet and ran behind the gigantic dome thing that I had been attached to. I rounded in time to see Elwin knock Ray's sword out of his hand. The sword clattered and slid across the roof. Ray pulled his wand out of his pocket and flicked it at Elwin. Elwin was thrown and landed on his back twenty feet away. He sprung back up like Jackie Chan and ran after Ray. Ray had picked up his sword and ran to the edge of the roof. He had an evil grin on his face when he saw me and pointed his wand at me. He flicked his wrist and I fell to the ground, clutching my head. Elwin dropped next to me. I screamed in agony, but that just made the pain worse. I curled up in the fetal position and covered my head; it was all I could do.

"Ba ha ha ha ha!" I could hear Ray laughing over the fever pitch pounding in my temples. "There's always more than one way to bind someone." My body levitated right out of Elwin's grasp and above his reach. I was still in the fetal position, unable to function through the pain. "When are you going to get it? I win! The king and queen are dead and when Sarette and I are bonded—"

"I am not dead yet." I heard Grandmother Paige's voice ring out as the pain in my head lessened. Opening my eyes a sliver, I saw that I was encompassed in a purple light. As the light faded, so did my pain. I was floating ten feet higher above the roof. From the spirit crystal at the top of Paige's wand, a purple light was stretched all the way around Ray's waist; it pulled him off the roof, holding him suspended eighty feet above the fey below.

"Ray, I told you, you are too late. Elwin and I have been mated by the queen," I said from my suspended position.

Ray looked at me and snarled. He started to move his wand when Elwin ran across the roof with his sword in hand. Ray was still looking at me when Elwin jumped off the roof, ran his sword through Ray's chest, and pushed them both out of my line of sight. I knew the moment Ray died, though. Whatever was holding me up popped like a bubble and I went crashing onto the rooftop. My only thought was of Elwin, who had fallen in the process. I saw a door on a turret on the other side of the roof. I started crawling until I managed to get on my feet and then I ran.

FORTY

I ran through the door in the turret and looked into the circular space. Stairs lined the wall going down, which reminded me of the inside of a lighthouse. I took the stairs two at a time, around and down. At the bottom, there was one door. I opened it and walked into the middle of a long hallway. Doors lined either side and steps went down on either end. I had no idea where I was going. With no point of reference, I took off at a jog to the stairs on my left.

On the next floor down, there was another hallway of closed doors like the one above. I went down another flight of stairs that ended in a wider hall with arches and openings. I ran down the corridor. Half way down the space opened up. To my right was a grand foyer with marble columns, a fountain in the middle, and arched double doors that were at least fifteen feet tall. Around the doors was a stained glass window depicting the different realms of Daearen. Across the hall on my left was the entrance to the ballroom. I ran through the opening as Elwin ran in from outside on the opposite side of the room. I ran down the center set of stairs and took the left circular stair to the ballroom floor. Elwin was faster than me and was almost at the bottom of the stairs. I still had a couple more to go, and I either tripped or launched myself off the steps toward him. Elwin wrapped his arms around me as I knocked him over. I landed on his chest and he let out "oomph" and closed his eyes.

"Oh my Goddess! Did I hurt you?" I looked Elwin over for injuries but stayed on top of him. I put my hands on either side of his face and looked closer.

"Survive a vicious battle to be plowed down by your mate."

I slid my hand under his head and brought it back, looking for blood. There was none. I moved my other hand under the other side of his head to check and said, "Yep, excellent queen I'll make."

Elwin quickly snaked his hand around my waist to my back and pulled me tighter to him. His other hand on the back of my head pulled me into his hard kiss. When the kiss ended, I put my forehead to his and took a couple of steadying breaths.

"I agree with your grandmother. You are going to be the most wonderful queen Daearen has ever had," Elwin murmured against my lips and gave me a light kiss.

"My grandma!" I got up quickly, causing another "oomph" to come out of Elwin, and started running toward the courtyard door. "What about my dad? What about all the other fey?" I shouted back to Elwin as I ran. He was answering me, but I didn't slow down long enough to hear what he said. There was a large silent crowd with their backs to me in the courtyard. With the intent of politely and inconspicuously walking through the crowd, I took a couple of steps, but I didn't look where I was going and tripped over my own feet. I caught myself before falling on my butt, but not before kicking a pile of discarded weapons. The clinking and clanging of swords, daggers, and who knows what else, reverberated through the courtyard.

All at once, hundreds of fey turned to me. I stood there looking like an idiot. I didn't know what to do. Wave and say hi? Pretend it didn't happen? Jump up like Mary Katherine Gallagher, Superstar from that *Best of Saturday Night Live 90s* DVD I had given my mom?

Standing before me were my fey who had risked everything for me, my family, and my kingdom. There were losses; we just didn't know how many yet. I was humbled in their presence. I placed my right fist over my heart and bowed my head to them all in respect and gratitude. I heard a rustling and when I raised my head, I found every fey had returned my gesture.

When the fey lifted their heads, they parted and created a path to the center of the courtyard. I began walking and nodding to the fey as I passed them. In the center of the courtyard was my dad. He was bloody and battered from his fight with Ray, but alive and standing. My grandmother had Will on one side supporting her, and the young fey I had saved on the other. I picked up speed and ran to remove the distance separating us. My father caught me and picked me up. We put a lifetime of hugs into that embrace.

"Daddy!" I croaked out and burst into tears.

"Princess!" My father, the king, was crying too. "I love you so much and I'm so sorry, Sarette. Please forgive me for not being there."

"There's nothing to forgive. I get the bigger picture. I love you too, Daddy." One last squeeze and my father set me down. I walked into my grandmother's arms next and her two supporting fey stepped away.

"I really wish we had time to get to know each other in this form. I've waited so long to meet you, Sarette," my grandma said.

"What?" I leaned back to look at her.

"It's time," she said.

Shaking my head, "Grandma, no, I just got here. I have no idea what I'm doing. I'm not ready." I began to sob. "And I've never had a grandma before. I don't want to lose you now." She pulled me to her and held me tight.

"You will be the *Spirit* queen, my dear. You *will* see me again." I sniffled and she pulled back again and put her hand on my cheek. "My beautiful granddaughter, you are going to change everything. It *is* what it *is*, you *are* who you *are*, and *who* you were *meant* to be, Sarette, the queen for a new age in Daearen." She wiped the tears from my face and stepped back. She looked past me and nodded. Elwin was at my side holding my hand.

"First, let's make this officially official by announcing it to the realms." My grandmother touched my pendant and then Elwin's with her crystal wand, smiled and took several steps back. Both of our pendants started glowing green and the light they emitted grew. It enveloped us and spread out. When it hit the fey closest to us, a purple light waved through the crowd like at a laser show.

"Trippy," I said.

"Wait for it . . ." Elwin replied. My pendant began to vibrate on my chest and the light from it got brighter. The ring of light around us flashed brightly and then left the courtyard, shooting out in all directions, expanding like a giant smoke ring.

"Wow!" I said.

"Sarette, please come here," Paige said. Elwin squeezed my hand and I stepped in front of my grandmother. She held out her wand to me and I took it. There was an audible noise around us in response—a mix of ahhhs, ohhhs, sobs, and sighs. I didn't look around. I had a feeling this was going to be the last time I ever saw my grandmother alive. These were the last moments of Queen Paige of the Spirit Fey's reign. She reached up and took her crown off. I bowed my head and she placed it over my head and straightened it across my forehead.

"I love you, Sarette," she said.

I looked up. "I love you too, Grandma."

She placed her hands near mine on the wand and her entire body started to sparkle like a disco ball. The sparkle was then concentrated over her heart before it moved through her arm to the wand and paused there, growing in brightness. The sparkle moved into my hand and spread throughout my body. I was a disco ball for ten seconds or so. Then, Queen Paige closed her eyes and started to collapse. The king was there to catch her and gently lower her to the ground.

As I knelt, the sparkle faded altogether. My grandmother's last breath was a loud exhale of a misty purple smoke. It floated above her, moved to me, and I inhaled it through my mouth. As soon as I closed my mouth, it flew open again and I screamed. A brilliant purple light released from the crystal wand. As it hit Ray's dead body and those of his fallen minions, and many of his survivors, they turned into purple smoke and "poofed" out of existence. The dark fey left standing fell to their knees and did the heart-fist-bow.

"Elwin, please come here," my father said. As Elwin walked to the king, I placed my grandmother's hands on her chest and stood up.

King Roland, my father, took his crown from his head and Elwin bowed his. My father placed the crown on Elwin's head. It fit perfectly across his forehead. My father then took a large gold ring with an inset amethyst off his right hand and placed it in Elwin's palm. Elwin put it on and my father said in a booming voice, "Long live King Elwin of the Spirit Fey."

The entire crowd, including me, repeated his words.

Will stepped next to the king and said, "Long Live Queen Sarette of the Spirit Fey." The entire crowd repeated his words.

The young fey that had watched over my grandmother stepped forth and said, "May the God and Goddess bless their reign."

"Blessed be," the crowd said and did the heart-fist-bow.

I'm not sure what made me do it or where the knowledge came from, but I suddenly knew what I needed do. I held my crystal wand up and said, "I am humbled by the presence of the sacrifices my brave and loyal fey have made today. I am honored to return you to your elements."

I closed my eyes and heard a gasp from the crowd. *Please, God and Goddess, let me honor them. Honor them. Honor them. Honor them.* I felt my chest start to warm and I opened my eyes. I was a disco ball again. I concentrated the feeling into my heart and pushed it into my wand. When the spirit crystal glowed brightly, I forced the energy out all at once. My knees got weak. Elwin caught me and tightly wrapped his arms around me. My fallen fey began to shimmer. They let out a flash of light as their bodies disappeared and they became one with their elements. Swirling spheres of water, air, earth, and fire danced where their bodies had been. They hovered for a moment before rising and dissipating into the atmosphere above us.

Gasps came from all around me. On the ground, wherever there had been a fallen fey a small disk appeared—white, green, blue, and red. There was one purple one and it was where my grandmother's heart had been. I picked up the disk and on the front was an etched picture of my grandmother, her name, and the dates of her birth and death. On the back were concentric rings of Celtic knot work leading to the center where there was the trinity knot. I held the disk to my heart and closed my eyes. *Soon*, I heard Grandma say.

I opened my eyes and had another moment of brilliance. "Is every fey ready to go home?" There was a slight murmuring amongst the crowd. "Elwin, why is every fey looking at me like that?" I whispered to Elwin.

"The Queen was the first fey to even attempt anything like that. Queen Paige was able to teleport herself and a few others with her. But that was very rare; it took an extraordinary amount of magic and left her in a weakened state for days. What she did tonight was one of the reasons she died. She must have exhausted almost all of her magic at once, leaving her only enough to mate us and make you queen."

"Then, how did Ray bring all of his fey here, then jump all over the hillside, and then do a bunch of magic on the roof, and still not even look tired?"

"By taking our magic," I heard spoken from the crowd.

"I'm sorry. What?" I asked and one of the remaining fey who had followed Ray stepped forward. "Those who went willingly with Ray had to give him some of their magic. That was his price for sparing their families. Those of us who resisted . . ." Tears fell from his eyes. "He found another way to be in control of half of my magic."

"Oh my Goddess, no," I said and tears welled in my eyes.

"He took my mazon, my Leah, right from our house. He left our children there by themselves. Not all of us had made it home before something bad happened to the little ones. Our mazons were back on their own porches the next morning in an almost catatonic state. They have virtually no magic left and it has not regenerated like it's supposed to."

I stepped away from Elwin and walked over to the fey. I put my hand on his shoulder and said, "I am so sorry. Is she gone now? Can you still feel her?" He looked at me and didn't say anything. "I know I would feel my heart rip in two if Elwin died. What do you feel?"

"I feel whole," he said and fresh tears formed in his eyes.

"I think you need to get home posthaste. I don't know what you'll find. But, don't you want to know now?" I asked. He nodded his head. "All the more reason to try to send every fey home."

"Sarette, I don't think that's a good idea. We have no idea how strong you are yet," my father said.

I rolled my eyes. "I'm stronger than I look. You said it didn't take *all* of the queen's magic to do it. She still had some left to mate us and make me queen. I have no intention of abdicating the throne. I just got here and unless there is a need for a royally sanctioned mating," I shrugged my shoulders and scanned the crowd. "I think I'm good. I thank you all. Godspeed." I raised my wand and thought, *Home.* In less than a blink of an eye, almost every fey was gone. The fey that were left were those who helped me get to the castle.

Mike and Tessa had their arms around one another. Lilly was leaning against the train car with Mica. Ethan and Meghan Conner and Paul were sitting on the ledge of a fountain that I hadn't noticed until now. Mick and Darius were standing near Elwin. My father was next to Will and he had his hand on the young fey's shoulder. I think I unknowingly gave him a royal assignment or something. That's okay, he's a sweet kid. I smiled at him and he broke his "o" face to smile back. Then, I took a closer look at everyone else and they all had the shock and awe face.

"What? I'm okay. See?" I asked the group. There wasn't a response from the peanut gallery. There was complete silence. "Could somebody say something please?" All I heard were crickets. "Did I just do something wrong? I don't know what I'm doing. I'm totally screwing this up, aren't I?"

There was a collective "No."

"Okay, then." I waited for somebody to say something.

Thank the goddess for Elwin. He put his arm around my shoulder and said, "Didn't I tell you she was amazing? She did not lose her magic or her health in accomplishing that feat." My stomach chose that moment to growl loudly. "Or her appetite!"

There were mostly smiles and I only heard a couple of chuckles until I elbowed Elwin playfully in the stomach then there was all out laughter.

"Seriously though, I'm starving. Anyone else hungry?" Can we order pizza? I really liked those pink and stripped purple thingies we had on it last time. Can we get that again?"

"Sweetheart, you're the queen of Daearen," my dad said.

"So?"

"You can get whatever you want, whenever you want it," Elwin said.

"Pizza." I nodded, turned, and started walking to the ballroom entrance.

"We have cake too, as long as the kitchen wasn't ransacked," my father said.

"Cake?" I turned around.

"It's your birthday," Dad said.

"Does there happen to be skee ball, a claw machine, or Time Cop in the castle?" I looked around at confused faces. "What? I always wanted a princess pizza birthday party at Chuck E. Cheese. A couple of arcade-type games in a castle doesn't seem like a far stretch. I don't expect a seven-foot-tall cartoon mouse to be walking around or anything but —" A horrible thought came to me. "There isn't, right?"

"Isn't what?" Elwin asked.

"A seven-foot-tall cartoonish mouse-like creature in Daearen?"

Everyone chuckled.

"No, there isn't. And you're too late," Lilly said.

"Too late for what?" Exasperated, I threw up my hands. "What else? Seriously."

"You're not a princess anymore; you're a queen." Lilly did the heart-fist-bow, then smiled and said, "No Time Cop or claw machine. There was Ms. Pacman though when I was a kid, it might still be here."

"It is," my father said and everyone looked at him. "I can have that and the skee ball machine moved out of my room into the arcade. Your mother taught me to play. I love those damn games." Everyone laughed.

"Queen Birthday pizza party at the palace arcade it is. And there's the added bonus of a wedding reception. Let's go." I turned and strode across the courtyard.

Elwin caught up to me and said, "We'll have time before the pizza is done to go over some intelligence."

I stopped, turned sharply, and looked at him. "No, none of *that* tonight. Tonight is our wedding night and I want to celebrate *that* with friends. Today is my eighteenth birthday and I want to celebrate *that* with friends. I just became a queen . . . not totally settled on how I feel about it but, regardless, I want to celebrate *that* with friends, too. We didn't fix anything tonight. We have not solved any of the real problems of Daearen. We stopped one turned fey from taking the throne, but it was not a problem-solving night. It was a distraction from the real war that has been raging here. Tonight, I want to celebrate the *good* things. I don't want to discuss how we won one small fight in a life-and-death battle with the fate of the world at stake—at least not for the next two or three hours." Elwin gave me a confused look. I stood on my tiptoes, he leaned down, and I whispered in his ear, "That's the plan until we go to bed. There, we should act like it's the last night on the planet. I think that could be fun, don't you?" I gave Elwin's earlobe a small bite and blew in his ear.

Elwin shivered, let out a throaty groan, and picked me up so we were eye to eye. "We could always have pizza sent to the room. Are you positive you want to celebrate tonight?"

I nodded and gave him a soft kiss. Elwin had fire in his eyes as he tangled his hand in my hair and pulled me into a hard, wanting, "holy crap" kind of kiss. He set me on my feet when the kiss ended. He looked into my dazed eyes and gave me a sly smile.

I shook my head to refocus. We were alone in the courtyard, everyone else had gone inside. "I can't not show up for my own party that I just threw for myself five minutes ago, but I'm sure nobody will mind if we leave early. Let's go." I tugged Elwin's arm to get him moving. "The sooner we get there, the sooner we can go."

Elwin pulled me back to him and cradled my face in his hands, "I love you, Sarette."

"Love you too, Elwin."

He kissed me again. This one was filled with a promise of our future together.

The Daearen Realms Series
Can you imagine a world where science is replaced with magic?

Bienn-Theine: Book Two of the Daearen Realms

Mathew has a lot on his plate. After finding out that his best friend Sarette is actually his cousin, a fairy, and destined to be queen, he also learns that he's a prince and an heir to the Fire Fey throne. Now instead of applying to colleges and sucking down Boston Coolers in Michigan, he must travel through Daearen to Bienn-Theine, the fire realm, to claim his birthright and fight the dark magic threatening to take all that Mathew holds dear— the woman he has come to adore, Sarette and the family he just found, the fey he has come to love, and the land that becomes home. Mathew must become both a man and a prince to defeat the dark fey threatening the balance between good and evil, not only in the Daearen realms, but on earth as well.

Eitlean: Book Three of the Dacaren Realms

Dark magic has spread, gaining traction throughout Daearen and threatening to destroy the balance within the realm—as well as that of Earth. But all may not be lost...

When Banee-Belle of the Air Fey discovers an ancient clue, one which could lead her to the most powerful spells ever written within the realm, hope returns to her heart. If she can employ her wits to decipher the clue, she will gain the ability to wield magic of unheard of power against the Light Fey's evil counterparts. But before her quest even begins, Banee learns she must team up with the one fey who broke her heart, leaving her to live an incomplete life—a fey never made whole.

Can Banee push aside her contempt and distrust to complete her most vital mission yet? Will she have the strength to face her own broken heart to prove she is so much more than the pretty princess everyfey assumes her to be—saving her fey in the process? Find out in the next thrilling adventure to restore balance within the Daearen Realms.

AUTHOR'S NOTE

Thank you for taking a chance on a first-time author. I hope you enjoyed reading Meanmna as much as I loved writing it.
Reviews are what make indie authors like me gain visibility and become successful. So if you have a moment, please leave a review at your online retailer and on Goodreads. Good, bad or ambivalent, I appreciate them all!

I'd love to connect and you can find me all over the place!

Facebook:
Author Emmy Gatrell:
https://www.facebook.com/authoremmygatrell/
Daearen Realms Series: https://www.facebook.com/emmygatrell
Nathanial Lupinski's Bitches Page:
https://www.facebook.com/LupinskiClan/
Emmy's Bad Ass Entourage (BAE):
https://www.facebook.com/groups/EmmysBadAssEntourage

Amazon: https://www.amazon.com/Emmy-Gatrell/e/B00HWCD4RA
Instagram : https://instagram.com/emgatrell
Twitter: https://twitter.com/emmyeg
Goodreads:
https://www.goodreads.com/author/show/7770821.Emmy_Gatrell

Website: http://emmygatrell.com/
Subscribe to my newsletter: http://emmygatrell.com/emmys-newsletter/

THANKS TO:

This experience has been humbling and rewarding. It wouldn't have been possible without some special folks.

My kids: For putting up with too many delivery pizzas and frozen dinners during the writing of the book.

Yvonne Perry at Writers in the Sky Creative Writing Services: I am walking away a better writer and will be forever grateful.

Craig Davis: Thanks for the first read and I look forward to kicking your butt in Words with Friends, at least sometimes.

Norman Wong: WOW! The cover is so beautiful. It's even better than I imagined! Thank you, thank you, thank you!

My parents, sisters, and friends: y'all are awesome and I love you.

Jon: You know. Bunches.

68323412R00100

Made in the USA
Lexington, KY
07 October 2017